EMPTY NEST

BOOK THREE: THE EUPHEMIA SAGE CHRONICLES

ROSY FENWICKE

WONDERFUL WORLD

CONTENTS

Prologue   1
Chapter 1   5
Chapter 2   14
Chapter 3   21
Chapter 4   32
Chapter 5   37
Chapter 6   42
Chapter 7   49
Chapter 8   55
Chapter 9   61
Chapter 10   67
Chapter 11   76
Chapter 12   85
Chapter 13   88
Chapter 14   95
Chapter 15   99
Chapter 16   103
Chapter 17   109
Chapter 18   115
Chapter 19   119
Chapter 20   123
Chapter 21   128
Chapter 22   134
Chapter 23   140
Chapter 24   143
Chapter 25   148
Chapter 26   153
Chapter 27   156
Chapter 28   166
Chapter 29   172

Chapter 30   176
Chapter 31   184
Chapter 32   192
Chapter 33   197
Chapter 34   200
Chapter 35   206
Chapter 36   211
Chapter 37   216
Chapter 38   221
Chapter 39   227
Chapter 40   231
Chapter 41   239
Chapter 42   243
Chapter 43   250
Chapter 44   254
Chapter 45   259
Chapter 46   262

Dedication and Acknowledgements   267
About the Author   269
Hot Flush. Book 1: The Euphemia Sage   271
Chronicles
Switched Up. Book 2: The Euphemia Sage   273
Chronicles
Coming Soon: No Retreat: Book 4: The   275
Euphemia Sage Chronicles
Cold Wallet.   277
Death Actually. Death. Love. And in Between   279

PROLOGUE

J OE K INCAIDE WASN'T EXACTLY AVOIDING Euphemia Sage. But he left Oakhill Station as soon as she arrived. He was merely, he thought, delaying the inevitable. In the meantime, the opportunity to revisit the Pounui Wetland Reserve and observe this season's spoonbill chicks as they prepared to leave their parents' nests was too good to miss. He looked forward to spending a quiet night alone tucked up in his sleeping bag in his shack and going to sleep to the sound of the waves on nearby Ocean Beach.

He needed time to settle his nerves before he faced her. His responses to her inevitable questions had been prepared weeks before but he needed time to practice them. He needed to practice how to sound truthful when he said them. It was vital for everyone's well-being that she believed him. Kenneth would accept what he said at face value. He was a man. But Euphemia would have no compunction calling him out if she thought he was being less than honest about the accounts. If only the events of the last year had not necessitated this deception he wouldn't be in this position. There was too much at stake to be caught now.

I regret having to lie to her; he thought as he walked along the levee to the shack where he did his bird watching. Kenneth and Euphemia had been his friends since their university days. He liked and trusted them. They were clever, and they were fun. For the last twenty years in April, they had made the trip over the hill from Wellington to Oakhill Station to go through the end-of-year accounts of Oakhill Station the property which had been in the Kincaide family for over one hundred and fifty years. Once the business was over, they spent the rest of the weekend enjoying themselves.

Not this year.

Joe looked up. He had arrived. The shack was a small but sturdy one roomed building made from plywood. To call it a shack was disrespectful because it had every modern convenience, money could buy. Powered by discrete solar panels, and covered in webbing woven through with branches and grasses, it was so well camouflaged, a pair of bitterns had nested alongside it last spring - their deep booming calls reverberating around the marshes in the mornings.

It had no windows, just small openings in the walls with shutters which he could raise and lower depending on the weather and which birds were where, on the massive wetland surrounding him. The furniture and fittings comprised a large chest, which doubled as a table, one chair, one high stool, a bed, a small stove which ran on wood pellets, LED lanterns and sink fed with filtered rainwater from a tank on the roof. There was a shelf of books, thrillers each one read many times over, and a pair of high-powered binoculars. Well-stocked with the necessities of life, he kept tins of baked beans, coffee, whisky and chocolate in the chest. His usual trip involved him stopping first at the Martinborough Bakery to purchase two baguettes and then at the cheese shop in Featherston to pick up a round of South Island Brie. He locked the shack when he wasn't there, to keep out the lost and feckless; the door bolted and padlocked.

Except today. The door was wide open. He put his backpack down and approached cautiously across the wooden causeway.

'Who's there?'

There was no answer. A gust of wind blew the door back on its hinges, slamming it against the wall with a loud bang. He listened, but heard nothing to indicate anyone was inside. Ready to confront an intruder, he stepped over the threshold and into the gloomy interior of his shack. There was no one there.

He heard footsteps behind him. He turned. It was too late. Joe didn't see the man who put the wet rag over his nose and mouth and held it there until he passed out.

CHAPTER 1

EUPHEMIA FLICKED OVER THE PAGE OF THE Architectural Digest magazine. Yet another photo of a glamorous woman leaning casually against a marble countertop in her designer kitchen. Why do people do that she wondered? Display their homes for people to gawk at. She pushed the magazine away and in the process almost knocked over the cup of herb tea she now didn't feel like drinking. It was three o'clock in the morning. Euphemia was exhausted. She was wearing an old t-shirt of Kenneth's and a pair of his hiking socks under the tatty dressing gown she had found in her room.

It was her second night with little to no sleep. Her eyeballs prickled painfully every time she blinked and the herb tea had not helped the growling in her stomach which had morphed into low grade nausea. She yawned and swivelled around on the bar stool to stare out the windows running the length of the front wall of the living room. In daylight, the Ponatahi Valley stretched below the house like a painting, the seasons reflected in the colors of the paddocks and trees dotting the rolling hills of Oakhill Station. Under the new moon, there was nothing to see - the countryside lay shrouded in darkness.

Joe Kincaide had brought them here many times over the years to discuss his plans for his dream house. The ridge was close to the old homestead, but far enough away to be private. He had the house mapped out in his head and knew which room would go where and the materials he would use to maximize energy efficiency. He had studied the location from every angle and knew exactly what would be seen at different times of the year, how the sun would warm his home in winter and how the breeze would cool it in summer.

Now built, the house was exactly as he had said it would be. The warm concrete floors primed by the sun released their heat through the night into the triply insulated home. Automatic shutters directed cool air under the eaves to keep the house cool in summer. Grey water irrigated the gardens and kept the grass roof flourishing while a composting system managed organic waste. Batteries lined up against the back wall in the shade, stored energy from the banks of solar panels on the roof. Everything that came onto the property had to be reusable or recyclable. It was called the New House for good reason, and it was the subject of much speculation in farmhouses up and down the valley.

Used to the carpeted floors of the turn of the century Thorndon villa where she and Kenneth lived, Euphemia immediately understood the appeal of polished, warm concrete under her feet and triple-glazed windows. The house was both modern and elegant. Not that she expected anything less. Joe had excellent taste and had furnished it with carefully selected pieces of both antique and modern furniture. The colors were light, the mood open and the artwork expensive. The New House was also unashamedly a bachelor's house. There were guest rooms downstairs where his close friends stayed, but he always made it clear an invitation was only ever for a couple of days. 'Any longer and like fish, guests lose their charm!' He was used to his own company and a firm believer in people not outstaying his welcome.

'I'm happy by myself,' he told Euphemia. The New House was still under construction and they were sitting in the living room of the old homestead looking out the bay windows to the trees at the back of the grass tennis court. Over eighty feet tall, the oaks had grown from acorns brought to New Zealand from Warwickshire by Joe's great-great-grandfather. He had planted them after he cleared the land of native bush in the 1850s. Now full grown, they sheltered the homestead from the prevailing wind, letting the sun shine through bare branches in winter and providing welcome shade in the hot dry Wairarapa summers. More oaks grown from the acorns of the original trees lined both sides of the mile long drive from the road to the homestead.

Old Joe had been brave to travel half-way around the world by sailing ship to an uncertain future in the Antipodes. Many times he wondered if he had done the right thing when the pull of the old country tugged at his heart. Could he make a success of farming this strange land with its unpredictable winters and drought-prone summers? According to Kincaide family legend, it was seeing the oak trees flourishing in this new environment, which gave him the courage to stay and build his fortune and it was why he had named his property Oakhill Station.

'Charlotte left six months ago,' Joe said. 'I've got used to living alone. Not here, though. This house is too big and there are too many reminders. I'll move into the New House as soon as it's finished.' He drained his gin and tonic and got up to refresh his glass. 'Ready for another?' he asked. Euphemia and Kenneth shook their heads. There was no such thing as a small gin when Joe was pouring.

'When will you move in?' asked Kenneth.

'Three months,' said Joe, sitting down again, the juniper fumes perfuming the surrounding air. 'Just as well, because Arthur's coming home. He and Ally called last week. They want the children to go to school in New Zealand. Elizabeth will go to Whanganui and Josh will go to the local primary until he's old enough to join her. Ally wants them to be able to come home for the holidays. She thinks Hong Kong is too far to travel. So long story short, they're going to move in here. Which is fitting. This house feels empty without a family living in it. Charlotte bolting has worked out well for all of us.'

'You don't mean that,' said Euphemia.

Joe shrugged, the ice cubes tinkling in his glass. 'We weren't getting along. Hadn't for years. You saw that last year. She made it clear then how she felt about me. Her running off with Derek was a bit of a bugger, though.' He sipped his gin. 'Good station managers are hard to find.'

'You haven't found a replacement, I take it?' asked Kenneth.

Euphemia wanted to poke her husband in the side. How could he be so… business-like, so callous?

'I've been advertising, but young people aren't interested in farming anymore. They don't like the isolation, or more to the point their partners don't. Even when I explain we're only half an hour from Martinborough, the smart ones aren't interested and I don't want the others.'

'What are you going to do?'

'Nothing I can do,' he said. 'Back in old Joe's day, there were thirty men working the place and Grandma Ruth had fifteen staff to help with the house. I've taken on a couple of laborers from town, but they only want part-time work. I'll get by. I have to. Arthur will help out when he gets home, but he's not the most practical fellow. He is also being very mysterious about a scheme he's got for in mind for the grazing block, next to the sanctuary. Another gin?'

'Go on then, but not too strong,' said Kenneth, ignoring Euphemia's stare.

Now, she looked down at Petal, fast asleep in her bed. The little pug was lying on her back, her soft tummy pink and bulging, her legs splayed in different directions, her eyelids flickering as she emitted a series of high-pitched wuffs, dreaming whatever pampered pugs dream about.

'You're lucky you can sleep,' said Euphemia.

She got up and walked through the pantry cum laundry and opened the back door. Cold air rushed past her and she pulled the dressing gown tightly around her before stepping outside. Flat clouds covered the dark sky. In the near distance, she could make out the smudged outlines of trees behind farm buildings at the side of the house. Nothing moved. The silence crowded over her as if the world had stopped.

In the distance a sheep bleated. The spell had broken. Below the house, the headlights of two cars appeared on the road snaking through the narrow valley. Cars travelling together on a country road at this hour of the night wasn't an unusual occurrence. The farmers in the valley were a social lot, willing to travel in to nearby Masterton or to a neighbor's farm for a night out. What was unusual was that as they got closer, the headlights went off—at exactly the same time — and stayed off. She heard their engines slow as the cars pulled to a stop at the bottom of the drive, opposite the entrance to the sanctuary. Car doors opened, footsteps. One? No two people crunched across the gravel to the sanctuary.

She tugged the dressing gown around her neck to seal in her body warmth and to stop the chill getting in. Footsteps again, one set heavy belonging to a man and another lighter set, a woman's or may be a child's. Car doors closed, engines started and still lightless the cars drove off towards Martinborough. Odd there had been no voices. She shivered in the darkness, pulled the dressing gown tighter and went inside.

Returning to the cozy warmth of the house, she shut and locked the door. If Joe had been there, he would have laughed and called her a townie. He never locked his doors. 'No need,' he said. 'We're miles from anywhere. Your average burglar wouldn't bother coming all the way out here.'

She tipped the rest of the herb tea, now stone cold, down the sink, put the mug in the dishwasher and tidied away the magazine. Downstairs, the muffled sound of Jane's snoring, which she had been trying so hard to ignore, reached another crescendo. In the silence which followed, Euphemia counted to four. The familiar pattern of throaty snorts started again getting louder and louder until, as if perilously teetering on the edge of something - they stopped. A wave of envy engulfed her when she looked at Petal—the little dog, blissfully unaware of the racket downstairs, rolled over and snuffled into her blanket.

Euphemia rubbed her eyes and opened her mouth wide to release the tension in her jaw. You brought this on yourself; she thought as she padded downstairs to her bedroom, slipped off the dressing gown and climbed between the sheets. Lying on her stomach, she buried her face in the pillow, wrapping it around her head and cursed herself for suggesting Jane come on this trip. Jane was a snorer and Euphemia knew it. If only she had remembered how badly, how relentlessly, and how loudly her friend snored. If snoring were an Olympic event, Jane would win the Gold, Silver and Bronze.

Euphemia rolled onto her back, stared at the ceiling, and willed herself not to listen. She counted to one hundred slowly. It was no good. She jumped a flock of sheep one at a time over an imaginary fence, then tried to picture each hair on her left big toe. Nothing - not even a droopy eyelid. Worse, the crawling sensation on her skin started as a familiar heat advanced across her chest and over her shoulders. Sweat enveloped her skin like plastic wrap under the sheets, which now became a cloying, unbearable burden and which had to be flung off immediately or she would suffocate. Her flushes got worse when she didn't sleep, and the less she slept the more flushes she had. The vicious circle of life for a midlife woman.

Her friends, also in their fifties, sang the praises of HRT. After taking it, their fatigue disappeared and once again they were the women they had always been. Euphemia believed them. She wished she could take it too, but Aunt Maree and now Barbara had made it clear there was no coming back if she did. Once the powers were hormoned away, they were gone. Forever. She was still struggling with the arrangement. On nights like this, the allure of any relief from her exhaustion was overwhelming. The nagging voice asking what was the point of having superpowers she barely used became louder, bolder and more insistent.

It was no good. She sat up, turned on the light, plumped the pillows behind her, opened her laptop and scrolled through endless junk mail automatically hitting delete until she got to Joe's email.

Kia ora Euphemia and Kenneth,

It was a fabulous wedding. Thank you. I was honored to be invited. I don't know who looked more beautiful, the bride, her sister or their mother. Kenneth, you looked passable. Old - but distinguished.

K, I'm sorry you won't be accompanying your wife on the annual accounts pilgrimage to the station this year, but no doubt we shall cope without you. Good luck on your trip to Asia.

E, the accounts seem fine at this end, so will only need a quick sign-off this year. BTW, the fatted calf is looking nervous. See you on the 15th.

Nga mihinui,

Joe

The email written on the 12th of March, a month after

Kezia's wedding was sent the day before Kenneth and Roger had left to go on their business trip to Singapore and Asia. She had hoped Kenneth would postpone leaving until after they'd been to Oakhill, but evidently this wasn't an option - something about meeting Barbara's contacts in Vietnam at a mutually convenient time. He tried his best to look contrite, but Euphemia saw straight through his sham regret. He couldn't wait to get away and start his big venture selling into the Asian market, his poorly concealed excitement oozing from every pore.

Ted, the chef at a well-known Wellington restaurant, had approached Roger and Kenneth for ideas on how to capitalize on his success, less than a year ago. Kenneth had leapt at the opportunity and the company *Desserts are Us* was formed without Euphemia having a say in the matter. He said he still enjoyed working at Sage Consulting, but it was obvious he didn't enjoy it as much as he had in their early days.

Kenneth loved challenges and once Sage Consulting had grown to occupy two floors in an office building in downtown Wellington, his enthusiasm waned. He was spending more time on the golf course and less time at the office. It was when his relationships with customers became less important than speed and efficiency. Kenneth was a people person. He enjoyed solving problems and coaching others.

Talents which were no longer essential after Kezia, their eldest daughter and self-confessed computer geek, joined the firm and took the consultancy online. A smart man, he understood computers and technology, but only enough to understand what he wanted them to do and not enough to make them do it. Computers and software were mere tools to him and not the gateway to the future. This attitude which didn't endear him to the start-up tech companies approaching Sage Consulting to access Kezia's expert assistance, and he felt sidelined.

That his change in attitude had also coincided with the onset of Euphemia's superpowers did not escape her attention. She had done her best to be discrete. She didn't want him to feel emasculated by her powers. It also defeated the point of having superpowers if everyone knew she had them. Knowing the pressure she would be under to perform and explain if her abilities were common knowledge gave her the collywobbles. It had made her anxious when Jimmy, the pesky journalist fresh out of journalism school, had filmed her saving the Wellington harbor ferry from sinking in a storm. When he threatened to go public, she was terrified he was going to ruin her life and the lives of her family.

Thankfully Barbara Scarsdale came to their aid. A prominent but elderly Sydney businesswoman, she provided the funding for Kenneth's business. The video was purchased from Jimmy and buried deep in the RS Holdings vault and Alison's father was finally taken to a place where he could do no harm.

Euphemia was still uncertain whether Kenneth's business had just been a convenient excuse for her to meet Barbara. Both women had inherited the genetic switch which triggered the powers from their common ancestor Rachel. Barbara's powers how ever were waning with age and she made it clear at their first meeting, that she expected Euphemia to continue the work of the family research foundation.

For the sake of peace on all fronts, Euphemia had agreed and put aside her doubts about the older woman. She had celebrated Kenneth's success as he devoted all his time to the new company. She was just pleased to see him so happy, even though it meant they spent less time together. In these months which followed the adventures in Sydney, she had been fully occupied running Sage Consulting and organising her eldest daughter's wedding to think much about the powers and what her future might be.

CHAPTER 2

Every April for the past twenty years, Euphemia and Kenneth had packed up the car, and driven over the Remutaka Hills to stay with Joe at Oakhill Station in the Wairarapa. Ostensibly, the trip was to get the end-of-year accounts in order. This was quickly done. Then the three friends spent a couple of days relaxing in the countryside. This was the first time Kenneth had not been able to come.

She hadn't planned to invite Jane, the receptionist at Sage Consulting and an old school friend, but once the invitation had been extended, there was no going back. It was nine o'clock in the morning. Kenneth had left at 5 AM to catch his plane and Euphemia had been for a twenty kilometre run to take her mind off his leaving. Showered and dressed for work in a plain black trouser suit and white trainers, her short hair freshly washed, she emerged from the elevator with Petal at her side.

It was a shock to see Alastair from HR, still wearing his fluorescent Lycra bike clothes consoling a sobbing Jane. His road bike leaned against the reception desk.

Petal had run straight over to Jane and standing on her

back legs pawed at her lap, her head cocked to one side. Jane reached down and fondled the little dog's head.

'What's wrong?' asked Euphemia.

'It's Dan,' said Jane. 'We broke up.'

Euphemia didn't miss Alastair's stifled smile as he offered Jane a tissue.

'I'm sorry. We're both sorry. Aren't we Alastair?'

Alastair jerked upright, caught in the act of not being very sorry at all and nodded solemnly. Jane reached blindly for his hand. 'You understand don't you,' she said her eyes leaking gratitude as she looked up at him.

'I do,' he replied. Before Euphemia could think of an excuse to leave, he uttered the dreaded words, 'Tell us what happened. Talking helps.'

Jane took a deep breath, swallowed, and started her story. 'Dan was, is, lovely, but he expected me to go tramping. Every weekend,' she said, paused and took another deep breath. 'In the bush. Up hills. Through rivers. Sleeping in huts with no electricity, with outside loos, which didn't flush. I tried to like it, Effie.'

Euphemia automatically rolled her eyes. She hated being called Effie and had told Jane this many times, but it hadn't sunk in and, sadly, she was getting used to it. It didn't mean she liked it, but she no longer saw the point of making a fuss. But Jane was the only person she allowed to call her that. Woe and betide anyone else who took liberties with her name.

'You're talking about Dan, the mountain guide, the one who rescued you from Mt Taranaki?'

A look of annoyance flashed across Jane's face. 'Yes, of course it's that, Dan.'

'Sorry, I had to make sure we were talking about the same person.'

'How many Dans do you think there are?' Jane said. 'Never mind.' She grabbed another tissue from the box and blew her nose. 'It was the possum's fault. It made me realize it could never work between us—not long term. Those bright red, mean little eyes staring at me when I opened the door to the loo. The noise it made. It was like this.' She made a sound in the back of her throat. 'A creepy gargling sound like... the devil choking.' She shivered theatrically. 'It was horrible. I knew right then I had to end it.'

'With the possum?'

Jane hurled another look at Euphemia before burying her face in a tissue.

'Dan must be devastated,' Alastair said. 'Losing someone like you.'

'You are sweet Alastair. A true friend.' Jane stared up at him as he gazed adoringly down at her.

'It's probably for the best,' Euphemia said.

Jane straightened in her chair. 'What do you mean? We were in love. Sometimes I wonder if you want me to be happy again. You made your feelings about Justin perfectly clear. Then you were mean about Kevin and now you're being mean about Dan.'

'Whoah, hold up.' Euphemia said. 'That's not fair. Justin, your husband of thirty years, was having an affair - with our receptionist Alison Sinclair. They kidnapped you to steal your jewelry so they could run away together. Then Justin tried to kill us before he set himself on fire and burnt your down your family home. I nearly died saving you. Ben was lucky to get out of the house alive. As for Kevin, he took you up Mt Taranaki to scare you into marrying him so he, too, could steal your jewelry. It was lucky for you he was afraid of heights. Sure, Dan is nice, but he is twenty years younger than you. And fitter. And he lives in the wilderness. He would never move in to your tiny apartment on the Terrace and you were certainly not going to go off and live in the wild. Alastair, tell her I'm right. Tell her breaking up with Dan is for the best.'

Alastair moved away from Euphemia to the other side of Jane's chair, his hand protectively across her shoulders. Jane smiled at him again as she turned away from Euphemia and put her hand over his.

'Have it your way,' Euphemia said. 'I've got work to do. Come on Petal.'

Petal arched her back, yawned, stretched one leg after the other, and without a backward glance at her mistress, jumped onto Jane's lap and leaned against her.

Normally after such a canine slam-dunk Euphemia would have popped in to Kenneth's office for a consoling chat or failing that would have gone up to IT on the floor above and chatted to Kezia. This time, she had no one. Kenneth was on his way to Singapore and Kezia was still on her honeymoon. Never had a Tahitian Island seemed so far away. She couldn't even call Nicky, her youngest daughter, and suggest they meet for lunch. Nicky had made it clear at the wedding she was going on a secret assignment for the police and was only to be contacted in emergencies. 'Life and death emergencies,' she told her mother firmly.

At least Euphemia had her work to distract her from the problems at the front desk. She was an excellent business consultant and enjoyed every aspect of her work, from meeting clients in the office to balancing their annual accounts. She didn't understand the bored restlessness, which had prompted Kenneth to set up a new business. His desire to take on a project without her had been disappointing, but she had gone along with him and even pretended she thought it was a good idea. The fact was she had no choice if she didn't want her husband to be miserable.

Meanwhile, she was perfectly content looking after the clients at Sage Consulting, many of whom were planning their retirements. Euphemia was becoming adept at succession planning and coaching the next generation into family businesses. Not that they needed coaching. They were so keen to develop and improve on the previous generation's hard work. She was pleased Kenneth wasn't ready to embark on their own succession plan, but she hadn't expected he would start a business with Roger, his best friend, and exclude her from their plans. Let it go Euphemia, she told herself for the zillionth time, but it was a hard thing to do.

It was later in the afternoon when Euphemia heard a knock on her door and looked up.

'I'm leaving,' Jane said. 'Stress, I can't cope. Besides, I have a hair appointment. Alastair said he will look after reception.'

Euphemia, her mind focused on a problem in the station accounts, had nodded without thinking. Jane had turned away when Euphemia called her back. 'I'm sorry about before,' she said. 'You're my friend and I do want you to be happy.'

Jane, her bottom lip quivering, smiled weakly.

'I have an idea,' Euphemia said. 'Why don't you come with me to visit Joe at Oakhill? Kenneth and I usually go together, but he's not here and it would be nice to spend time with you away from the office. On second thoughts I'll be doing the accounts, but Joe can show you the station.'

'Didn't his wife run away with their manager?' asked Jane, visibly brightening.

'Either the manager or the head shepherd - I can never remember.'

'Definitely the manager,' replied Jane. 'It was hot gossip at the Golf Club. That poor man.' She nibbled her bottom lip. 'I've seen photos, and he's very good looking, isn't he? And rich.' Jane sat down in the chair opposite Euphemia. Is he still single?'

'Yes and he is comfortable, not rich,' Euphemia said. 'His money is tied up in the farms, which are locked up in family trusts. He and Arthur, his younger brother, owns half of the station each,' she added.

'No children?' said Jane.

'Joe doesn't have any, but Arthur does. Two I think.'

'And they're all beneficiaries of the trusts?'

Euphemia shifted in her chair. 'That's privileged information. Look, I'll understand if you don't want to come. It will be boring stuck out in the country. Not much to do for a city girl like you.'

'No. I'll come,' said Jane. 'To keep you company. I know what it's like to be abandoned.'

'I haven't been abandoned.'

'They aren't here, are they?' Jane stood up. 'Besides, I know you. You'll bury yourself in the work if Kenneth isn't there. I'll cook, that is, unless Joe has staff... which he probably does, so I won't...' Jane giggled. 'An old station homestead, which has been in the family for generations. I can picture it now - deep wooden verandas, a country kitchen with an Aga, of course. There will be an enormous dining room with a table big enough to seat twenty. The drawing room at the front of the house will be full of saggy sofas and raggedy armchairs, paintings of ancestors, rugs and antiques. I bet there's lots of silver. The upstairs bedrooms will have feather quilts and four-poster beds and the loos will have pull chains and be down the hall. I bet there's a big overgrown garden.' She paused and bit her bottom lip. 'I had a garden, the work I put into my borders. You never saw them, did you?'

'You never invited me.'

'Yes, I should have. Sorry. Blame Justin. He didn't like you and now I know why. You always saw straight through him. Anyway,' she paused. 'Oakhill - there'll be a vast lawn, probably a tennis court and definitely a pool. There has to be. All those big stations have them. The best thing is I can wear my jewels and not feel like I'm showing off. This is going to be such fun. Thank you.'

'You're welcome. I'm looking forward to having you there.'

Jane stopped at the door. 'I have to tell Alastair the good news.' She clapped her hands together. 'Joe Kincaide. Think what this will mean.' Jane had skipped down the hall.

Euphemia woke with a start, sending the laptop on her knees, sliding off the bed and onto the floor with a thud. A cool breeze wafted through the open window along with the sound of a ruru, the little New Zealand owl hooting softly in a tree over by the sheds. Maori believed the ruru has special powers and comes to warn and protect those it guards. She smiled, knowing it was there, and reached down to pick up the laptop and put it on the bedside table. Next door - all was quiet. It was a mystery to her why Jane never snored between four thirty and six thirty in the morning. The window of opportunity was small, but it was reliable. Euphemia turned off the light burrowed under the duvet and went to sleep.

CHAPTER 3

'I'm going to be sick. You have to pull over.'

It was the second time Jane reported feeling unwell on the drive over the steep and winding Remutaka Hill road. It was the second time Euphemia had pulled over to the shoulder and stopped the car. Jane had insisted on sitting in the back seat 'to be a comfort to Petal' so Euphemia considered she had brought the nausea largely upon herself. The problem could also have been the tiny three-door sedan. Better suited to city streets, the little car made hard work of the hills and it wasn't great on corners, worse if you were sitting in the back seat. Jane refused to be told. The fourteen kilometres of tight bends hugging the hillside as the road first climbed then just as rapidly descended 550 meters was the problem, not where she sat.

'I wouldn't have come if I'd known. It's the car,' she added. 'It's just too small. Kevin had a lovely big car. Dan drove a Land Cruiser. I'm not used to being this close to the ground.'

'Why drive a gas-guzzler if you don't have to? Think about the environment,' said Euphemia.

'Environment, phooey. Look around. Trees as far as you can see. New Zealand is the greenest country in the world. Everyone says so.'

'Maybe, but it won't stay that way if we all drive monster cars which pump carbon dioxide into the atmosphere.'

'You are so preachy. You were like that at school,' Jane said, the color slowly returning to her face. 'I do my bit. I recycle. I walk to work.'

'You walk because it's close and because you don't have a car.'

'Maybe if my employer paid me more, I could afford a car.'

Suddenly, a white Volvo hatch rounded the corner almost on two wheels, and veered towards them. Jane, clutching Petal to her chest, ducked down and braced for impact. Just in time, the driver, a woman wearing huge sunglasses, yanked the wheel and pulled her car back to the centerline to make the corner. Jane sat up and together they watched open-mouthed as she swerved wildly around the next sharp bend and disappeared.

'Now there's someone who doesn't care about the environment,' said Jane, letting Petal go.

THE SMALL TOWN of Featherston and the gateway to the Wairarapa sits at the base of the Remutaka range. In the old days, coaches and trains used to stop there for refreshments before carrying on with their journeys north. As travel became easier, fewer people stopped. Recent efforts by the locals to smarten up century old buildings were paying off. Several of the shops stocked a charming variety of food and collectibles. There were cafes with excellent coffee and a playground for bored children. A farmer's market on Saturday mornings had grown in popularity, such that customers would travel from the neighbouring villages to take advantage of the variety of fresh fruit and vegetables on offer.

Some enterprising inhabitants had worked hard to rebrand Featherston as a Booktown. There was now a plethora of bookshops selling old and new books, a festival held each year in May/June drew readers and writers from all over the country.

Euphemia stopped the car outside a row of old wooden shops shaded by verandas over the footpath.

'C'est Cheese'. The best cheese shop in New Zealand,' she announced, pointing to an oak door set back between two white painted bay windows. 'We'll get the bread at the bakery in Martinborough. They make the best baguettes and pastries, but we'll buy the cheese here. Joe likes Stilton, so we always stop on our way to Oakhill.'

'I like Stilton too,' said Jane, undoing her seatbelt and pushing the passenger seat forwards out of her way. 'This is getting spooky, right?'

'What do you mean?'

'Joe. Me. We have so much in common.' She smiled and ran her fingers through her light brown hair. Euphemia noted the recent cut and color, done yesterday after she left work. The length below her ears suited her and showed off her diamond cluster earrings. The Breton t-shirt, the Hermes scarf knotted at her neck, the casual above ankle jeans and loafers complimented her slim body. It was good to see her looking as she did in the old days, before Justin died. Back then, Jane had been the envy of her friends, not only for the style she injected into everyday outfits but for the smart way she matched her clothes with the right piece of jewelry from the collection left to her by her mother. The fire had destroyed most of her clothes, but thankfully her jewelry had survived. Judicious purchases on vintage sites and a regular military-like patrol of the local op shops had returned her wardrobe to its pre blaze-splendour.

Before Euphemia could tell her how nice she looked, Jane climbed out of the car. She adjusted her trousers and, without waiting, pushed open the heavy door of the cheese shop and went in.

'I was going to suggest we take you for a walk first,' said Euphemia, reaching back to fondle behind the pug's ears. Petal harrumphed, put her head down and closed her eyes. 'Or not.'

Inside, the shop was cool; the lighting dimmed. A series of softly lit glass cabinets filled with cheeses of all shapes and sizes occupied one side and hanging above the cabinets were skinny and fat salamis, dried cheeses, and bunches of aromatic herbs. The wooden floorboards creaked under foot just as they had reacted to customers for over a hundred years. On the other side of the shop, narrow wooden shelves stocked with jars of delicacies sourced locally and from overseas lined the walls. If something tasted delicious, it was here. In the rear, a glass window looked into the cold room where the largest cheeses were stacked on metal shelves. Jane was standing at the counter, sampling small cubes of Gouda on toothpicks. She nodded at Euphemia and pointed, 'It's so good. Get some of this as well. Joe will love it.'

'How can you say that? You don't know him.'

Jane smiled mysteriously. 'Trust me. I have the strongest feeling Joe and I have more in common than even you would suspect. Buy the Gouda. You won't regret it.'

Euphemia did as she was told. It was easier and she wouldn't hear the end of it otherwise. While the woman behind the counter was retrieving a block from the cabinet, she surveyed the shelves behind her picking up several packets of crackers, a tin of local olives and a bottle of truffle infused olive oil and putting them in a pile on the counter along with a length of venison salami. The woman, Sally, told her it was made locally from farmed deer. From the cabinet Euphemia chose a brie from Canterbury and a tub of dill-laced Drunken Nanny goat cheese. Sally recommended they would go well with a fig log and quince jelly, so she added these to the pile. Finally she selected an English Stilton and waited while the woman sliced a thick wedge from the round, weighed it and wrapped it in waxed paper. She hadn't meant to buy so much, but she justified her extravagance by telling herself this was a holiday as much as a work trip. She had just tapped her card on the machine to pay when she heard screaming outside on the footpath.

'Stop. Give that back. It's mine.'

She looked out to see Jane wrestling with a young man wearing a dark hoodie, low-slung jeans and high tops, the laces undone. The car door gaped open beside them. Petal had stirred herself to peer through the window, her goldfish eyes black in alarm. The man had Jane's handbag under one arm while she clung to his other arm as he tried to push her away. On the road a car slowed, the passenger pointing, staring open-mouthed as she passed by. From, the garage across the road, a man called out something unintelligible but threatening while he waited for a break in the traffic to come across to help. The thief gave Jane one almighty heave, sending her backwards, but still she didn't let go. Right then his low-slung jeans turned traitor and slid down over his skinny hips. He tripped, falling sideways towards the shop window, taking her with him.

Euphemia was out the door. In one swift movement, she whisked the handbag off his shoulder and hauled on his hoody to swing them both away from the glass. She pushed Jane back and knocked her attacker face down on to the pavement. Euphemia knelt beside him. 'Don't move,' she said.

'Or what?' he said, struggling to yank up his trousers and

saggy underwear to cover the pale hairy buttocks which were on display for all to see.

'Or this.' Euphemia obliged with helping tug and he recoiled as the crutch of his trousers jammed up between his legs.

'And this,' she added, gripping him hard around the elbow of his right arm and digging her fingers into the nerve. He howled with pain and stopped struggling, a look of astonishment on his face when his arm flopped powerless by his side.

Sally came out to ask if Euphemia needed any help, adding, 'The cops are on their way. The station is around the corner across the railway line,' she said, pointing. 'Two minutes' walk. Can I get you anything?'

Euphemia readjusted her position and her grip on the young man. 'I was going to order a coffee before I got interrupted. Don't suppose you could manage a long black to go?'

'Make that two,' added Jane. 'I don't appreciate having my bag stolen,' she said, bending over and poking the guy in the back to emphasize each word.

'I don't appreciate you poking me,' came the muffled reply. 'I have my rights. As soon as Eliza gets here, I will tell her to charge you women with assault.'

'She will do no such thing. Eliza is the policewoman,' Sally explained. 'You're kneeling on Daryl Matthews, Featherston's own village idiot. And because you saved my window, the coffees on me. I'm still trying to figure out how you moved so fast.'

'Me too.' It was the man from across the road. 'I've never seen anything like it.'

'I run a lot,' Euphemia said.

'Oh.' The man sounded unsure. Euphemia was hoping she wouldn't have to go into details when Daryl started whining.

'You're for it too, Sally. I'll tell Eliza you defamed me.'

Euphemia pinched the nerve a little harder, and Daryl yelped. Sally sighed loudly and went back inside the shop. The man from the garage waited to make sure he was no longer needed. Hands in his pockets, he sauntered back across the road.

A few minutes later Eliza arrived. She tsked when she saw Daryl. Bulked up in her stab-proof vest, and wearing navy blue loose-fitting trousers and solidly unflattering black lace-ups, she crouched down beside him. 'Not again, mate,' she said. 'This is the third time this month. Why do you do it? You get caught every time.' She straightened up. 'Let him go,' she said to Euphemia. 'You'll come quietly, won't you?' She nudged the prostrate Daryl with her foot.

He got up slowly, rubbing his right elbow and flexing his fingers, all the while sending accusing looks at Euphemia.

'Stand over there,' ordered the policewoman. 'And don't run like you did last time or I will have to Taser you. Like I did last time. Now ladies, I need your names and contact details.' Daryl pulled his hood up and over his face and slumped against the corner of the building, waited with his arms crossed in front of him.

Eliza took her notebook out of her pocket and looked expectantly from Jane to Euphemia.

'I need to pay,' said Euphemia, and she ducked back inside the shop, leaving Jane to give her the required information.

* * *

LATER, as she slowed the car to look at an enormous billboard standing alone in the middle of a paddock, Euphemia said, 'You didn't need to say we were passing through on our way to an emergency.'

'She would have made us come to the station to give our statements otherwise,' said Jane. 'We would have been there all afternoon. I'd rather be with Joe. I know we're going to be soul mates and I don't want to waste time with unnecessary form filling. She's got our contact details. Sally saw what happened. That's all she needs. Why have we stopped in the middle of the road?'

'That,' said Euphemia, pointing. A huge billboard had been erected at the bottom of a paddock. It featured a grey-haired couple wearing hiking clothes. They were standing in sunshine in a patch of native bush, looking adoringly at a pair of tui in a kowhai tree in full bloom.

Jane read aloud, *"Live the rest of your best life at the Oakhill Sanctuary Estate. Give back before you give up. Advanced Care Ward Available. Properties selling now. Contact Arthur Kincaide."* A phone number followed.

'Give back before you give up?' Who wrote the marketing, the grim reaper?' asked Jane. 'Why would anyone want to spend their last days out here in the middle of nowhere?'

'Because of that,' said Euphemia, pointing to an area of dense bush behind a high fence.

'What is it?'

'That,' said Euphemia, 'is Joe's pride and joy. It is the Oakhill Sanctuary. And probably the reason Charlotte left him. I'm surprised you haven't heard of it. He's a conservationist, but I don't need to tell you, his soul-mate that. He has plans to return all of Oakhill Station to how it was before his great-great-grandfather arrived and burned off the bush. Behind that fence is Stage One, and it has cost an absolute truckload of money.'

'Oh.'

'But when you truly love native plants and birds, the cost is irrelevant. Right?'

'Right. The bush. The birds. Trees. And bushes. Flax is

great too. Joe and I are on the same page when it comes to nature.'

'Sure?'

Jane nodded.

'Then you just might be his soul mate, after all. Arthur, however, is less into conservation and more into making money by the looks of that sign.' Euphemia drove a short distance and stopped in front of a pair of tall iron gates with Oakhill Station emblazoned across them in peeling gold lettering. The gates swung open silently in front of the car. She drove through and they closed again.

'How did that happen?'

'Joe programmed the gate to recognize my number plate. He loves gadgets.'

'Of course he does. We both do. We love native trees and native birds and stuff. I love tech and gadgets. So does he. And we both adore Stilton and Gouda.'

'Didn't Kezia have to show you how to work the remote on your smart TV?'

'She helped, sure, but I've done it since. Without Justin around, I've had to figure out a lot of things. You'd be surprised.'

A single lane limestone drive curved up the hill in front of them. It was littered with acorns dropped from the oak trees still in their summer green, which formed a shaded arch. After driving a short distance, Euphemia registered a flash of red between two tree trunks higher up the hill, but it was gone before she could work out what it was. The courting calls of cicadas and the noise of the acorns crunching beneath her tires almost obscured the sounds of gravel and dirt hitting the grass verge. She had time to swerve the car off the road and prevent the collision, but that was all. A red Tesla S swooped over the rise and sped straight past where her car had been only seconds before.

In her rear vision mirror, she saw the Tesla's rear lights come on as the driver braked, before he reversed quickly to stop alongside her. Joe Kincaide lowered the passenger window, took off his aviator sunglasses and elbow resting on the door smiled at her. Age had been kind to Joe, enhancing the good looks he carried from his youth. Lightly tanned, his thick grey hair swept back over the top of his head to fall into line at the top of his neck. His broad shoulders and slim physique were a testament to not only his healthy diet, but to regular daily exercise and his undisputed masculinity.

'That was close,' he said. 'Sorry.'

'Good to see you too,' she replied. 'You're not slowing down in your old age, I see.'

'As we're the same age, I'd hold back on your ageist comments if I were you Mrs Sage. Haven't switched to an EV yet? When you do, get one of these. Marvelous cars. Go like the clappers, especially in the insane mode. Here is the only place I can let rip. On the open road, there's always some moron in a people-mover smugly driving at 50 mph believing they're saving the planet by holding everybody else up.'

Jane, stuck in the back seat, was struggling to undo her seat belt. She pulled herself forward and wedged her face between Euphemia and the open window. 'I'm Jane French,' she called, ducking around so Joe could see her. 'I'm here to help. You have a beautiful... '

'Joan, is it?' said Joe. 'Righty ho. Good to meet you Joan.' He turned to Euphemia. 'Sorry, but something's come up at the Lake farm. I have to go over and sort it out. I'll be away tonight, maybe tomorrow as well. You don't mind, do you? As I said, in my email, it's pretty straightforward. Hardly worth you coming all this way.'

'Of course I don't mind,' Euphemia replied. 'I know where everything is. We'll look after ourselves and I'll have the accounts ready by the time you get back.'

'Excellent. I knew I could rely on you. Right, I'll be off,' he said, replacing his sunglasses. 'See you the day after tomorrow. You saw the sign? Bloody Arthur has jumped the gun. We can talk about it when I get back. Good to meet you, Joan.' He wound up the window and was gone - the red car disappearing behind a cloud of lime dust and crushed acorns.

CHAPTER 4

'This isn't it. It can't be,' Jane said. 'This is a hill with a door in it. It looks like we have arrived in Hobbiton.'

'This is it,' replied Euphemia, turning off the engine and getting out of the car. She stretched and took a deep breath of fresh country air, then popped the hatch, grabbed their bags and deposited them in front of luminous lime green door flanked by two stark black ceramic urns.

'But, but... where is the homestead? Where is Oakhill House?'

'Joe doesn't live there. He lives here.'

'You said he lived at Oakhill House.'

'I didn't. I said he lives at Oakhill Station. Which is here. He lives in the New House and this is the New House.'

'So he doesn't live in the homestead where the Queen Mother stayed? Where royalty always stays when they come to the Wairarapa?'

'You're thinking of the family homestead. The house Joe's great-great-grandfather built in the 1860s—that Oakhill House,' said Euphemia. 'Joe moved out after Charlotte left.

But that wasn't his main reason. He's always wanted something smaller and easier to look after, something modern and eco-friendly. His brother Arthur and his family live in the homestead now. They moved in when they got back from Hong Kong, so it's worked out well for everybody. Come on, we've got a lot to do.'

'But... but...,'

Euphemia didn't wait to hear what Jane was going to say. She picked up their bags and, leaning on the perfectly counter-balanced front door, which swung back when she put her weight on it, went inside. Jane had no choice but to follow. Petal, asleep on the back seat, didn't notice she was alone until the sound of a dog barking in the distance woke her. She opened one eye, sniffed the air and, finding nothing of interest tickling her nose, went back to sleep.

The view of the Ponatahi Valley below the house greeted Euphemia as she walked down five wide stone steps taking her from the entrance hall into the living area. As always, she had to stop on the bottom step to take in the beauty of countryside spread out in all its glory in front of her. It was late summer and the grass on the surrounding hillsides had dried off to a muted golden-brown, a colour which reminded her of the fur on her childhood teddy bear.

Built with no expense spared, the New House had floor to ceiling triple-glazed doors and windows on the front walls on both floors. The rear of the house had been constructed into the hillside for both stability and insulation. The green door, the only clue the house was house there. Joe ensured trees planted around the farm offset the carbon used during the build.

Every room top and bottom except for the service areas opened on to two balconies, running the length of the house - vertical shutters screening them were retractable in winter to let the sun in. Racks of solar panels fenced off from the goats provided the house with power. Toru and Wha, two very surly goats, keep the sward on the roof, manageable. It was the beginning of a dry autumn and thankfully they weren't there when Euphemia and Jane arrived. Last year, Wha had tried unsuccessfully to butt her as she unpacked the car. She hoped Joe had locked them in a paddock, out of butting distance.

A dedicated solar panel on the roof of the garage powered the Tesla. Joe used the car for town trips and fun drives. 'I'm pragmatic. I'm not a fanatic,' he explained when Euphemia and Kenneth queried the diesel flatbed truck and the ATV parked beside the shiny fire-engine red car.

A spring-fed creek running down the shallow valley between the two houses provided water, via gigantic tanks sunk into the hill higher up. Food waste went to Toru and Wha or along with the organic waste, was composted and stored until Joe removed it once a year for UV treatment. It returned to the farm as fertilizer.

'A man living alone doesn't produce much rubbish,' James said. 'I can only wear one jersey at a time, one pair of pants, one pair of boots.' Euphemia had kept silent rather than point out that each item of clothing he wore was made from the finest cloth and the strongest of leathers. They always looked brand new and were thus unlikely to wear out. 'I'm a man of few needs or desires,' he said. 'The smaller the footprint I leave behind on this tired old planet of ours, the better.'

Jane stomped head down through the front door but looked up when she came to the steps. Her eyes widened when she saw the view. 'That is incredible,' she said. 'And this is a beautiful room.' Descending the steps, she circumnavigated the long room, her fingers brushing black marble kitchen counter-tops, and running along the backs of two long sofas positioned to face each other in the middle section. She had noted the Scandinavian dining table and chairs before stopping in front of a painting, which occupied the entire wall at the end of the room. 'That's a...'

'McCahon?' said Euphemia. 'Yes. It's one of them—the rest are downstairs.'

Jane, fingering her chin, regarded it thoughtfully. 'I've always preferred this one,' she said. 'Others say it's not his best, but I like it. I can't wait to see the rest. Modern houses are so much better than old houses. Haven't I always said that? They're elegant and how shall I put it? Considered.'

'Considered is an excellent description. Well done Joan,' said Euphemia. 'Come on, this way. Let's unpack and then I'll organize dinner. I'm starving.' She led the way downstairs, carrying their bags. 'Take your pick,' she said in the hall, which ran the length of the back of the house downstairs, the bedrooms opening from it. 'You choose.'

There were three guest bedrooms, and they were all the same—large enough to accommodate a queen sized bed, a wardrobe, and each had an en suite bathroom. Euphemia dumped Jane's bag on her bed before she realized she'd lost her. Retracing her steps, she found her in the master bedroom admiring the view from the balcony. 'I don't think we should be in here. Invading a man's privacy when he's not here to defend it is not appropriate.'

'I'm only looking. You can be so old-fashioned.' Jane followed her out of the bedroom, Euphemia firmly shutting the door behind them.

'It's bacon and egg pie for dinner tonight,' said Euphemia when they met back upstairs. 'I had one in the freezer at home and thought it would save cooking.' She put the dish in the oven and set the controls to reheat. 'And I brought this,' she said, holding up a bottle of chardonnay.

'Now you're talking,' said Jane, searching for and finding glasses in a cupboard.

They ate the pie sitting side by side at the table looking

down the valley, the changing colors as the land progressed into darkness, absorbing their attention and making conversation unnecessary.

'Petal! I forgot Petal.' Euphemia leapt up and ran out to the car. Petal, an accusing look on her face, allowed herself to be picked up and carried inside. Then she allowed herself to be fed and watered. When Euphemia brought her dog bed inside and put it down on the concrete floor, still warm from the day's sunshine, Petal stepped into it, turned three times and curled up with her back to Euphemia. It had been an exhausting day.

CHAPTER 5

Euphemia opened one eye, then shut it quickly to protect her retina from a mushroom blast of morning sunshine. She groaned and pulled a pillow over her face. 'What time is it?'

'It's late. A quarter to seven,' said Jane. 'I made tea.'

'I've only just got to sleep.'

'Don't be silly. You're normally at the office by now.'

'I normally sleep the night before.'

Jane put the mug on the bedside table and plumped down companionably on the side of the bed. 'I didn't sleep well either. It's the silence. You can't get away from it.'

'You could have fooled me,' muttered Euphemia, throwing off the pillow and hauling herself into a sitting position.

'I mean it. I've been awake half the night expecting to hear something—a siren, a rubbish truck, a street sweeper - normal night sounds.' Jane wrinkled her brow. 'I heard a possum, though. They're everywhere making their creepy crak-crak-crak sounds. Why you don't we see possums in daylight?'

Euphemia lifted the mug to her lips, the hot tea a godsend, and opened her eyes. 'What on earth are you wearing?'

'Running clothes.' Jane stood up and did a twirl. She was wearing hot pink trainers, little pink pompoms attached to her socks rested pertly on the backs of her shoes, pink leopard, spotted leggings and a matching singlet under a bright pink and white striped jacket. She accessorized the outfit with diamond earrings and an array of rings on the fingers of both hands.

'But you don't run.'

'I do. I started a month ago. You should keep in shape as you get older, use or lose it, I've always said.' She stood up and started jogging on the spot. 'Come on. Get your gear on. You can't stay in bed on such a beautiful morning.'

'But I run alone.'

'You don't have to now, do you? I can keep you company. We can chat, talk over any problems you're having at the office, and plan the day. Anything you want to share, I'm here for you. Kenneth has left you and you can't shoulder the burden of Sage Consulting all by yourself. It's not fair. I've been reading the business magazines in reception. Did you know that the most successful CEOs exercise in the mornings? It helps them strategize.' She stopped jogging and waggled a finger at Euphemia. 'But we won't get any strategizing done if you stay in bed.' She collected the now empty mug and jogged out of the room.

Euphemia had never looked forward to a run less. Runs were her alone time. Her me-time. They always had been. Before the onset of her superpowers, before the girls were born, before she met and married Kenneth, before university, way back when she was living with Aunt Maree, and school bullies were making her life hell, she had taken up running. In the mornings. Alone. When she got older and the girls were at school, she tried to fit another run in later in the day. Alone.

The endorphin release was part of the attraction, but the rest was pure selfishness. A run gave her time to let her mind wander to whatever she wanted to think about that day, and she guarded this time with herself.

The trails in the bush reserves behind their Thorndon home gave her a place to connect with nature - to ground herself on the planet. She was forever grateful to the far-sighted Wellingtonians who had saved corridors of native bush from development. Introduced predators like Jane's hated possums and rats, mice, stoats, weasels, even hedgehogs were slowly being eliminated and as a result native trees had regenerated and the native bird population was thriving. It was this mutual love of the New Zealand bush and its wildlife which had brought Joe Kincaide and Euphemia together at university. Because of this connection, when he inherited Oakhill Station, he asked Sage Consulting to help manage his affairs.

For the past ten years, Joe had worked tirelessly to establish his sanctuary. Charlotte, his wife, had been less than impressed. At the outset, she attributed the time and money dedicated to his passion as a passing phase. 'He's always had them,' she told Euphemia when she phoned to have another sizeable sum transferred into her personal account. 'Remember when he took up ballooning and had to be rescued after he got blown halfway to South America?'

Euphemia remembered.

'And the time he got lost on the car rally in the Australian desert and we didn't hear from him for a month?'

Euphemia remembered that too.

'This whole save the planet buzz is another one of his mad ideas. He'll stop when he finds something new to distract him. He'd better because there's only so many dead possums left lying about the place a girl can stomach.'

Two months after this conversation, Charlotte made good with her threat and ran away with the station manager. The relationship didn't last and Euphemia heard later that Charlotte had moved to Australia. She thought it a pity because, despite their differences, Charlotte and Joe worked as a couple. Joe had loved his wife. Her betrayal hurt him deeply. To cope with his pain, he devoted even more time and money to the sanctuary, which meant his farm and associated business interests suffered. It was only when Arthur and Allie returned from Hong Kong and he had people to talk to that he seemed to take any notice of what was happening. Kenneth told him he hoped it wasn't too late.

'Arthur and Ally,' said Kenneth. 'They never struck me as a couple who would consciously choose to live in the country. Not after the bright lights of Hong Kong.'

'I thought that too,' said Joe, helping himself to a second hefty gin. 'But they seem happy about it. He says he can work anywhere as long as he has access to the Internet.'

'What does he do exactly?' asked Kenneth.

'Money, property, shares that sort of thing. Financial gobble-de-gook. God, I don't know. Done well, whatever it is. He wasn't much use on the farm when he was a kid. Accident-prone. Not good with his hands.'

They were again sitting in the big comfy armchairs looking out over the tennis court to the trees. The sun had suddenly set, the autumn chill descending with a thump. 'Dinner is in the kitchen tonight. I know you won't mind.' Joe finished his gin and got up. 'There's a pair of kaka nesting in the sanctuary, you know. They arrived at the beginning of the year.' He had smiled and headed off to the kitchen shaking his head as if he couldn't believe his good luck.

Euphemia got out of bed and pulled on her cool weather running gear. It was the same as her hot weather gear, but it had sleeves and was thicker. Just in case, she added a vest. She always wore the same black merino top and leggings, black socks, trainers and a black wool vest, preferring to stick to the tried and true rather than indulge in the latest fashion. She sent Kenneth a quick text saying she was missing him and that she was off for a run—in case he called straight back. A quick glance at her inbox made her wish she hadn't bothered. Twenty-five messages. They could all wait.

Jane was nowhere to be found when Euphemia went upstairs. Petal had moved from her basket to a patch of sunshine on the floor in front of the window. She didn't get up when she saw Euphemia, just raised one eyebrow, yawned and shut her eyes.

'Don't think you're going to lie there all day, Petal Sage,' Euphemia said, bending down to stroke her head. 'You're going for a walk later.' Petal shuddered.

'Joe has a brilliant composting system,' said Jane, coming in through the back door. 'I would have one, but living in an apartment in the middle of Wellington means it's not worthwhile.'

'You could have a worm farm. There are small ones designed especially for apartments.'

'What would I do with the stuff from the worms?'

'Give it to me to put on my garden.'

'Good idea. I might discuss it with Joe when he gets back. He'll know the best one to buy.'

'Or you could ask me. I've had a worm farm for years.'

'I'll ask him if you don't mind.'

'I don't mind at all,' said Euphemia, holding the front door open. Jane broke into a slow jog as soon as she left the house and they set off down the drive. Running together felt more comfortable than Euphemia had expected. Maybe this could work after all, she thought as they reached the halfway mark.

CHAPTER 6

Euphemia keyed the code into the pad beside
the station gates. A door in the wall swung open. Jane wiped
away the sweat dripping into her eyes and went through first.
Directly across the road were the padlocked gates of the sanctuary bearing a sign, which read 'Private Property - Keep
Out'.

'Let's run around the perimeter,' said Euphemia, pointing
to one side of the mesh fence as it snaked up and over the hill
opposite. 'It's challenging, but it's fun. Lots of ups and
downs. Fifteen k's so it won't take long.'

'Give me a minute,' Jane panted. 'I need to check my
laces.'

Euphemia jogged backwards and forwards across the road,
while Jane methodically untied and retied her laces, then stood
up again. 'Cross-country running is something I could be very
good at,' she said, swinging her arms in a horizontal arc over
her hips. 'There's something about the fresh air. It is so good
for the lungs.'

Euphemia coughed to stifle her laughter.

'I heard that,' Jane said. 'Typical. I'm supporting you and

you don't support me. You wonder why you don't have any friends. Run by yourself. I know you want to. I'll go this way. By myself.' Without waiting to hear what Euphemia might say, Jane made a ninety-degree turn and jogged down the road towards town.

There was no point in going after her. Okay, so she laughed when she shouldn't have - so what? Jane didn't need to press the nuclear button. If anyone has the right to be offended, it's me, thought Euphemia feeling offended. I have friends. She doesn't know them, but I do. That's what matters. I don't see them very often because of work, but I have friends.

The sudden urge to run as fast and as far as her super-powered legs would go overtook her. She was now so tightly wound up she was afraid she would burst if she couldn't get rid of her pent-up energy. She checked to make sure Jane had already crossed the brow of the hill and was out of sight. To be absolutely sure no one would see her, Euphemia ran slowly beside the fence until she couldn't see the road. As soon as she crested the hill and was safe from prying eyes she let rip, rocketing down the steep slope into the next gully, her legs a blur as she leapt rocks and vaulted gaps in the trail where the earth had fallen away under the feet of one hundred years of grazing sheep. She zoomed past the top of the sanctuary, up the hill and down into the next gully where the grass had given up growing two months before. She kept running on dry dirt until she stopped on the summit and turned around to see a cloud of dust suspended in the air behind her.

Normally she wouldn't have minded, but at this height her trail and black silhouette would be visible to anyone driving by. That there were no vehicles on the road was a relief. The stock had been moved off the paddocks weeks ago, which meant there was no reason for farm workers to be out and about. That only left the sanctuary. She had no way of knowing if anyone was inside or if they had seen her. She listened for voices and footsteps in the bush, but heard nothing.

It is what it is; she rationalized. But vowed not to be so careless in future. The freedom to use her super powers depended on her remaining anonymous. Not for her, the flashy capes, latex body armor or the cinched waist bodysuits of your comic book female super heroes. She could think of nothing worse than having to find a place to change each time her services were called upon. In the movies, the transformation to superhero happened by CGI. This was the real world. She had to make do with the every-day clothes an ordinary fifty-four-year-old woman would wear. Plus, she was too old to wear latex, let alone anything with a cinched waist. One benefit of the powers being activated at menopause - there were no stupid costumes - just running gear and comfortable shoes. The invisibility attached to middle-aged women who, in almost every culture, are routinely under-estimated and over-looked, provided the only cover she needed. Anonymity had protected her ancestors' exploits and as a result, they lived well-balanced lives.

The widespread adoption of smartphones irrevocably changed the odds of remaining undetected. Euphemia simply had to be more careful. There was no point in her cursing the technology or the social media platforms disseminating videos worldwide; she had to accept and work with the reality. Despite her senses being tuned to the infinitesimally sensitive end of the scale, despite super-strong muscles and lightning fast reflexes, despite her healing abilities and despite having superpowers she still didn't know she possessed, she had to act as normally as possible. She had to be who she was: a fifty-four-year-old business consultant, a wife and the mother of two grown daughters, who lived in a pleasant suburb in Wellington, New Zealand and who enjoyed long distance running. Until she needed to use her super powers, when she had to be as discrete as it was possible to be.

Jimmy Abrahams had not been the only threat to her anonymity encountered in the last year. Her ex-receptionist's father, a man with so many aliases he didn't have a name, had been on her trail for years. A geneticist, he changed his identity as often as she changed her socks. He had inveigled his way into her mother's life to study her genetic make-up after she let slip the family secret when she was drunk.

Known throughout the nightclubs of Europe as Wild Freddie, her mother ran away from her home in New Zealand as soon as she had turned eighteen, determined to wring the most out of life. Gorgeously beautiful, tall and uninhibited, she earned her living as a model featuring in the glossy magazines of the day. It was a surprise to everyone, including Freddie, when she gave birth to a daughter. The identity of the child's father was never revealed. Freddie's lifestyle caught up with her, her modeling work dried up and after three years, she could no longer support herself, let alone a child. She returned to New Zealand, left her daughter on her sister Maree's front step and, without a word, went back to Europe. Euphemia's earliest memory was standing alone, clutching Ducky and waiting for the door to open.

Freddie died when Euphemia was still at school. Initially Maree kept the details of her death confidential, judging correctly that Euphemia's feelings about her mother were too raw.

In her will, Maree instructed the family solicitor to send a series of letters to Euphemia on significant birthdays. These revealed as much as Maree knew about the powers. Freddie, according to the coroner's report, died in a car accident in Coldsham, a village in Warwickshire in the United Kingdom. There were rumors she had been drinking, but the post-mortem reported no alcohol in her system. A mysterious puncture mark on her arm was noted, for which there was no explanation. They had buried Freddie in the churchyard in Coldsham. One day, Euphemia planned to visit her mother's grave and find out as much as she could about her death and the man who she suspected had caused it.

In the meantime, she had accounts to audit. She jogged steadily down the hill at what she considered to be a normal middle-aged woman's pace until she reached the cover of the trees and the fence line. She stopped and listened again for anyone inside the sanctuary. Silence. A relief, but strange there was no birdsong. This early in the morning, any self-respecting bird sanctuary would have been alive with the sounds of birds marking out their territories, calling to their neighbors and mates, as they decided what they were going to eat that day and where. The morning chorus should be ringing around the valley, but the only noise was from the road.

Below her, a school bus rumbled up the rise and stopped outside the station gates. Euphemia watched a young boy, dwarfed by a huge backpack, climb on board. The other kids jostled him as he made his way to a seat at the rear. As the bus jerked into gear and drove off. She saw him sitting alone staring forlornly out the window.

A single fantail darted in front of her face, and she reared back. It chirped and swooped around her head flicking its tail this way and that with the skill of a Parisian courtesan. It flew down the inside of the fence and landed on the ground next to a gap in the mesh. Joe had once taken great pains to explain the finer points of predator fence construction. There weren't supposed to be any holes. There wasn't supposed to be a gap at the bottom either, because the mesh was designed to be buried six inches deep into the earth.

She bent down to get a closer look. Someone had cut the thick wires clean through. A pair of standard pliers or wire cutters wouldn't be sharp enough to leave such a clean edge.

Someone had come here with the specific intent to cut such a hole in this type of fence wire. Which meant that person or persons had purposely sabotaged the perimeter. A shallow trench in the dust showed a lever or even a crowbar had been used to bend the cut section of mesh up and out of the way. More concerning were the footprints around the hole —each one leading inside the sanctuary. Small animals had passed this way and so many that the prints overlaid each other. Two caught her attention. One looked like five long skinny toes and the other had four fat pads extending from the back. The first was definitely a rat. She recognized it from similar ones near her compost bin at home. She didn't know what the second one was. She hadn't seen it before, but she offered a silent prayer that it wasn't a ferret or a stoat. Joe hated these animals with a passion bordering on insanity.

She stood up and brushed the dust off her hands. The fantail now sitting on the top of the fence cocked his head and fixed her with a look from a brown eye as if to say, what are you going to do?

It didn't take long to find three large stones in the paddock, stack them against the mesh, then wedge them into place with dirt. She checked to make sure there was no one around, then scaled the twenty-foot fence and dropped down on the other side. The fantail chirruped and darted around her feet before disappearing into the undergrowth as she barricaded the hole from the inside. Back on the outside of the fence, she inspected her work. It wasn't perfect, but it would do until she could organize someone to come up and repair it properly.

The rest of the fence looked intact - all fifteen kilometers of it. She was certain, because she inspected every inch as she ran the perimeter once more and made sure. She was thinking about her first cup of coffee for the day as she was running quietly up the last hill between her and the road when she heard two men arguing.

'You said a hundy.'

'It was a simple job, and you buggered it up.'

'Yeah, well. She wouldn't let go. A hundy or I'll tell.'

'Tell what? To who? Fifty and you're lucky I'm feeling generous.'

There was something about one voice. She'd heard it before and it had grated then, as much as it did now. The speech pattern, the whininess, who was it? Whiny voice muttered something under his breath before he climbed onto a motorbike, kicked it into life and roared off in the same direction as the school bus. By the time she thought it was safe to come out from under the trees, she was alone. The other man had gone.

CHAPTER 7

'Kenneth called,' Jane yelled from the kitchen, where she was drinking coffee and eating toast. 'Your phone was ringing, so I answered it.'

'Thanks,' said Euphemia. She checked the coffeepot. It was empty. 'I'll ring him back after a shower.'

'No need. He said he's fine. They are flying up to the Cameron Highlands with the CEO of something or other. I forget. Anyway, it's not important. They're going to play golf and he'll call when he can.'

'I was looking forward to talking to him.'

Jane shrugged, got up, rinsed her cup under the tap, brushed the crumbs off her plate and put both in the dishwasher. 'He'll call back.'

'I know, it's just... never mind.' Euphemia straightened her shoulders and sighed.

Jane settled back on her stool, licked a finger, and leafed through an *Architectural Digest* magazine. She was in the same place looking at the same magazine when Euphemia returned, ten minutes later showered and dressed for the day. It was nice not to have to wear make-up and a sheer luxury to wear her second best running gear instead of a business suit. Euphemia had never been interested in fashion or her appearance, much to her eldest daughter's disappointment. She had enough smart jackets and trousers to rotate through the days of the week, but she changed out of them as soon as she got home. She only wore make-up at the office - usually a light foundation, mascara and lipstick and only because these were quick to apply and the clients seemed to expect it.

'I'm sorry, okay?'

'You don't need to apologize,' said Jane still not looking up. 'I had a perfectly good run by myself. You were right. We should each do our own thing while we're here.'

Euphemia poured hot water over the coffee and replaced the plunger. 'I'm glad you see it that way. More coffee?'

'That would be very nice, thank you.' Jane put down the magazine. 'I met Ally, Arthur's wife, on my way home. She'd driven her little boy, Joshua, down to catch the bus. I'm invited for drinks this evening.'

'Not me?'

'She hasn't met you.'

'No. But you told her I was here?'

'Actually, your name didn't come up. We didn't speak for long, but I can call and ask. I'm sure she wouldn't mind if you tagged along.'

Euphemia poured two cups of coffee and handed one to Jane. The rich smell of caffeine hit the nerve endings at the top of her nose with a jolt. Dialing down her olfactory sensitivity, she took a sip. 'No, it's okay. I'll stay here and work. There's plenty to do. Speaking of which, shall we get started?'

'Where? I've been through the house from top to bottom and I can't find anything resembling an office?'

'Ah,' Euphemia said. 'Follow me. I will reveal all.' She slung her bag over her shoulder, picked up her coffee and walked over to the bookcase lining the wall at one of end of the living room. Jane and Petal followed. 'Hold this please,' said Euphemia, passing her cup to Jane. She searched the spines of the books on the middle shelf and when she found '*East of Eden*' by John Steinbeck, pulled it down. A section of shelving separated from the others, and silently swung towards them to reveal a room. Euphemia smiled and stood back indicating Jane and Petal should precede her. The book shelf/door swung shut behind them.

They were now standing in a square room at one corner of the house. Floor to ceiling glass windows on two sides met at the apex, making them feel like they were standing on a platform overlooking the valley. Two desks positioned to face each other were in the middle of the room and under them was a huge red oriental carpet spread over oak parquet flooring.

'Is that what I think it is?' Jane was staring at a portrait of a tattooed Maori woman on the back wall hung in a recess, surrounded by yet more books.

'Sorry to disappoint.' Euphemia said. 'That is not a Goldie. It is a Sim.'

'What is a Sim?'

'Karl Sim. He forged remarkably excellent copies of Goldie's work and sold them to unsuspecting buyers. Sadly, the law caught up with him. Convicted of forgery, they sent him to prison. He had duped many people out of a lot of money. His talent could not, however, be denied. When he was released, he changed his name by deed poll to Charles Feodor Goldie. Honesty pays. They accepted his new forgeries signed by the new Goldie for what they were, and now a genuine Sim is worth quite a lot. Not as much as the original Goldie, but enough. You're looking at an original copy of the original. Joe's father commissioned Sim to make a copy of his authentic Goldie, which is on permanent loan to the Auckland Art Gallery.'

'That is my favorite Goldie slash Sim, or is it a Sim slash Goldie?'

'Not sure, but it's mine too,' Euphemia said. 'It's the dignity with which the subject holds her head. How you paint dignity I do not know, but he has done it. I could look at it all day but,' she sighed, 'we have work to do. You take that desk and I'll take this one,' she said, plugging in her laptop. 'I nearly forgot. I have to call Joe.'

Her call went straight to voicemail, so she left a message. 'Hi Joe, I found a hole in the fence this morning. It's been there a few days, by the looks of it. Would you get back to me with the details of who I should call to get it repaired?' She hung up and opened her laptop.

'That's not good,' said Jane.

'It's not. I saw rat tracks too, maybe a ferret.'

'Dan hated ferrets,' Jane said. 'And rats. He said they breed so quickly that once they get a foothold somewhere, they're really hard to get rid of. Disgusting fact. A mother ferret will mate with her male offspring if there are no other males around.'

'That is disgusting. See those files on the shelf under the painting,' Euphemia said, swiveling around in her chair to point to them. 'Would you start at A-E and go through the invoices, putting them in order of payment? April, then May and so on. I'll go through the bank statements.'

They worked for two hours, each one concentrating on their separate tasks until Euphemia's, then Jane's nose wrinkled and they looked up. Petal lay sound asleep under the desk.

'That much smell from such a small dog.' Jane said fanning her nose and standing up. Petal, oblivious to the disruption she'd caused, snuffled and stretched but didn't open her eyes. 'How do we get out of here?'

Euphemia searched the bookcase, found 'Westward Ho'

by Charles Kingsley, and pulled it down. The door swung back into the living room.

'Leave it open. I'll put the kettle on,' said Jane.

Euphemia grabbed her phone and followed. A Sage family photograph, including Kezia's new husband Ben and his father looking resplendent in their wedding finery, Petal at Nicky's feet and wearing a white bow around her neck, was her screensaver. There were no missed calls from either Joe or Kenneth. No texts. Nothing. She keyed in her code and checked apps and email addresses. Nothing. Joe should have received her message by now. She had expected him to call back immediately to tell her what to do about the hole because it needed repairing, and the predators tracked down and killed before they did any more damage, but who was going to do it?

'Gouda sandwich?' asked Jane.

'What did you say?'

'I've made sandwiches,' Jane said, pushing a plate across the bench towards her. 'You didn't eat breakfast.'

There was a scattering of paws on the concrete floor and Petal barreled into the room before screeching to a halt next to Euphemia, where she sat down and, eyes alert, looked up expectantly. Still puzzling why Joe hadn't called her back, Euphemia absentmindedly peeled a piece of crust from the sandwich and dropped it straight into Petal's mouth. Petal swallowed, and repositioned herself on her haunches closer this time, brown eyes sliding from the sandwich to Euphemia and back again as she waited quivering, for the next morsel.

'Something doesn't feel right,' she said. She called Joe again. This time instead of voicemail she was advised, his number was not currently in use and she should check she had the correct details. Never in all the time she had known him had she ever received this message. Joe, wedded to his phone, loved getting calls. It made him feel less isolated, living in the country where farming could be a lonely business. His phone was always with him and always on. Always.

'No answer?' asked Jane, finishing her sandwich.

'No, which is silly because there'll be a simple explanation. There always is. In the meantime, you didn't come across any fencing invoices in the files, did you?'

'Not so far. Feed merchants, tractor suppliers, but nothing from a fencer. Maybe you could ask Arthur who he uses?'

'That's a brilliant idea,' said Euphemia. 'I'll pop over now. You're a genius, Jane.' Euphemia picked up her sandwich. She was hungry after all and finished it in two bites, much to Petal's disgust.

CHAPTER 8

JANE TOOK THE LEAD ON THE WALK DOWN THE DRIVE to the homestead. 'You'll need someone to introduce you', she explained.

'I met them both at Joe and Charlotte's wedding, but that was a long time ago. Hopefully, they will remember me.'

Oakhill Station Homestead was rather grand. Built in the style of an English Georgian manor house but with the addition of wide verandas surrounding it on three sides, it sat well on the land. Two storeys, it had a pitched corrugated iron roof which had recently been painted dark green. The walls were a soft white and the windowsills and doors picked out in full gloss black. The verandas were demarcated from the garden by closely trimmed box hedges. A white gravel driveway encircled the house with a large area for cars to park at the back, the only side of the house without a veranda. To the left, there was a tennis court, its sagging net bifurcating shaggy grass covered in leaves. Beyond that, steps led down the side of the hill to a swimming pool.

It had astonished Euphemia to learn the pool had no filtering system. Built in the 1950s after a particularly good wool payout, there was a tap at one end and a drain at the other. 'It's spring fed. When the water gets green like it is now,' Joe had explained. 'We open the valve. An hour later, it's empty. A quick hose down, close off the drain and we turn on the tap. Look, I'll show you'. He lifted the top off a small hatch in the ground, reached in and fiddled with a lever. Next minute, water gushed out of a pipe set in the pool's side and within minutes, it was nearly full. He reached down and fiddled with the lever again, and the gush turned to a dribble.

'Isn't that a waste of precious water?'

'Not really,' replied Joe. 'We don't have to add any chemicals to the pool or spend money on electricity to run a filter. The old water irrigates the home paddock where we keep the chickens and Boris the pig.'

'The same Boris who just had eleven babies?'

'All our pigs are called Boris. It saves a lot of angst organizing the Christmas ham. Lucky for this Boris, she was pregnant when we got her. Her piglets literally saved her bacon.'

That had been the year before last and Euphemia was wondering whether Boris had lived to breed again when a tiny dog, ears as flat as the fluff allowed, barking furiously, burst through the box hedge, hurtled towards Petal and stopped inches from her nose. Petal stood her ground, albeit behind Euphemia's legs. Her eyes bulged as the dog first sniffed her bottom and then under her belly before getting to the all important nose area. Petal stopped shivering and sniffed back. Their eyes held, they circled each other twice more. Petal dropped onto her front paws and barked. The Chihuahua, its fluffy ears now fully perked, barked back and took off with Petal in hot pursuit as they disappeared behind a white Volvo parked beside the open back door.

'Petal,' hissed Euphemia running after her. 'Come back now. Now. Come and sit.'

'Brutus. Inside.'

A woman Euphemia recognized as the driver who had overtaken them on the Remutaka road stood in the doorway, her hands on her hips pointing to a spot on the floor in front of her, which she expected Brutus to occupy. Seeing Jane, she relaxed. 'Joan, it was this evening, wasn't it? Or am I getting muddled in my old age?'

'Hi Ally, it's actually Jane, not Joan, and yes, we did say tonight. This is Euphemia Sage. You've met before, I think.' Ally was wearing jeans and a blue cotton shirt with a darker blue sweater draped over her shoulders, the sleeves knotted at the front of her chest. She had rolled her shirt-sleeves to below her elbows. Her tanned arms showed off many gold bangles worn with a heavy gold watch, which drooped over her right wrist. A large solitaire diamond on her left hand flashed in the sunshine. Medium height, slim and toned, Ally was not beautiful, but she was attractive. She knew how to make the most of the assets she had. Her highlighted blonde hair, cut in a short bob, grazed her shoulders and she was wearing just enough makeup to bring out the blue of her eyes and the whites of her dentally curated teeth.

'We met at Joe's wedding,' said Euphemia, leaning forward to shake Ally's hand. The dogs erupted through another hedge circled behind the women before the Chihuahua took the lead and in one joyous bound hurdled the back steps and sped inside the house with Petal in hot pursuit.

'It's good for Brutus to have a friend,' said Ally, laughing. 'He's been so mopey since he got out of quarantine. You'd better come in.'

They followed her inside down a wide hall past a loaded coat rack, which had assorted pairs of gumboots lined up underneath it, and into a roomy kitchen. There was an Aga at one end, a seating area at the other, and a narrow pine table with benches on either side squarely in the middle. A man was sitting on a sofa facing a large flat screen TV watching a cricket match, seemingly unconcerned by the dogs doing laps of the coffee table in front of him. Ally walked over and removed an ear bud. He turned to protest. When he saw the women, he jumped to his feet, a huge smile lighting up his face. 'Good,' he said, clicking the remote to mute, 'company.'

Arthur Kincaide was as Euphemia remembered him. He looked nothing like his brother. His dark straight hair was long and parted on the side so it fell over his left eye. This meant he had to flick it back out of the way to see properly. Tall and elegantly proportioned, Arthur had none of the strength implied in Joe's broad shoulders. Based on family photos she had seen, Joe was the spitting image of his paternal great grandfather and Arthur took after their mother's side of the family. She was from a family of bankers and shipping merchants who had settled Otago, a province on the South Island of New Zealand. Feisty, smart, and an excellent tennis player Sheila Kincaide had met her husband on one of his stock buying trips to Dunedin. Two months later, they were engaged. Six months later, they were married. And eight months after that, Joe arrived. Early, the one and only time of his life.

'Brutus,' Ally called sternly. The fluffy dog stopped chasing Petal and trotted over to sit meekly and expectantly at her feet. Petal joined him. Ally tossed them treats, which they gulped down and looked up for more. There was an awkward silence as everyone focused on the dogs and waited for someone to speak. Then they all spoke at once.

'A cup of tea,' suggested Ally.

'That would be lovely,' said Jane, taking a seat at the table. Ally busied herself with filling the kettle and getting mugs out of the cupboard.

'Not for me, thank you,' said Euphemia. She scooped up Petal and turned to Arthur. 'I have come to ask you if you know who Joe gets to work in the sanctuary. I was running around it this morning and found a hole in the mesh. I saw tracks, so I think animals might have already got inside.'

Arthur frowned. 'Of course. Let me see what I can find. I'll be back in a tick.' He disappeared down the hall, which led to the front of the house.

'Don't you and Kenneth usually come together?' Ally asked Euphemia.

'He's in Malaysia exploring opportunities to supply restaurants.'

'You should get him to talk to Arthur. He knows Malaysia well and might help. You didn't want to go with him?' The kettle boiled and Ally turned away to fill the teapot.

'Unfortunately, it's a busy time of year at Sage, so it wasn't possible. Maybe next time.'

'I loved living in Hong Kong,' Ally said. 'Such nice people, so much to do and the food.'

'You came back so your children could go to school?' asked Jane.

'And because Arthur had a project, he wanted to get off the ground here.'

'Talking about me?' Arthur stood in the doorway. 'We came back so Josh could go to the same school the men in our family went to. I'm a great believer in tradition.' He walked over to collect his tea from the bench and took a sip. 'Elizabeth, our daughter is there already. This is the man you want,' he said, passing Euphemia a piece of paper. 'Call Sandy.'

'Thank you. The project is the retirement village, I take it? I didn't realize planning permission would be granted so quickly for such an ambitious project. Some of my clients' developments have taken years to get to the selling stage.'

Ally flicked her husband a worried glance.

'We haven't actually got planning permission yet. Expressions of interest, rather than actual sales, are what I'm aiming for now. Then, if I can build enough enthusiasm, the council will have to come to the party. It'll be great for the local community. Jobs for starters and it will boost the profile of the sanctuary.' Arthur walked over to Ally and put his arm around her shoulders.

'It surprised me Joe agreed to it,' said Euphemia.

'He could see the sense of it. Retired greenies who want to give back in their old age - a free, educated and passionate workforce who pay to live close by. What's not to like? They get to live in the perfect place to show off their talents and expertise. It's win, win.' He paused. Ally took that moment to duck out from under his arm. 'We need the council to fast-track planning permission and we're good to go.'

'They have to give it and soon,' Ally said. There was desperation in her tone. Sensing Euphemia's stare, she brightened. 'I hope you'll pop over for a drink later. Around five.'

'That would be lovely,' Euphemia replied. 'Thanks for the number,' she said waving the piece of paper at Arthur as she called Petal.

'They're good people,' Jane said as they walked back to the New House. 'Giving up their lives in Hong Kong for the sake of their children.'

Euphemia was silent. She was thinking about how desperate and panicky Ally had looked when they talked about the sanctuary.

CHAPTER 9

Euphemia noticed the size of his hands first. They were huge. His fingers, which were flexed slightly at rest, were rough skinned, the cracks ingrained with dirt, but when she shook his hand, she immediately felt his inner gentleness. Sandy Martin, fencer, was broad shouldered, thin-hipped, muscled, tall and with a full head of hair. He climbed out of his battered Land Rover in one fluid practiced movement and walked towards the house with an easy familiarity. His tanned skin, weathered by the elements, highlighted his brown eyes ringed with thick lashes, the fullness of his lips and his even teeth. Euphemia appreciated a good-looking man when she met one. She was married, not dead.

'Thank you for coming and so quickly,' she said, her voice cracking traitorously as she attempted to still her beating heart. This man even smelled wonderful—leather predominantly with a hint of thyme, both aromas overlaying a remnant of soap covering engine oil.

A wet nose brushed her hand. She glanced down.

'That's Fergus,' said Sandy. The dog, a black and white Collie, had mismatched eyes, one blue the other brown, which made him look slightly mad. Petal was doing her best to get the collie's attention, but to no effect. Fergus only had eyes for Sandy. Not used to being ignored, Petal pulled out all the stops. She whimpered, her corkscrew tail beating like a metronome. She scampered coquettishly forwards, then back and bent down, her hind-quarters raised. Fergus, immoveable, sat calmly at Sandy's side.

'Sorry about Petal,' said Euphemia. 'She's not usually like this.'

'He gets it all the time, especially from bitches. If he's interested, he'll let her know.' Sandy looked at his watch. 'If you're going to show me what needs fixing before it gets dark, we'd better go.'

Euphemia had to remind herself why this man was standing in front of her. 'Right, of course.'

'We'll take mine,' Sandy said, walking to the driver's door of the Land Rover. Fergus automatically leapt into the back. Euphemia looked down to find Petal unusually trotting at heel confidently, assuming the expedition included her. She picked up the little dog and climbed into the passenger seat.

'Did you bring her muzzle?' asked Sandy. He reached around to attach two straps behind Fergus's ears.

'Petal won't need one. She's a harmless town dog.'

'They're the worst. No discipline. No experience of the bush. They get excited by all the smells,' Sandy replied. 'Dogs are worse than ferrets. If they get the scent of a Kiwi, they'll track the bird back to its nest and kill it, and nothing you can say or do will stop her.'

'She's a lapdog, not a hunter,' said Euphemia. 'I'm surprised she wants to come at all.'

'Without a muzzle, she stays here. Inside.'

Sandy meant what he said. Rather than argue, Euphemia carried an astonished Petal into the house.

'Right,' said Sandy, turning the key when she returned. 'Show me this hole.'

He parked the Land Rover at the sanctuary gate. He was as fit as he looked. Their walk up the hill took less than twenty minutes. He said nothing when she showed him the gap in the fence and he said nothing on the drive back to the house. Turning off the engine, hands on the steering wheel, he sighed. 'It's not good. I'll be back first thing in the morning with the right equipment.'

'You saw the tracks. Do you think whatever is in there has been there long?' Euphemia asked.

'Three days, I reckon. That was the last time it rained. I'll fix the hole and set some traps inside. We'll catch the mongrels, won't we, boy?' Fergus's mismatched eyes misted over with pleasure when he heard his master talking to him.

'Is there anything you need?'

'Nothing. You won't even know I'm there.'

Just what I was afraid of, she thought realizing the best run on the farm was now off limits.

'Who was that?' Jane asked when she went inside. She was wearing a black fitted dress and fixing an emerald earring in one ear. Euphemia recognized it as part of the emerald set. The other earring and the rather spectacular matching necklace dangled from her hand.

'That was Sandy Martin. He's going to fix the fence tomorrow morning,' she replied. 'What have you been doing?'

'I had a nap. My bed is so comfortable. I lay down for a second and next minute it's nearly time for drinks. You should try it, you're looking peaky.' Head tilted to one side, Jane attached the other earring. The stones matched the color of her eyes perfectly and looked fantastic against the pale skin of her neck.

'Why is Petal looking so put out?' Jane asked.

'Fergus, Sandy's dog, ignored her, and she doesn't have a muzzle.'

Jane shook her head, the drop earrings flashing in the dull light of the late afternoon. 'I don't know what you're talking about and I don't want to know. We've got drinks at Oakhill House in fifteen minutes. You'd better get ready.'

'I am ready. It's not formal, is it?'

'No, but you can't wear the same clothes you've been wearing all day.'

'There's nothing wrong with them.'

Jane rolled her eyes. 'Your shoes aren't clean.'

Euphemia bent down and brushed the dust from her trainers. 'There,' she said. 'We're in the country. I don't get dressed up when Joe is here.'

'That's Joe. Arthur and Ally are more sophisticated. It's your call. I'm not your mother. Just as long as you don't mind being the odd one out, wear what you like. Can you help me with this?' She held out the emerald necklace and turned around.

'Do you think your mother would have worn the emerald set to casual drinks on a weeknight?' she asked. 'In the country?'

'Mmmm, maybe you're right. Mummy always said it was better to be understated than over-emphasized. The earrings will be enough.' She turned on her way downstairs. 'You could put on lipstick? Make a bit of an effort?'

Euphemia poked out her tongue.

'Very grown-up,' said Jane.

Euphemia fed Petal, then wandered into the office and opened her laptop. They had got little done today. Joe ran each of his farms as separate companies, each one owned by the Kincaide Family Trust. His accounts were therefore more complicated than they needed to be, and there was a lot to do. Without him to answer her questions, and without Kenneth's help, it was going to take longer than usual to sort everything out. The organization to get the hole in the fence repaired had slowed things down. She planned to make her excuses to Arthur and Ally and leave early so she could get back to work.

In the bottom of her handbag, she found a pale pink lipstick she had forgotten she owned. She put it on. Jane was right. It was only polite. There was a crumpled tissue in the bag too and she used it to give her shoes another clean. After dusting off her leggings, she pulled her merino top into place. Next, she brushed out her hair and tucked it behind her ears. The cut she'd had for the wedding had lasted. Now she preferred the shorter, slightly darker style to her earlier blonde shoulder-length style. She was too old for longer hair and the darker streaks meant she could transition to grey without it being so obvious. It was so unfair her body's ability to heal quickly did nothing to take away her wrinkles or stop her hair from going grey. What was the point of only feeling young on the inside?

Normally, she preferred to avoid social occasions with people she didn't know well. She attended the smaller work functions and enjoyed going out for dinner as a couple with Kenneth, or with friends, but that was it. She preferred interacting with people on a one-to-one basis and left the schmoozing side of the business to her husband. He was more outgoing and got along with everyone. As a lone male, he was welcome at any function. He lapped up the attention he got from women, but he made it clear he loved his wife, who was waiting for him at home.

Euphemia checked her phone. Still no calls. Euphemia missed her husband. Thirty years of marriage, give or take, and this was the longest they had spent apart. Euphemia wasn't used to sleeping alone, or staying awake at night alone listening to Jane snore. She missed him in her bed. That and the day-to-day contact with her mate, the hugs and handholding, the kisses in passing, his wry comments about all manner of trivia which made her laugh. Mostly, she missed being able to talk over her day with him and listen to him talking about his day. Ally had been right to ask why she hadn't gone with him. She could have, and she should have. Sage Consulting was big enough to manage without either of them for a short period. The girls no longer needed her, and Jane would have looked after Petal. She damped down the sneaking suspicion she hadn't gone because she was still coming to terms with Kenneth starting his business with Roger and not with her. Had she played the martyr because she was jealous of what he and Roger had achieved?

Now, she had to make nice with the Kincaides. The only consolation for what she was about to endure was the possibility they could tell her where Joe was. Better still, they might tell her what time he was coming home.

CHAPTER 10

'I HAVE NEVER BEEN SO EMBARRASSED IN MY LIFE,' said Jane, holding on to Euphemia's arm, as they walked up the drive. Euphemia was using her phone to light their way.

'I can understand that,' said Euphemia, hauling Jane back to the vertical. Despite her best efforts, Jane's legs kept sliding off to the side threatening to pull them both over.

'Ally didn't say much, did she? Well, she didn't get a chance,' Jane added, answering her own question. 'Arthur was going on and on about Hong Kong and how well he did there.'

'He's a successful man. He's used to talking about himself.'

'You're successful,' said Jane, reaching up and patting Euphemia's face. 'You don't go on and on about yourself.'

'There's a difference,' replied Euphemia. 'I'm a woman.'

The sensors detecting movement at the front door activated the outside lights. Jane reeled back, putting her hand up to shield her eyes. 'Why do they have to be so bright?'

Euphemia redoubled her grip and pushed open the door. Recessed hall lights at calf level lit their way down the steps into the living room. Jane disengaged from Euphemia, staggered over to the sofa and fell straight onto it. Petal, woken by the noise, jumped on top of her and licked her neck.

'Not now, Justin,' murmured Jane. 'I'm tired.'

Euphemia put Petal in her basket and draped a rug over the now sleeping Jane. Next, she propped a cushion in front of her to make sure she didn't roll onto the floor. In the kitchen, she filled two glasses of water, put one on the table next to Jane and took the other through to the office and sat down at the desk. Lit only by the screen on her laptop, she started work. At midnight she closed the lid and sat in the dark to wait, Jane's soft snoring from the living room keeping her company.

At twelve-fifteen, there were footsteps on the drive outside. Walking on fallen acorns in autumn is like walking on bubble wrap, fun but unavoidably loud; nature's perfect warning system. The slower the person walked and the more carefully they tried to place their feet, the louder the scrunch. The footsteps moved to the far side of the house. She heard fumbling, then a switch being turned off.

It was time to move. Euphemia tiptoed past the sleeping Jane, noting that Petal, never one to miss an opportunity, had cuddled in beside her. The stair lights didn't turn on when they should have. Given the short time spent at the side of the house, she guessed the intruder knew how to shut off the power supply.

Waiting in the dark had allowed the cells in the back of Euphemia's eyes to boost the supply of rhodopsin, the protein in the retina, which processed light. Enhanced protein production inside her body's cells was the key to her super powers. The living room was now visible in minute detail, albeit in forty-nine shades of grey. She heard the intruder climb the back steps. She saw the handle turn slowly and the door swing open. A man dressed in black had a leather satchel slung over one shoulder. He was wearing thick woollen socks, rather than shoes.

She stood still as he slid noiselessly over to the sofa. What a pillock, she thought when she saw him smile down at Jane, touch his finger to his lips, then to hers. Still unaware of her presence, he tiptoed downstairs. She followed. Clearly familiar with the layout of the house, he went past Joe's room, past Euphemia's room, and into Jane's room. Quietly, she locked all the doors except Jane's before returning to the living room. While he searched through Jane's belongings, she popped outside and re-connected the power.

On her return, she went to the sofa, put her hand over Jane's mouth and shook her friend awake. Jane's eyes flared open in fright and she struggled until she heard Euphemia whispering in her good ear. Petal growled before huffily scooting to the end of the sofa.

Properly awake, Jane sat up and ran her fingers through her hair scratching her scalp loudly and vigorously until Euphemia glared at her, a finger to her lips. Together they sat in silence, staring into darkness and waited.

When she saw the first wooly sock on the top stair, Euphemia clicked the remote. The room lit up like a sports ground at night. One foot up, one foot down, the man reeled back and would have fallen down the stairs if Euphemia hadn't leapt forward and grabbed him by the arm.

'You bastard.' Jane advanced towards him, her hands curled into fists. She punched him in the chest three times, one punch for each word. 'How could you?'

Euphemia prevented a fourth punch by grabbing Jane's hand and tucking it in hers as she led her away. 'He gets it. Don't you?'

Kevin unhooked the bag over his head and nodded pathetically.

'Do you?' Jane hissed.

He nodded again.

Kevin, of Mt Taranaki fame, had been happily ensconced in the library overlooking the tennis court when Jane and Euphemia arrived for drinks. It turned out he was Ally's much older brother and had been staying with the Kincaides for a month in exchange for help ingwith farm work. Euphemia's quick glance at his hands showed he hadn't been doing anything of the sort. They were pale, pink, and manicured but his grip on his whisky glass was decidedly firm.

Kevin was the first man Jane had gone out with after Justin died and within six weeks of their relationship beginning, he had inveigled his way into her life so much he persuaded her to climb Mt Taranaki with him. It was totally unlike Jane to do any strenuous exercise, let alone climb an extinct volcano, but Kevin had her in his thrall.

For the first time in her life, Jane was enjoying sex. Unlikely though, it seemed, the corpulent Kevin showed Jane what she had been missing in the years she was married to Justin. It didn't surprise Euphemia to learn that Justin was selfish in bed. She was delighted Jane had been liberated from her orgasmic desert, but it was regrettable that the person doing the liberating was Kevin.

The trip up the mountain did not go well. Jane was fine, but Kevin's ham-fisted attempt to scare her into marrying him failed miserably when he froze short of the peak. He found out he was afraid of heights at the two thousand three hundred metre mark. A flaw in his machinations he didn't know about until he was standing on the steep scree slopes near the summit looking out across the Tasman Sea towards Australia. He panicked. Jane called Mountain Rescue and Kevin had to be prised free from a boulder before they helicoptered him off the mountain. Jane never spoke to Kevin again. She fell promptly in love with Dan, her rescuer. All subsequent subsequent references to Kevin were verboten.

Until tonight.

His shamelessly hearty welcome to the woman he had tried to marry so he could get his hands on her jewelry, greeted them as they walked into the living room for drinks. Jane was surprised, then shocked. However, she had been brought up by a mother who had instilled good manners in her daughter. No matter the situation. Jane smiled and chatted amiably to Kevin at the beginning of the evening. Euphemia, unable to forgive Kevin's betrayal of her friend, sat quietly in a corner observing him; any hope of leaving early to go back to work dashed.

'I'm sorry,' Kevin mumbled, rubbing his chest where Jane had punched him. Then he made a break for the front door, his feet sliding out from under him in different directions, his socks giving him no purchase on the floor. He was determined. He nearly made it. His hand was on the handle and he was pulling himself towards it when Euphemia pressed the remote - the thunk of a bolt dropping inside the door sealed his fate. He looked around wildly, panic in his eyes.

'Come here. Now,' said Euphemia, commanding him with her voice. He slid across to stand beside her next to the table.

Of all her super powers, the voice command gave her the most satisfaction. It was both spooky and rewarding, being able to make people do her bidding. Unfortunately, it didn't always work, but when it did; it made her smile on the inside.

'Open your bag,' she ordered.

He unzipped the bag.

'Now tip everything out.'

Jane's emerald necklace, two strings of fat pearls - one short and one long — a pair of drop diamond earrings and a diamond pendant on a gold chain tumbled onto the table. Jane gasped.

'Is that everything?' asked Euphemia.

'I didn't bring the important pieces,' said Jane. 'You said we were only going to be here for a day or two, so I thought these would be enough. I didn't bring the sapphire suite. Do you think I should have?'

'I was talking to Kevin,' said Euphemia. 'I want to know if he put anything in his pockets.'

'Wait,' said Jane. 'The emerald earrings, they aren't there.' Jane's voice rose an octave. 'I bet he's stuffed them inside his, you know what?' She made a grab for the back of his pants.

'Stop, stop.' Kevin yelled. 'Just. Stop. It's not what it looks like.'

Euphemia had to pull Jane away. Kevin, with a tight grip on his waistband, faced them. 'How dare you,' he said, pulling himself up to his full height of five foot ten inches. This only emphasized the size of his gut hanging over his trousers. 'I don't have your emerald earrings because you're still wearing them.'

Jane's hands flew to her earlobes, and she looked suitably abashed. 'Okay, sorry.' She pointed to the pile of jewelry on the table. 'But this,' she said. 'I will never forgive you for this.'

'I can explain.'

'I doubt that. You only went out with me to get your hands on my family jewels. I remember Mt Taranaki. You should be grateful I didn't humiliate you in front of Ally. When I walked in tonight and saw you sitting there as if you owned the place, I was shocked, but I didn't want to embarrass you. I kept your shameful actions to myself and this is my reward.'

'Ah,' said Kevin, still keeping a tight grip on his trousers. 'When you say you didn't shame me in front of my family, that's not quite accurate, is it?'

'Meaning?'

'You told my nephew, little Josh, about our relationship. And after your third gin you told him what a great lover I was, and you said you hoped he would learn to be as good a lover as his uncle when he grew up. Thank goodness Ally intervened and told him to do his homework.'

Jane tossed her head. 'The boy lives on a farm. He's eight. He has a smart phone. There isn't an eight-year-old on the planet who hasn't googled sex.'

'Not now there isn't,' said Kevin.

'It's Arthur's fault. The gins were too strong, weren't they, Effie?'

'I stopped after the first.'

Jane clicked her tongue against her teeth. 'All right, it was a mistake. How was I to know he's only eight? He looks nine. Ten even. Yes, I drank too much, but stress drinking is a recognized medical condition. I'm a victim. I'm the first to admit it. But and this is a big but, that doesn't mean you may sneak in here and steal Mummy's jewelry.'

'I wasn't stealing it.'

'Yes, you were,' said Euphemia.

'I wasn't. I was borrowing it,' said Kevin emphatically. 'It's because I missed you so much. You were the best thing that ever happened to me. When you walked into the library tonight, you looked so beautiful, so young and so damned sexy. I had to win you back. So I made a plan. A stupid plan, I see that now, but you can't blame a man for trying to get back the woman he loves.'

'Puleese,' said Euphemia. 'Jane, don't believe a word he says.'

'Ssshhh Effie,' Jane said. 'Ignore her. What are you trying to say?'

Kevin puffing up visibly with the encouragement took Jane's hand and pulled her away from Euphemia.

'It was just a silly plan,' he murmured.

'Tell me,' Jane said.

'Okay, but don't laugh. I thought that if your jewels went

missing and after a day or two, I was the one who found them. You would be so grateful that we could start back where we left off.'

Euphemia raised her eyebrows, rolled her eyes, shifted her weight, crossed her arms across her chest, and snorted. Loudly. None of this made any difference. 'Earth to Jane,' she called. 'Earth to Jane. You cannot believe that load of codswallop. The man is a thief.'

'I think he's telling the truth.'

'He isn't. Remember the mountain? The helicopter? Dan?' Euphemia moved around to stand in front of Jane, forcing her to look away from Kevin. 'I vote for isn't.'

'It makes sense Euphemia. He was borrowing the jewelry so he could return it later. It's the most romantic thing anyone has ever done for me.'

Kevin realized he was out of the woods and let go of his pants. He took her hands in his and raised them slowly to his lips, his eyes locked on hers. Jane shivered, then flushed bright red. Euphemia could feel the heat rippling off her. Kevin pulled her into his arms and kissed her on the mouth. Deeply and for a long time. With tongue.

Euphemia felt a tiny bit of sick rise and settle in the back of her throat. The kissing stopped. There was whispering, then giggling.

'I can't,' whispered Jane. 'I came to keep Effie company. Not you.' Jane poked him playfully in the stomach.

'Do whatever you want,' said Euphemia. 'I wash my hands of both of you. Go. I'll be fine. I've got Petal.'

'See,' said Kevin, who was now running two fingers up and down Jane's spine.

'I'll get my things,' said Jane.

'You're fine as you are,' Kevin said, herding her quickly towards the door. Euphemia beat him to it and stood in front of them blocking their escape.

'Your earrings,' said Euphemia, holding out her hand. 'They'll be safer with me.'

Jane did as she was told while Kevin rolled his eyes. In two seconds, the lovers were out the door and gone.

'The only good thing to come out of this sorry story about a woman in lust is this. Tonight Petal, I will get a good night's sleep.' Petal was already curled up in her basket.

CHAPTER 11

The following morning Euphemia Sage was a
woman restored. A dream-heavy sleep had kept the hot flushes
at bay and she woke with a vigor she hadn't enjoyed since
arriving. There were still no messages from Joe, but happily,
there was a text from Kenneth. He was missing her and
looking forward to seeing her. He had something important to
tell her, but wanted to wait until they were face to face. And
good news; they had signed a twelve-month contract to supply
desserts to restaurants in Malaysia and Singapore. *Our hosts
insist we spend the next week playing golf. This is how they do
business here. We can't get out of it. K xx.*

In all their years of marriage, Euphemia had never
begrudged her husband playing golf. An outstanding rugby
player in his teens, Kenneth had been up for selection to the
All Blacks until a knee injury had destroyed his dream. Golf
became his exercise and the channel for his competitive energy,
and she was delighted. As the girls grew up and became independent, he played eighteen holes twice a week. He went to
tournaments at weekends, enjoying the social aspects of the
game and the sport itself. Never once did she worry about him

with other women. He was a man of integrity. She would not have married him otherwise.

Staying an extra week to play golf was, however, taking it too far. That he left a message when he knew she would be asleep rather than tell her what he was going to do smacked of marital cowardice. She thought about her options. He wasn't here to know how she felt, but she took satisfaction in knowing he would know. Just as she knew that he was enjoying himself when he should be flying home, would be difficult for him to do. There was no point in feeling irritated or resentful or any of the other negative emotions, because what could she actually do? But on further reflection, she hoped he was enjoying himself because she loved him and was pleased he did what he wanted to do, confident knowing that their relationship was strong enough to always want the best for the other. Always. Having tied herself in thought knots, Euphemia knew what she needed to feel straight again. She needed to run.

Sandy was probably already at work repairing the fence, so running near the sanctuary was out of the question. Instead, she followed a dirt road, taking her into the hills on the home-stead side of the valley. The rutted ground hardened by the dry summer meant she had to watch where she put her feet if she didn't want to rick an ankle, but this diversion was exactly what she needed. One foot in front of the other, she kept running. A skylark rose twittering from the grass and she stopped, following it with her eyes until it caught the breeze and flew away.

It was hard to admit she was missing Kenneth more than she thought she would. She wasn't so dependent on him that she pined for him, or at least she didn't think she was. She had her own life and her work to occupy her. But Kezia's wedding had changed how she thought about herself and her future. Two words spoken by her daughter on the happiest day of her life had rearranged her family relationships. From now on, Kezia's next of kin would be Ben. Not her and not Kenneth. They were no longer the most important people in her life. They were Kezia's yesterday. Ben was, her tomorrow. Then Nicky left to go undercover for goodness knows how long. Her instructions that she wasn't to be contacted only added to Euphemia's feeling she was nearing her use-by date. Once, that would have been fantastic. Now it was a big huge giant horrible letdown and Kenneth wasn't here to support her and tell it would be all right. He was playing golf with Roger.

She kicked the dirt. Twice. Then again, for good measure.

It. Is. Only. A. Week.

Get over yourself. Be happy for Kezia and Ben enjoying their honeymoon in Tahiti. Stop being such an old grouch. She started running again slowly, forcing herself to focus on her surroundings. The farm was looking very rundown. Empty paddocks, which should have been grazing sheep, and broken fences beside dry troughs. It was a depressing sight. Gorse bushes were making a comeback - it looked untended and in places derelict.

Oakhill Station comprised three farms and this one - the home farm - was the largest by several thousand acres. Her early perusal of the accounts showed that in the last year, it was also the least productive. With almost no flat land, cropping wasn't an option and years of intensive grazing by sheep and beef cattle had contributed to the loss of fertile topsoil through erosion. Joe had planted trees, but keeping each one irrigated until established was expensive and many died. His ancestor's burn-offs had opened up the land, but subsequent generations were bearing the cost of the depleted soil. Global warming wasn't helping.

The sanctuary was the only place in the valley where near - original vegetation had survived. His plan to restore the rest of the property to its pre-European state was all very well, but it would cost money, a lot of money, and the farms were barely financially viable. Kenneth had explained this to Joe the previous winter when the downward slide started. Joe seemed either unable or unwilling to hear what he was saying. Only the income from the farm bordering Lake Wairarapa and the cropping land further up the Featherston valley prevented him from having to declare bankruptcy. Euphemia dreaded being the one to tell him what the current accounts revealed.

Fists lightly clenched, arms and legs a blur, Euphemia ran straight uphill, hurdling the gate at the top with no idea what was on the other side. She soared through the air like a ski jumper landing twenty feet below the ridge, right in the middle of ten scrawny steers, searching for anything green to eat. Startled, they looked at her for a microsecond, then scattered in all directions. The sound of their hooves thundering down the hill away from her and the clouds of dust billowing up in their wake distracted her until she noticed one hadn't moved. He had horns. Sharp, pointy ones. Better nourished than the others, his black hide looked glossy in the morning sunshine.

His brown eyes rolled back and when he lowered his head and started pawing the ground, Euphemia searched for cover. *It had to be the one with horns,* she thought. Agile and fast, steers can easily outrun a woman. Once they got going, they were almost impossible to stop. An old headline flashed in front of her eyes. *'Cattle - New Zealand's most dangerous farm animals.'* The article referred to cattle plural. What about cattle singular? Because the beast which had her in his sights looked like the most dangerous of all, the most dangerous of all the farm animals in New Zealand, if not the entire universe.

The closest safe refuge was below her, two hundred metres away- a fence with a stream behind it. Uphill wasn't an option, even with superpowers, because that was where the rest of the herd had ended up. The other nine steers had circled back to line up along the fence line, facing her like an All Black front row, only bigger. She was in the middle of the worst game of bullrush ever devised. The odds of surviving were not in her favor.

The cattle behind her were getting anxious, judging by their noise. The 'horned one' hadn't moved. Euphemia hadn't moved. Whoever made the first move had to be quick because once committed, there would be no going back.

Euphemia was in heaven. Mind and body were on high alert. She positively zinged with fear and exhilaration - every part of her activated at the same time. Danger thrilling her deep to her core. She was supremely confident she could handle the beast. In fact, she relished the challenge. So much so she almost didn't want it to begin. Because then it would be over and she would have to go home, shower, sit down at the desk and finish the farm accounts.

She put aside the woman who hated rodeos because she considered them cruel. Euphemia pawed the ground and not for one moment did she unlock her eyes from the eyes of the horned one. A wash of honesty swept over her. She was this person. She could do this. She pawed the ground again and snorted. This is a contest of equals and I, Euphemia Sage, am the most equal. She lowered her head slowly and deliberately this time. Stretching her foot out in front of her, she dragged it back through the dust, declaring her intention to engage.

The 'horned one' snorted and pawed the ground in reply, his dust cloud bigger and nastier than hers. Behind her, the moans of the other animals got louder as the wires in fence rattled and pinged against their hides.

The 'horned one' committed. He lowered his mighty skull, his horns pointing straight at Euphemia like two powerful beams of light. He drew his front right hoof through the dust, once, twice, three, four times. His back end sank, as his hulk bunched to prepare for the charge.

Euphemia roared. The steer in front of her roared, the steers behind her roared, and the noise reverberated around the hills. Arms wide, she put one foot in front of the other, standing sideways to minimize the size of the target she presented. The 'horned one' unleashed his massive haunches and launched himself from a standing start, his feet thundering up the paddock, getting closer and closer. Closer. Closer. Closer. Nearly there. Closer. She felt his hot breath on her cheek. She jumped. Straight up. High. As his back passed underneath her, she stepped once, twice, and then off his bulk, pirouetting in midair to land facing uphill. The steer, deprived of its target, charged at full speed towards the rest of the herd, now scrambling past one another to get out of the way. He stopped just in time. And turned. He pawed the ground again and this time with gravity on his side, he thundered back down the hill. Straight at her. The steers behind him regrouped. They charged too - in a line - directly at her.

The ground shook under her feet growing into a bone-shattering earthquake. Forty hooves thundered down the hill. Nine skinny cattle beasts led by a maniac steer, all with the same agenda — her destruction. Shoulder to shoulder, rump against rump, the row of steers charged her with the sole intent of trampling her flesh, eviscerating her lifeless body and tossing it into the air, before grinding her into the dust.

Again she waited, crouched side on to the beasts and again she jumped high above their heads, coming down with her foot on the bony spine of one. She was going to use its back as a springboard like she had before, but her placement wasn't good. Her foot slipped off the galloping animal and down between bellies of two rumbling beasts.

Desperate, she reached for anything to hold on to. She had to stop herself from falling further. Bounced between bones and bellies, she slid lower, her fingers scrabbling for grip as the steers galloped full speed to the bottom of the hill. Buffeted between them, she stayed up for a few seconds, but the inevitable happened. The beasts separated. She hung on for as long as she could, then sunk to the level of pounding hooves, where the dust clogged her nose and mouth and she couldn't breathe. Sharp stones kicked up by flying hooves penetrated her clothing and lodged in her skin.

The steers stampeded onwards; the fence loomed ahead. At the end of the line, the beasts panicked. There was no way through. Her face smashed against ribs as she twisted around, trying again to get an arm over the back of the animal on her right. She tried to breathe but couldn't. Fence wires snapped and pinged around her. She heard bones snapping, her bones. The pain in her chest seared a narrow path straight to her brain.

Euphemia woke half propped up against a fencepost, one cheek jammed into a broken batten. Blood dripped from her forehead into her right eye. She flicked her tongue around her lips, found a cut and the loose tooth behind it. The sickly taste of her blood in the back of her mouth made her want to gag. She leaned forward to spit, but the pain in her chest surged and she froze—a string of bright red saliva dribbling from the side of her mouth and over her chin. With the back of her hand, she wiped it away. Carefully she lifted her head degree by slow degree to see where she was and found she was on one side of the busted fence. On the other side, ten starving steers tugged at the green verges of the stream trickling merrily over stones down the gully. The bucolic scene would have made a brilliant poster advertising the farming sector.

Euphemia tried to move again. She had to. Painful spasms in the muscles encircling her snapped ribs blocked her, freezing her position until gradually the muscles relaxed, the spasm passed and she could ease back against the post. *No one knows you're here. Help is not coming.* The sun was free of the horizon, a yellow circle in a light blue sky. It sent fingers of soft autumn light to brush the hills below her. *Focus.* The ground moved up to meet her in a series of rolling waves. She blacked out.

And woke to see a woman standing beside the stream, among the cattle - sunshine reflected from her hair formed a halo of light around her head.

'Kezia?'

The woman had Kezia's eyes - crystal blue, intelligent, knowing, but when Euphemia looked again, she knew it wasn't her daughter. It was Rachel, the woman in the drawings in the attic. The woman who villagers attempted to drown as a witch only, for her to survive and give birth to twin daughters, each with their own version of the switch. The mother of them all smiled and walked up the slope, arms outstretched. At that moment, and in so much pain, Euphemia desired nothing more than to abandon her broken body and be enveloped in the proffered embrace. It was too hard being a fifty-four-year-old super woman. It hurt too much. In the last year, she had been shot, knocked unconscious, and nearly burned alive. For what? How long could she go on punishing her body?

Rachel bent down and laid her hands softly on either side of Euphemia's face, her touch soothing. *You can do this and more. You will survive and you will find your purpose.* Rachel stood up then, rising higher and higher, as she faded into the sky.

Euphemia slept.

The considered munching of cattle eating grass woke her. Every inch of her body hurt when she moved, the nerves jangling in her limbs and head. Her doubt was gone. It was going to be all right. She lay staring at the clouds scudding across the sun, at peace while her cells continued the process of repair. Torn tissues and blood vessels cobbled together.

Snapped bones and ripped tendons rejoined stronger than before.

When she felt able, she tentatively took a breath then slowly got to her feet. No pain. A deeper breath. She felt fine. Her tongue slipped between her lips and teeth. No cut, no blood, no loose tooth. Tick. Tick. Tick. The cut above her right eye was gone.

Loud bellowing made her spin around. The cattle stood knee deep in the stream facing her, grass encapsulated in drool hanging out of their mouths. They looked content. The 'horned one'? Not so much. As if for old time's sake he pawed the ground, but with a full belly, his heart wasn't in it.

'I'll be baaaaack,' Euphemia drawled.

The 'horned one' flicked his tail and dropped his reply into the water with a loud splash.

CHAPTER 12

'WHAT IS THAT SMELL?' EUPHEMIA LOOKED UP FROM her laptop. Her nose wrinkled, his lips puckered as she tried not to breathe.

'I can't smell anything,' said Jane.

'Petal can. Look.' Petal, her tail beating twenty to the dozen, was whining and scratching at the bookcase, all the while throwing beseeching 'open-it-now-or-I-will-die' looks at the women. As soon as she opened the door, Petal in a flurry of paws scrabbling to find purchase on the concrete floor bolted straight through the living room and up the steps, only to be brought up short by the closed front door. She whined and scratched, desperate to be let out. Euphemia, still trying not to breathe, went after her, followed closely by Jane.

Sandy was standing on the drive, Fergus at his feet, the Land Rover parked behind them. Petal yelping with delight made a beeline for Fergus dancing around him, her tail leading her bottom towards him, her eyes bright with pleasure. Fergus, unmoved, yawned. Petal, unwilling to concede defeat, lay down, legs akimbo, her round stomach on display, her tongue lolling lasciviously to one side and wriggled in the dust.

'Pathetic,' Euphemia said. But she kept her hand over her nose and mouth, staying as far away from the source of the smell—Sandy—as she could. Jane stepped outside, brightening when she saw Sandy, then reeled back as if struck into the house and slammed the door. Euphemia heard gagging and groaning. She wanted to be where Jane was.

'You get used to it after a while. I did.' Sandy walked around to the back of the Land Rover.

'Please don't move,' Euphemia said. 'It's worse when you move.'

'Ferret urine,' he said. 'Mixed with a bit of rat. I was lucky to get it and on the first trap, no less. I've fixed the hole, but it's temporary.'

'You got a ferret?'

'First trap. I told you. I laid a line through the sanctuary to get the bastards. There are signs of both rats and ferrets, not sure how many, but I'll get them.'

'I shouldn't ask, but why do you reek of ferret urine?'

'That was an accident.'

'I'm pleased you don't smell like that on purpose.'

'I don't mind it.'

'You are joking.'

Sandy looked momentarily hurt. 'Fergus likes it, don't you, boy.' Fergus, looking embarrassed, stood up and resettled himself a short distance away. Petal moved over to sit beside him.

'Anyway, it's all in a good cause,' Sandy said. 'I was baiting the traps with the dead ferret's bladder and it broke, if you must know. Best bait there is. The little critters love it so much they'll come from miles away to get as close as they can to the source. Pheromones.'

'Great. I can't smell the attraction myself.'

'I'm going to Masterton to order a replacement for the damaged section. It'll be expensive. Not just the mesh, but the helicopter and the labor we'll need to lift it into place. The sections are very heavy.'

'How much are we talking?'

'At one thousand dollars a meter and each section is six meters long, so six thousand right there. It has to be sent down from Auckland. It's not something farm supplies keep on hand. I'll email you when I get the quotes.'

Euphemia almost wept with relief when she heard her phone ringing inside the house. 'I'd better take that. Important call. Thanks for letting me know.' Inside, she rushed to an open window and filled her nostrils and lungs with sweet smelling air. Only it wasn't sweet smelling. It smelt of ferret urine. It wasn't as bad on the far side of the house, but it was bad enough and no matter how much she dialled back her olfactory sensitivity, it clogged her nostrils with vileness. Blasted super-powers.

CHAPTER 13

THE ACCOUNTS FOR THE GRAZING BLOCK, WHICH operated under the company name of Oakhill Number 3, were almost done. Kenneth had advised Joe to buy this property ten years ago, and it had paid off. However, it wasn't enough. The other farms showed substantial losses. Euphemia checked and double-checked, but the figures didn't lie. Joe and Arthur were living beyond their means and would have to call on their dwindling reserves of capital to pay what they owed. If they were to survive the year, they would need bridging finance, hard work and a lot of luck. Euphemia understood why Arthur had suggested the retirement village development. It made financial sense to capitalize on the sanctuary and, if done properly, it could also be good for the wildlife.

The run this morning had reinforced her impression of a farm in need of resuscitation. It was depressing to see broken fences, poorly maintained water troughs, patchy grass cover and the few animals remaining hungry. Where was the supplementary feed needed to get through the autumn? It was expensive but vital if stock were to be in good enough condition to breed in the spring. She understood the sanctuary cost money to run, but it was built now, the costs sunk and the outgoings were minimal. So if money wasn't going into the farms or the sanctuary, where was it going? Sizeable sums of money had disappeared from the balance sheets, but where to and why?

Only Joe could answer these questions, and she still hadn't heard from him. She tried calling this morning and had again received the same message. His phone was switched off or out of range. It couldn't be the latter because cellphone towers surrounded Lake Wairarapa. She tried leaving a text, but the little red exclamation mark appeared in its circle with *message undelivered* printed underneath. It was possible he had lost his phone or broken it, so she emailed hoping he at least had access to that account, but it bounced back with an out-of-office message. *Joe Kincaide will be away for a few days and will contact the sender on his return.*

Euphemia checked the spreadsheets one last time and sent them through to Sage Consulting, where her staff would re-check them before formatting the report into the end-of-year templates required by Inland Revenue. She expected the final report to land back in her Inbox by the end of the day. In case she had missed something, she forwarded a file to Kenneth so he could try to see where the money had gone.

What if Joe wasn't back tomorrow? What then? She had only planned to stay for two days. She could stretch it to a third day, but she needed to get back to the office. It was a busy time of year and there were many clients who needed her attention. If only Kenneth had come home instead of playing golf. She was about to indulge in a spot of *'it's-not-fair. Me-stuck-here-working-while-you-go off-and-enjoy-yourself'* type of thinking, but stopped before her pity party re-booted. Logically, rationally, organizationally, she only had herself to blame for her current predicament.

'How about a coffee? A proper coffee,' she said to Jane. 'In town, at a café?'

'I thought you'd never ask,' Jane said, grabbing her handbag.

Euphemia pulled open the front door. Petal, reeking of dead ferret urine, lay curled up on the mat looking very shame-faced. With her tail between her legs and her ears back, she attempted to sidle past them into the house. Euphemia was having none of it. 'You acted like a hussy with Fergus so you can wait outside until we get back.' Petal's mouth drooped. She hung her head and tail still between her legs, she picked her way delicately over to a patch of grass in the sunshine and lay down, her back firmly towards Euphemia.

Euphemia parked her car on the main street of Martinborough outside the only café with an open sign. A couple of elderly day-trippers helped each other across the pedestrian crossing as a woman with two Jack Russell terriers on long leads crossed from the other side. There was a polite standoff in the middle as she reined in her dogs against their considerable will to allow the couple to pass.

'Martinborough is so quiet,' said Jane, slamming her car door shut.

'It is at this time of day because everyone is at work,' said Euphemia. 'It's busier at the weekends and in summer it's really busy. I've seen traffic backed up to the service station.'

'You mean half a block?'

'Don't be so rude. This is a great little town. Wonderful restaurants, lovely shops and the best bookshop in the South Wairarapa. It's over there behind the wine center.' She pointed to a row of shops on the other side of the street.

'As long as the coffee is as good as it is in Wellington, I'll be happy.' Jane pushed open the door to the café, and a bell tinkled merrily. There was a scattering of people sitting at long and small tables chatting quietly.

'Let's go through to the garden at the back,' said Euphemia. They found a seat at a small round table under a tree.

'How can I help you ladies?' asked the server.

'Two large flat whites please.'

'Anything to eat?'

'Do you have any red velvet cake?' asked Euphemia. 'I had some the last time I was here, and it was superb.'

'Two pieces?'

'Not for me,' said Jane. 'It's my Paleo day.'

'Two forks,' said Euphemia.

The coffee was exactly how Euphemia liked it - strong, not overwhelmed by milk and hot. Too many café coffees were over-frothed with milk and lukewarm.

Their server, Meghan, according to her name badge, returned with a generous slice of cake and the forks. 'Enjoy.' She left them to take the orders from two women sitting down at a table on the far side of the small courtyard.

'Excellent cake,' said Jane, taking a third forkful. 'This buttercream icing is to die for.'

'Are you here for the day?'

Euphemia looked up. A woman at the other table was talking to her.

'Sadly, only a couple of days,' said Euphemia. 'Work trip.'

'What do you do?'

Euphemia liked friendly people, but this was verging on the intrusive. 'Nothing interesting,' she said.

'Are you from Wellington?'

The woman would not give up.

'Yes,' replied Euphemia. She forked a large mouthful of cake into her mouth and hoped that would inhibit further enquiries.

'We heard someone was doing the accounts at Oakhill. Is that you?'

Euphemia nodded.

'Tell Joe Kincaide to get his house in order.'

The second woman fired a stern look at her friend. 'Jocelyn, that's enough.'

'No, it's not. My husband has been waiting for his account to be paid and he's not the only one. The Kincaides might have been good for it once, but not now. Joe only cares about that sanctuary. He doesn't give a hoot for the rest of us. Tell him to pay what he owes.'

'I'm sorry, she's not normally so rude.' Jocelyn's friend stood up. 'I think we should leave these ladies alone. You've made your point. Let's go inside.'

Jocelyn pushed back her chair and followed her friend without looking back.

'Awkward' sang Jane, chasing the last crumbs of cake around the plate with her fork.

'Very.'

'What should we do?'

'We can't do anything. Joe's the only one who can sort this out, and if he isn't back by the time we get home, I'm going to talk to Arthur about calling the police.'

'That's drastic.'

'What if he's been in an accident? You saw how fast he was driving. A few months ago someone drove off the Remutaka Road. The car hidden by the bush wasn't found for weeks. Imagine if Joe is lying at the bottom of a hill injured, unable to call for help.'

Jane put her fork neatly on the plate. She took a deep breath. 'I understand what you're saying.' She took a deep breath. 'Kevin said that Ally said that Arthur said that Joe has been behaving strangely. Could he have done a runner?'

'Absolutely not.'

'I'm only saying. People behave differently under stress. I should know. It can't have been easy when his wife ran off with the manager. Kevin said he hasn't paid her out yet, and it's been over two years. The farm is run down, debts are piling up. I know these old families and how they think about the land. I bet Joe would be mortified if he had to sell Oakhill after one hundred and fifty years of his family's hard work. No one wants to be known as the one who lost everything through poor management.'

Euphemia paused. 'Maybe, but I don't think so. I know Joe. He pays his bills. He wouldn't leave people in the lurch. And he is not a coward. I'll talk to Arthur and find out what he meant by strangely.'

'Okay, but don't tell him how you know. I'm going to the bookshop. See you back at the car.'

Meghan leaned over the counter as she was processing Euphemia's payment. 'Don't listen to Jocelyn. She's known for getting upset over things, which are none of her business. I don't know how Sandy puts up with her.'

'Sandy? Not Sandy Martin?'

'Yes. He's furious about the hole in the fence. He cares about the sanctuary as much as Joe does. Sandy helped build it and don't tell anyone I told you, but he didn't charge Joe for the time he spent putting up the fence. Jocelyn doesn't know. She would have a fit if she found out.'

'How do you know this?'

Meghan blushed as she handed Euphemia her receipt. 'It's surprising what a server overhears. Especially in a small town.'

'You don't know where Joe might be, by any chance?'

'I haven't seen him around for a couple of days. Is he missing?'

'Maybe. He left as we arrived. He said he would be back today.'

'Give me your number and I'll let you know if I hear anything.'

Euphemia took a business card out of her wallet and

handed it to Meghan, who tucked it into the pocket of her apron.

At the door Euphemia turned to say thank you, but Meghan was talking to someone on the phone. She was frowning, the muscles in her back tense. Euphemia focused on what she was saying, but all she heard was 'Joe's missing' before an elderly couple in matching rain jackets and white trainers coughed politely waiting for her to move out of their way. She stood back to let them in.

CHAPTER 14

'You're quiet,' said Euphemia. They were on their way back to the station and driving through vineyards in their full autumn glory, the reds and yellows of the grape leaves burnished against the sky by the afternoon sun.

'Jocelyn got me thinking.'

'Meghan said she's well known for stirring up trouble.'

'Where there's smoke, there's fire.'

'And some people are just mean.'

'The New House, the homestead, the paintings, the car. Joe is a wealthy man. Isn't he?'

Euphemia pulled into the verge to allow a fully laden truck to cross the narrow bridge over the Huangarua River on the edge of town. The driver raised his hand in salute as his truck lumbered past.

'Let me ask you a question. Are you wealthy?'

Jane burst out laughing. 'Me? No. I don't own the flat I live in. Everything I inherited went to pay Justin's debts. You know that.'

Without taking her eyes off the road, Euphemia reached

sideways to touch the drop diamond earring dangling from Jane's right ear. 'How much? Five thousand?'

'More. But I can't sell them. Mummy left them to me and I will leave them to Justine.'

'What will she do with them?'

'She'll wear them and leave them to her daughter.'

'What if she's out of work and starving? What if she doesn't have a daughter?'

'Maybe she could sell one piece until she got back on her feet. I suppose I could do that if I needed to, but I'm not that desperate. Not yet.'

'Justine is focused on her career. She might not have any children. What then?'

'I guess I'll be dead, so I won't know, will I? Personally, I think a career is overrated. I wish the young would do what we did. Get married and have children and forget all this work nonsense.'

'I did both.'

'You're the exception. You were the same at school and you also got lucky with Kenneth. Justin used to say he didn't know how poor Kenneth put up with seeing you all day at work and then all night at home. Justin was very clear when we married. It was his job to earn the money and my job to run the house. And entertain his business associates. Oh, and look pretty when he got home.'

'You can't still believe that? Not after everything he did to you?'

Jane sat in silence for a while and then quietly asked, 'What does it say about me and my life if I don't believe it?'

Euphemia was uncertain what to say next. She wasn't good at this sort of thing. She didn't enjoy talking about the inner workings of other people's marriages. It was enough that she knew what was happening in her own marriage. Kenneth was her best friend, and they discussed everything, even arguing, but the arguments were always civil and always produced an outcome they could both live with. He knew better than to play the 'man-card' and demand obedience. She couldn't imagine what it would be like to be married to someone who stifled your potential and insisted that this was what you wanted. Jane was right. She was lucky to have married Kenneth.

'It says,' said Euphemia after they had travelled another kilometre, 'that you loved Justin very much.'

Jane nodded. 'I suppose it does.' She touched the diamonds in her ear. 'I have been thinking, though, about what would happen if Justine doesn't have children. I am going to leave the collection to Te Papa, the Museum of New Zealand. It will be called The Watson Family Bequest.' She paused. 'Watson was my mother's maiden name.'

'And Justine will agree with that?'

'I don't know. She's doing so well in New York. She can buy her own jewels.'

'You know you will have to tell her or she will contest the will.'

'Maybe, but when the time is right. You know how she gets. No need to cause a fight before I need to. She might surprise me and have ten children. I doubt it. She's a lot like her father, bless her.'

'Getting back to what I was saying about wealth,' Euphemia said. 'You are wearing super expensive earrings and a diamond pendant... ,'

'That's not expensive. Only a few thousand.'

'The rings?'

Jane made a fist and rubbed her rings on her jeans to polish them. 'Yes, these are expensive. Daddy, my real Daddy, spent a fortune on Mummy's engagement ring.'

'Adding them all up then,' said Euphemia, glancing at

Jane. 'You're wearing between twenty and twenty-five thousand dollars' worth of jewelry.

'More.'

'Over twenty-five thousand dollars? Wow! We need to talk about your finances when we get back home. But the point I am making is,' said Euphemia pulling up in front of the gates to Oakhill Station. 'You look like a rich woman, but you have no money and live accordingly. Joe is the same. He looks wealthy to other people, but the accounts tell a different story.'

The gates swung open and Euphemia drove through. In the two days they had been there, the trees lining the drive had changed color. The leaves on the trees were yellow and red while those carpeting the drive lay brown against the green verges. It was beautiful and the oak arch was more typical of something you would see in the northern hemisphere than in a country at the bottom of the Pacific Ocean.

'Maybe Arthur could help,' said Jane. 'He says he's done well. He'll have lots of money.'

'I'm not so sure. In my experience, the ones who talk the loudest often have the least to talk about.'

'So, will they have to sell Oakhill?'

'That's what it looks like and sadly sooner rather than later. Please don't tell anyone. And by anyone, I really mean Kevin.'

CHAPTER 15

'WE HAVEN'T HEARD FROM HIM,' SAID ARTHUR, closing his laptop and pushing it to one side. 'When did he say he would be back?'

'Yesterday,' said Euphemia. She was sitting at the kitchen table in Oakhill House. Arthur sat opposite. He was wearing a light blue cashmere jumper over a checked shirt, the collar up and one button open at the neck. His closely shaved face and expertly cut hair emphasized he was a man more accustomed to life in the city than in the country. Today Ally looked as if she was country born and bred. She was wearing thick socks, baggy jeans, and an old denim shirt over a black turtleneck sweater. Combs held her loosely bundled hair in place on the top of her head. The only sign of wealth was the gold Rolex watch and collection of battered gold bangles jangling on her wrist as she chopped carrots at the bench.

'Joe does this,' said Arthur. 'Goes off for days. Comes back. No explanation. I wouldn't worry if I were you.'

'But where does he go? If there is a number, I could call him.'

'Look,' said Arthur, laying his hands flat on the table. 'I

don't mean to be rude, but is Joe's whereabouts any of your business? I mean, really. Your visit is a tradition, not a necessity. You could do everything online from Wellington. Why don't you go back to town and finish whatever you have to do there? Let his family worry about Joe.'

If only the almost undetectable tremble at the side of Arthur's mouth hadn't betrayed him, his reply might have offended her. That and the way Ally kept her back to her as she quietly put down the knife.

'What's really going on?' asked Euphemia quietly.

Ally's shoulders collapsed. When she turned around, there were tears running down her cheeks. She wiped her hands on a kitchen towel and looked at her husband. 'Tell her.'

Arthur stared at the Aga at the far end of the room, his eyes narrowed, the muscles in his jaw clenching and unclenching.

'Our daughter, Elizabeth,' said Ally finally. 'She's not at school. She's in a rehab facility in Auckland. That's why we really left Hong Kong. She got involved with drugs, so we came home so she could get treatment.'

Euphemia felt the woman's pain. 'No parent wants their child to go through that. I'm sorry,' she said. 'I hope she's getting the help she needs, but I don't understand what it has to do with Joe not being here.'

'He's angry with me for putting up the sign before we have planning permission. He thinks it will jinx it and that if the project doesn't go ahead, then the other greenies will think the sanctuary was a ploy to make money. Joe doesn't understand the urgency. We need to pay for Elizabeth's treatment, Josh's schooling. Believe me, none of it is cheap. The bank is funding us in the meantime, but the farm isn't paying its way and they will not keep pouring money in forever. Every time we want to discuss what we're going to do, he gets in that bloody Tesla and disappears.'

'The treatment can't be that expensive, surely?'

'Well, it is,' snapped Ally. Arthur looked at her and shook his head. With a huge sob, Ally ran out of the kitchen. Euphemia heard the door to the library slam shut.

'As a mother yourself, you will know what she's going through. She's sick with worry. We're both worried and Joe playing silly games doesn't help. The retirement village is a good idea, and it's our only hope.'

'I don't disagree with you. I think the sanctuary as a retirement project could work well for all concerned. There are plenty of greenies getting on in age who would be happy to devote their later years to saving the birds and bush.'

Arthur perked up. 'It is a great idea. Win. Win. Win. Nature wins. People win and our finances win. You'll help me persuade him?'

'On two conditions. You help me contact him and you change the sign. You can't have that "Give Back before you Give Up" slogan. It's ghoulish.'

'I thought that up myself. It's honest.'

'It might be, but not if you're serious about the idea.'

'Hm, I'll think about it. And before you say anything else. I don't know where he is. I would tell you if I did. Especially now that you're on my side.'

'I'm not on anyone's side. I don't want to see the family have to sell the station.'

'We agree then,' said Arthur. He pulled his laptop towards him. 'Is there anything else because I have work to do? Councils put no end of rigmarole into this planning permission stuff. It is wearing me down.'

'The farm,' Euphemia said. 'Who should I talk to about the stock?'

'What stock?' Arthur asked.

'There are ten steers in a paddock up the back of the farm. I found them when I went for a run this morning. They're starving. Correction. They were starving until they stampeded through a fence into a stream. Anyway,' she said feeling his irritation growing, 'someone needs to go up and bring them down.'

'I'll do it this afternoon. Anything else?'

'No, that's all.' She smiled, but he did not return her smile. That man runs hot and cold, she thought as she walked up the drive. No wonder Ally is on tenterhooks.

CHAPTER 16

KEVIN PUSHED OPEN THE FRONT DOOR AT FIVE o'clock. He had a bottle of wine under one arm and Brutus under the other. Petal, freshly bathed and smelling of Jane's hair shampoo, wagged her tail as soon as she saw him. Brutus might not be Fergus, but he was a dog, and he was a dog who wanted to play. Skitters of paws on smooth concrete followed as they tore across rugs and bounded over furniture before Euphemia called enough. The dogs stopped in their tracks, checking to make sure she really meant it and that this wasn't an extra part of their game. They could see she was serious, so flung themselves down under the table where pink tongues too big for their mouths dripped saliva onto the floor.

Jane was delighted to see Kevin. Freshly showered, she was wearing a camel cashmere turtleneck over jeans, ankle boots and pearls: pearl earrings, a triple strand opera length pearl necklace and a matching pearl bracelet. Her slick city hairstyle prevented the country chic from ageing her, that and her smile. Euphemia, feeling distinctly *de trop*, made her excuses and disappeared into the study, shutting the bookcase firmly behind her.

Happily, she found a text from Kenneth asking her to call him. He answered on the first ring. It was a relief to see him, even if he angled his phone to show his forehead more than his face. Behind the top of his head, she saw a screen of tropical plants and tables where people were eating and drinking. Music played over a tinny sound system.

'Hello,' he called.

It was so good to hear his voice. 'Hello back.'

'You should be here with me. Not slaving away at home. You'd love it. Look what you're missing.' He picked up his phone and rotated it above his head so she could see the road outside the restaurant. It was midnight, but there were lots of people about. Noisy motorbikes whizzed past through the crowds. She could almost feel the humidity. She was suddenly lighter, knowing he was missing her as much as she was missing him.

'I don't know why we still go to Oakhill,' said Kenneth, bringing the phone back to face his chin. 'It makes more sense to do the books online. Anyway, how is it going? Has he been entertaining you?'

'Joe isn't here. He left as we drove in and I haven't heard from him since. I'm getting worried because he's not answering my calls.'

'That's not like him.'

'According to Arthur and Ally,' she said. 'It is. He's been going off by himself for days at a time with no explanation, then turns up and acts as if he hasn't been away.'

Kenneth tilted his head. 'If they aren't worried, you don't need to be. He might have a secret girlfriend stashed away, and he's gone off to see her.'

'I suppose,' Euphemia said.

'I'm interested you took Jane?'

'She broke up with Dan and needed time to heal. Just a pity about the snoring. I barely slept for the first two nights and was about to put a pillow over her head when she debunked to the homestead to sleep with… You'll never guess who? Kevin.'

'Not Taranaki Kevin?'

'The man himself. He is Ally Kincaide's older brother, and he's supposed to be helping around the farm, but I haven't seen him actually do anything. He told Jane he was sorry, and he wanted her back and she believed him. I think the Dan thing made her vulnerable. She's forgiven Kevin and they're back together.'

'Didn't you say anything?'

'I tried, but she ignored me. I figure if he makes her happy, and I get to sleep, then it's the proverbial cloud. He tried to steal her jewelry, so I've got that in safe-keeping until we go.'

'He did what?'

'I'll tell you the long version when I see you. She knows, and she still decided he's the one for her. She's changed since Justin died, for the better, so I can't see her putting up with Kevin for long.'

'Women! You use us men. Then you toss us aside when you get what you want.'

'Hear! Hear!' The phone jiggled and Roger's face loomed into shot. 'You ladies, you're a mysterious lot. I'm looking at you, Euphemia. Don't worry, your secret is safe with me.' He raised a bottle of beer, clinked it against the phone.

Roger, Kenneth's oldest friend, was the best man at their wedding. Their company and family lawyer, he was Kenneth's partner in their new business, but when he wasn't giving a legal opinion, he behaved as if he was still in his twenties. He drank more than was good for him and, rather than being the life of the party, he could be a liability. He was only serious on the golf course and only because he was determined to beat his oldest rival, Kenneth. It was proving difficult, but Roger had seen a new coach for tips, and had invested in a new set of clubs. His handicap stayed at eight. Kenneth was closing in on four.

Euphemia couldn't abide the game. She resisted every attempt to get her to play. Roger might be annoying, but he was doing her a favor. His obsession with beating Kenneth had taken the pressure off her to play and let her get on with her own life. She had one problem with Roger, apart from his drinking. Kenneth had admitted he may have hinted to him that Euphemia had special powers. He assured her it was only a hint, and that Roger hadn't believed him. But Roger's less than subtle digs, which he kept dropping into every conversation, were close to the bone. She hoped he didn't have one gin too many and share his jokes with the wrong person.

There was a tussle, the sound of men grunting. The ceiling and overhead fans came into view. Then Kenneth's face.

'Hold on,' he said. 'I'll go somewhere quieter.' She watched the floor of the restaurant judder past, then his forehead reappeared. He was sitting in the lobby of a hotel. White shutters, potted palms and whicker furniture, a typical tropical design now behind him. 'Are you missing me as much as I'm missing you?'

'More,' replied Euphemia. 'Tell me you won't go away without me again.'

'I won't be going away again. Period,' Kenneth said. 'A weekend with Roger is one thing. A week is bearable, but two weeks? No. I've only just realized my best friend of thirty years can be an annoying idiot. If I go away, you're coming with me.'

'Deal. Sage Consulting is not the same without you here.'

'Ah, I get it. You miss me for my accounting skills and business insights. And I was thinking you were missing me for my body - the abs of flab, you know, and love.'

'You didn't let me finish,' she laughed. 'I miss those abs of flab more than you know. When do you get back?'

'Five days. I'd be back sooner, but I can't leave Roger alone. It's not fair.'

'I suppose you're right. He shouldn't do all the work.'

'I meant to the clients and the business. Roger would be fine anywhere with a bar. He wears them out and the clients agree to anything to make him go away. I need to stay close to make sure he doesn't promise more than we can deliver.'

'That's good, isn't it?'

'It will be when we employ more staff. I'll take on a director's role and you and I will have more time together. If that's what you want?'

'I do, and I've been thinking the same. I have even been looking online for golf clubs.'

Kenneth's face froze.

'Not a good idea? Forget I said it.'

'Screen freeze,' he said. 'What have you been looking at?'

'Nothing. We'll talk when you get back. On a more mundane matter, did you have time to look at the file I sent?'

'I did. I agree with you about the missing money. There's no point in you staying if you can't talk to Joe. He's the only one who can tell you where the money has gone. You don't think he's done something awful, do you?'

Euphemia replayed their last encounter in her mind, searching for any micro-expressions which would betray Joe's true state of mind. The problem with micro-expressions is they are just that. They are over in a flash, gone too fast for most people to interpret them consciously. Her powers gave her the ability to recall situations perfectly and replay them in slow motion. She analyzed Joe's face frame by frame. After a few seconds, she shook her head. 'No, he was perfectly happy the last time I saw him and definitely not suicidal.'

'It means the most rational and obvious explanation will be the most likely. There has to be a woman, and he went to meet her. He'll be back and will explain where the money is and it will be fine again.'

'You're right. I'm being silly. There is also a police matter, but it can wait. You know how much I love... ,'

'Police matter?'

'Effie!'

The yell came from the living room.

'Effie. We need you. Now!'

'You'd better go,' said Kenneth, but he was talking to the ceiling in the office.

CHAPTER 17

She was shaking. Jane had one arm around her and Brutus was on full fluffy ear alert, one paw resting protectively on Ally's shoe. Josh, his little chest rising and falling faster than it should be, was standing beside his mother biting back tears. Kevin was fussing over cups and tea bags in the kitchen.

'Can you help?' asked Ally. 'It's Arthur. He took the ATV up the back of the farm two hours ago and he hasn't come back. He's not answering his phone and it'll be dark soon. Anything could have happened.' Her voice faded.

'I'll stay and look after things here,' volunteered Kevin. 'Don't worry, I've got this.' Three women and an eight-year-old boy turned and looked at him. 'I can't go. I'd be next to useless because of my acrophobia.'

'What is acrophobia?' asked Josh.

'It's the name of a very serious condition. It means fear of heights. Jane knows.'

'Is a hill a height?' asked Jane.

'Looking down, it is.'

'What if we need you for man-stuff? What if Arthur needs you?' asked Ally.

'Call me and I'll call emergency services. They're trained for that sort of thing. That's what they do. Now, who would like a nice cup of tea?'

Euphemia had left the room and now returned wearing her vest and carrying a backpack. 'I found some stuff in the cupboards, which might be useful. I'll run ahead. Jane, you and Ally, take the ute. Josh, stay here with your uncle and look after the dogs.'

'He's my Dad. I'm coming too,' said Josh. Legs apart, his skinny arms folded across his puffed out chest, Euphemia knew he was going to come no matter what anyone said.

'I'll look after the dogs and everything else. Don't worry about us,' said Kevin.

Ally sent him a withering look. 'You really are a ...,' She stopped and put her hands over Josh's ears. 'Tosser,' she finished.

'We'd better go. It's getting dark,' said Euphemia.

Jane grabbed jackets from a hall cupboard and threw one each to Ally and Josh. 'Ally, you're on gates,' she said as they headed out the door. 'See you there,' she called, but Euphemia had already left.

Not having to worry about being seen or, worse, identified in the fading light, Euphemia vaulted fences and dodging the occasional rabbit burrow powered up the hills. Five minutes after leaving the house, she had reached the top paddock and, slightly out of breath, stood perfectly still and listened. A rising wind played an eerie tune in the fence wires on the ridge-line as low clouds scudded across the sky, bringing with them the possibility of rain.

'Arthur,' she called, peering into the shadows.

Down by the stream, the cattle stirred restlessly on hearing her voice. One snorted and set off a cascade of alarmed noises as their outlines, black in the evening gloom, moved restlessly around each other.

'Arthuuur,' she called again.

No reply. Tracks in the dirt confirmed he had driven through the gate and down the hill towards the stream. She followed them, wondering if the steers would remember her as this morning's intruder or as the person responsible for getting them to food? She prayed it was the latter because she had had enough injuries for one day. A quick check of the other side of the ridge found nothing, so she zigzagged her way down the slope to the stream. Keeping her voice calm, she called out Arthur's name repeatedly. A day's gorging on fresh grass had filled the steer's bellies, their roundness momentarily lit by a sliver of moon escaping from behind the clouds.

Slowly she circled up and to the rear of the herd, giving them plenty of room to escape past her as she followed the stream to where it dropped under another fence and into the next paddock. The animals' legs slurped in the churned up mud, their heads rearing up as they bunched together away from her. Closest to her was the morning's nemesis, his horns shining white in the gloom. Taking a high route past them, she jumped across the stream and climbed the hill opposite to get a new and better vantage point. The herd backed up, keeping their collective eye on her. Then one moved. She spotted the ATV upside down in the stream, balanced precariously against the fence at the bottom of the paddock.

'Arthur,' she called again, aiming her voice at the ATV. Nothing. Arms flapping to shoo the steers away, she ran to the machine, taking care where she put her feet. Piles of sloppy manure were everywhere. She could cope with running shoes full of mud, but running shoes full of cow poop were another matter entirely. The cattle backed further up the narrow valley, some more frightened than others, their eyes shining white against black hides. Thankfully, the 'horned one' stayed with the rest of the herd.

She put her hand on the upturned machine. It was still warm. Either the accident had just happened, which she doubted because she would have heard it on her run up the hill, or the engine hadn't stopped when it overturned and it had run out of fuel in the last ten minutes. She squatted down and searched for Arthur underneath, but saw nothing. She stood up. Had he been thrown clear? Her foot slipped from under her and she sprawled across the ATV tipping it forwards. Mud squelched as the rear chassis sucked free. Wedged against a fencepost, the machine slid forwards slightly. The post creaked, then snapped, the machine started slipping slowly and inexorably towards the drop. She scrambled backwards, her foot slipped again, but this time it wasn't on a rock. It was on something round and soft and it was moving. In horror, she saw a leg dragged away from under her through the water, towards the fence and the sheer drop on the other side.

Euphemia had a moment to grab first one foot, then the other. She had less time to wedge her feet against the rocks in the streambed and haul back with all her strength. The remaining fence posts groaned and creaked as they slowly ratcheted out of the ground. Her heels dug deeper into the bottom of the stream. She tucked a leg under each arm and leaning back with all her might, tried to pull Arthur free.

The machine jerked forwards, exposing first his pelvis followed by an arm, then his chest and the other arm, his shoulders and head. Thankfully, he had been lying face up. He wasn't face down in the water and so hadn't drowned. Freed from the weight of the machine, his chest movements jagged, he gulped air and struggled, twisting against Euphemia loosening her grip on his legs. His mouth opened, but no sound came. A black strap tightened under his chin. His eyes blazed with fear as he stared up at her. Still attached to the ATV by a strap, he was being dragged towards the edge of the drop.

Two fence posts gave way with a loud cracking and splintering of wood. The ATV teetered on the edge, then tipped and disappeared. In a microsecond Euphemia threw herself forwards unhooked the strap of Arthur's binoculars from under his chin and landed beside him in the water. There was a humongous crash followed by three loud thuds as the ATV landed, then somersaulted down the hill spraying broken bits of metal and rubber in its wake. The silence which followed, was broken by the sound of a woman's screams.

'He's all right,' Euphemia yelled, her voice booming across the valley.

Arthur lay in the stream, his eyes closed, his face a sickly greyish white, his breathing shallow. As if he wasn't wet enough, a squall of rain brushed over them. Euphemia picked him up in her arms like a baby and carried him past the cattle mess to an area where the grass was dry. She put him down gently and checked his pulse. Weak and too fast. He was cold from being in the water for so long. She found the emergency blanket in her backpack and tucked it around him. The cattle standing on the opposite bank watched them. The ute, straining in first gear, made its way through the last gate. Euphemia, looking up the hill, saw the headlights scoping the sky. Leaving Arthur in the recovery position, she ran up to meet it and showed Ally where to park.

'Josh stays here,' she warned. 'You stay with him, Jane. Ally, come with me.'

'Wait, I can't see you,' Ally called.

'Sorry, forgot.' Euphemia switched on the headlamp she'd put on earlier and handed Ally a spare. 'There are ten steers down there and I've only just got them settled. Another stranger is going to set them off, so keep close.' Ally didn't need to be told twice. Euphemia took her hand and guided her carefully down the rutted hillside.

'Arthur.' Ally dropped her hand and galloped down the hill to the silver blanket glinting in the gloom and knelt beside her husband hugging him. The cattle stirred on the other side of the stream. Nine backed away. One didn't. Head down, back flexed, he snorted and pawed the ground.

'Now? Really?' said Euphemia. She crossed the stream to get between him and Ally. 'This time, I'm ready, you inconsiderate bastard.' Standing in his sight line, she waited, legs apart. He charged. When his horns were within reach, she grabbed them, stopping him in his tracks, then using the horns as a lever, she twisted his head around and down. Using every ounce of strength, until he was brought to his knees, then she turned him on his side where he lay, huffing into the mud. She tied the rope from her backpack, around his legs. That's where she left him, surprised, trussed, and powerless to hurt anyone.

Ally, focused on her husband, didn't see what had happened. But someone did. Euphemia heard a gasp from above. She looked up to see a pale eight-year-old face duck out of sight. Dammit. He'll have to wait. She splashed back across the stream and joined Ally beside her unconscious husband.

CHAPTER 18

THE TRIP DOWN THE HILL WAS FRAUGHT. NOT ONLY because it was dark, and the paddocks were steep, but because Jane was driving while Ally looked after her husband. Being a farm, the gates still had to be opened and closed, notwithstanding the unconscious man desperately in need of medical attention lying in the back of the ute between his wife and small son. Euphemia ran ahead, letting Jane through one gate, closed that and then hurrying past the ute and opening the next. By the time they reached the house, the ambulance was waiting.

They lifted Arthur into the back and, with the paramedics working to get lines in and bloods off, and with sirens wailing, the ambulance disappeared down the drive to the nearest hospital in Masterton.

'She'll easily beat the ambulance,' said Euphemia, as they waved Ally off in the white Volvo.

'Yup,' said Josh.

'As the point man coordinating our response, I think that went smoothly. Well done team,' said Kevin, putting his arms around Jane and Euphemia's shoulders.

Euphemia shuddered and stepped out of his embrace. Jane stayed where she was, looking thoughtful. 'Credit where credit's due, Kevin,' she said finally. 'You did a good job calling the ambulance.'

'I did, didn't I,' he replied and planted a kiss on her forehead.

'We need to talk. Not here. At the homestead, okay?' Jane cocked her head towards the yawning Josh.

'You two go,' Euphemia said. 'Young man, let's get you fed and into bed. You've got school tomorrow.'

'School?'

'What else did you think you'd be doing?'

'Visiting my father.'

He had a point. Keep calm and carry on might not be the best policy after all. 'Fair enough,' she said. 'Hope you like bacon and egg pie, because that's all I have. Eat first, then bed. We'll talk in the morning.'

Getting Josh into bed proved to be quite a process. First, he insisted he have a shower because that's what he did at home. Then cross his heart and hope to die. Yes, Brutus did sleep in his bed and he slept beneath the sheets. The way the Chihuahua enthusiastically burrowed under the bedclothes, leaving only his fluffy behind exposed on the pillow, seemed to confirm this assertion and, without evidence to the contrary, Euphemia let it go. After such a busy evening, she didn't need a stressed Chihuahua and an exhausted eight-year-old, both unable to sleep. Next, she had to read him a story, or rather a chapter, in the book he was reading on his Kindle. *Treasure Island* by Robert Louis Stevenson seemed rather a mature selection for such a young boy, but she let that go, too.

She read two chapters and, thinking he had fallen asleep, turned out the light. She was tiptoeing out of the room when his sleepy little voice piped up, 'What you did to that steer was incredible, Mrs Sage. I've never seen anything like it—not even on YouTube.'

'I did nothing to the steer,' she said. 'Now go to sleep.'

'Okay. Night.' He paused. 'Mum and Dad will be amazed when I tell them.'

'They will say you have an overactive imagination. I suggest you say nothing. They have enough to worry about.'

'You're right,' he said. 'I uploaded it to TikTok so they can look at it when Dad gets better.'

Euphemia switched on the light. 'What did you upload to TikTok?'

'The video of you wrangling the steer. That's the right word? Wrangling?'

'It was dark.'

'That doesn't matter. I set the camera on night mode. There's enough to make it very interesting. It hasn't gone live yet but I only need to click one button.' He paused again. 'Unless... ,'

'Unless what?' She couldn't believe this sweet little boy, his freshly washed face resting on the pillow next to the fluffy bottom of his beloved dog, could be about to blackmail her. Whoever put cameras into phones had a lot to answer for.

'Ten thousand dollars, in my bank account by the end of the week.'

Just like that. What do they teach kids in school nowadays? Euphemia stared at the ceiling, avoiding the bright blue eyes shrewdly assessing her.

'Oh, you were talking to me.' Euphemia said. 'Because for a minute I thought there was a millionaire in the room.'

'You are a millionaire. You're a boomer. Your generation has all the money. You've had the benefit of years of government subsidies, which my generation won't get. And you own a business. So please don't play the poverty card, Mrs Sage. It's beneath us both.'

'Who are you? I mean, really?'

'My name is Kincaide. Josh Kincaide. Don't underestimate me, Mrs Page. I have the video. It's on TikTok and it will go live. Unless you pay up. Now would you mind if I went to sleep? It's been a long day. And could you please leave the hall light on?' He added, his voice suddenly sounding less confident. 'In case there are monsters.'

CHAPTER 19

Euphemia slept well, despite being in a room next to a pint-sized blackmailer. Eight years old and extorting money from an adult, that Kincaide Kid was some piece of work. He could wait. She needed proof the video existed before she did anything. He knew that. And she knew his greed trumped his desire to achieve TikTok infamy. Time would be her ally. She intended to use it to full advantage.

She woke at dawn to see Jane carrying her shoes, her head down and shoulders drooping, tiptoeing past her door. This was a different Jane from yesterday. Yesterday she had sauntered in after breakfast, chin in the air and smiling smugly as she completed a post-coital-victory lap of the kitchen. Maybe the lustre of Kevin's charms had worn off - disappearing into the night along with his gumption. Euphemia hoped so. Jane could do so much better.

There seemed little point in going back to sleep. Arthur was in hospital and there was still no message from Joe. It meant there were decisions to be made. She made her best decisions outside after a run, so she pulled on her merino running gear number twos and slipped out of the house.

At the top of the hill, she stopped to admire the view. The valley floor was blanketed by mist, while in the distance, the deep blue silhouette of the Tararua range marked the line between land and sky. The dense green bush-clad hills of the sanctuary across the valley colour-blocked against the yellow grass in the surrounding paddocks. A light flashed from inside the sanctuary. She waited, but it didn't happen again. She focused on where it had been, right in the middle and halfway up. Maybe Sandy was checking his traps - and the sunlight had reflected off the surface of something shiny. That would explain it.

Magpies in the trees around the homestead rose through the mist, their wings thumping the air until they settled again, their calls reminding her of the poem -*The Magpies* by Denis Glover, the first New Zealand poem she had liked at school. His made-up words resembled their calls: the quardles, oodles, ardles and the wardles, reminding her she was a long way from her home in the city.

She shook herself. She hadn't come up here to admire the view. The cattle needed to go into a safer paddock. She didn't want to have to call the vet to come out and euthanize a beast which had fallen over the unfenced drop, or got tangled in loose wire. She also planned to check the scene of last night's drama. In daylight, before anyone arrived to muddy the evidence. As it was a farm accident, the authorities would have to be notified. The hospital had probably entered the details into the WorkSafe website last night. Inspectors would likely be here to conduct a scene examination either today or tomorrow, and she guessed they'd take the ATV away to have a mechanic to look over it.

She changed into her gumboots and put her trainers in her backpack. Calmly, she moved around behind the herd then walked forwards her arms wide. All ten went into the adjacent paddock without a fuss. Even her nemesis was docile this morning, trotting past her like the lamb he definitely wasn't. There wasn't as much grass in the lower paddock but from the looks of their bellies, a day on hard rations would do them good.

She secured the gate, then followed the tracks of the ATV to the top of the hill and down again. The churned-up mud and cow poop on either side of the stream made the ground slippery, and she was pleased she was wearing gumboots. As the sun climbed over the ridge line, a ribbon of mist formed on the surface of the stream. For a few minutes until it cleared, she felt as if she were floating above the ground in a magical world of nebulous shapes and uncertain surfaces.

The tracks of the ATV down the side of the hill, marked out by the morning dew on crushed grass, ran in a straight line before veering away near the bottom. An exposed surface on a half-buried rock had been ground away where the ATV hit it. Deep impressions in the mud confirmed that it had rolled several times before stopping upside down in the water, with Arthur pinned underneath.

Thankfully, the water was shallow, so he didn't drown, but being spring-fed, it was freezing. He stayed warm while the engine was running, but it was sheer luck she found him before cold and hypothermia claimed him. Shading her eyes with her hand, she looked back up the slope. There were no brake marks, just the tracks leading straight downhill.

She splashed down the stream and peered over sagging fence wires to the fifteen-foot drop into the next paddock. Fifty yards away, the ATV lay where it landed, on its side and surrounded by metal and broken bits of plastic. She vaulted the wires, almost losing her footing on the slimy surface below, then steadied herself and walked over to the machine. The handlebars were buckled. One of the front tyres had a hole in it, the wheel rim bent out of shape. Mud and strands of green slime coated the body.

Euphemia was no mechanic. Any interest she had in cars was based on color, and even this was negotiable. She did, however, understand the workings of small engines because she mowed the lawns in Thorndon every week and liked to keep the mower running efficiently.

Both brake cables on the ATV were loose when they should have been encased in solid plastic sheaths. This can't have happened in the accident or the sheaths themselves would have been damaged. They only looked the way they did because someone had gone to the trouble of sliding the cables out before the accident. Without brakes, Arthur had no chance of controlling the ATV on the downhill slope.

A grid search revealed nothing else, so she hauled herself back up to the stream and searched its banks, then the stream bed itself. Glimmers of wet steel caught her eye. A wing nut was wedged under a rock. The other one had landed in a pile of mud and cattle poop. Holding her breath, she took it out and quickly rinsed it in the stream. Her suspicions were confirmed when she saw the inner threads on both nuts had been filed smooth. With the sheaths pulled back, the bare nuts would have easily jiggled free as Arthur drove up the hill. When he applied the brakes, there was nothing for the cables to strain against. No wonder there were no skid marks. Someone had sabotaged the ATV.

CHAPTER 20

'Joe? It's Euphemia. Don't worry, but Arthur's had an accident, and he's in hospital. He'll be okay, but you have to come home. If you don't call back, I'm calling the police.'

Jane looked up from her plate of toast. 'What are you going to do if he doesn't... you know?'

'I will call the police.'

'If he doesn't and you do, does that mean we have to stay?'

'We don't have a choice. Someone has to look after Josh.

As if on cue, Josh appeared at the top of the stairs in his pajamas, his blonde hair sticking to one side of his head, with Brutus hung over his shoulder. 'Where's Mummy?'

'He is the most gorgeous little boy.' whispered Jane.

'Isn't he? And so enterprising.'

Jane frowned. 'Not a word I would have used, but whatever.'

Euphemia almost gagged when Josh put his thumb in his mouth and, still holding, Brutus came over to Jane and put his hand on her knee. 'Will you give me a cuddle?' he asked. His blue eyes stared up at her, and Jane pulled him into her arms.

'Oh my God - he is so cute,' she mouthed over his head to Euphemia.

Josh, his little chin resting on Jane's shoulder, fixed Euphemia with a steely glare and rubbed his thumb and fore-finger together in the age-old gesture for money. Euphemia didn't gag, but she spluttered. It took all her self-restraint to stifle her desire to reach out and pat his sweet little cheek—hard and more than once. Before she could succumb to the temptation, Brutus wriggled out of Josh's embrace, jumped down, and started barking. Petal leapt up and rushed to his side and joined in. Their eyes met, and they knew what to do. They egged each other on in a hysterical chorus of the small dog symphony, which stopped only when the door swung open to reveal Sandy and Fergus. Brutus and Petal couldn't stop. They had worked themselves up into such a frenzy that they sprinted over the furniture, circled the living room and burst out the door onto the driveway, then like a pair of tiny greyhounds ran as fast as they could to wherever they might end up.

Sandy, disgusted at seeing two dogs out of control, yelled after them, telling them in no uncertain terms to behave and get back inside. One circuit of the LandRover later and Brutus and Petal did as they were told, leaping the steps and lapping the kitchen island before skittering to a halt next to Euphemia.

'Are they always like that?' asked Sandy. He raised an eyebrow in disapproval as Fergus sat quietly at his side.

'It's the country air,' Euphemia said.

'If you say so.'

Jane unwrapped Josh's arms from around her neck and held out her hand. 'Jane French,' she said. 'We haven't met.' With her head tipped to the side, she gave him her best Princess Di smile.

Automatically, Euphemia bridled. *I saw him first,* she

thought. *'Oh God. Did I just think that? Where are you marriage-policewoman? Tell me to think about my husband. About Kenneth. He's good looking too - in his own sweet way. Yes, but even you, Constable Straight'n'Narrow, has to admit, Sandy Martin is one of the best-looking men you have ever seen or will ever see in your entire life.'*

She sighed.

Then Jane sighed.

Then they both sighed loudly together at the same time.

Thankfully, someone was thinking about something other than the man's good looks. It was Sandy.

'I've got the quote for the helicopter,' he said. 'They can fit us in on Friday.'

'I want to go in the helicopter,' Josh said.

'It's a working helicopter. It's not for little boys,' Sandy said.

'Mrs Sage,' Josh said. 'Tell him I can go in the helicopter.'

'You heard Mr. Martin. He says you can't. So you can't.'

'But I want to.'

Euphemia wondered whether a little tap on the bottom constituted child abuse in today's PC environment. Surely a tap wouldn't warrant a conviction. A fine possibly, but nothing more. 'Jane, would you help Josh get dressed?'

'I'm eight. I can dress myself.'

Euphemia stepped away from the boy, putting the kitchen bench between them for safety's sake. 'Okay. Why don't you have breakfast and then get dressed? Mr Martin and I have work to do in the study.'

After what had already been a stressful morning, it was a relief to come into the study and sit down. Euphemia sat at her desk while Sandy pulled Jane's chair around and sat beside her. So close she could see little hairs poking out above the buttons on the shirt, which strained across his manly chest.

'Why is Josh here?' he asked.

'Arthur was in an accident. The ATV rolled. Ally is staying with him at the hospital.'

'Is he okay?'

'I think so. We're taking Josh in later, so we'll find out then.'

'Demanding little bugger, isn't he?'

'More than you know.'

Sandy pulled a notebook and pencil out of his pocket and flicked through the pages until he got to the one he wanted.

'This is the all-up cost of hiring the helicopter for the morning - weather permitting. This is for the mesh and for a couple of men to help position it in place after we lift the damaged section out.' He passed her his notebook.

Euphemia couldn't believe how much it was going to cost - over twelve thousand dollars. For a sanctuary which didn't earn its keep, it was too much.

'Joe should make this decision.'

'Have you heard from him yet?' he asked.

'No, but if I don't soon, I'm calling the police. I'm worried something has happened.'

Sandy was sitting so close to her their faces were almost touching. She smelled coffee on his breath and felt the warmth of his body radiating against her. Their eyes met and held. She coughed and leaned back in her chair. She wanted to fan herself, but that would be too obvious.

'Joe will be fine,' he said. 'It's not the first time he's gone AWOL. But the sanctuary won't be fine if we don't fix this hole. It's been there longer than I thought. No wonder it's so quiet. Luckily, the birds aren't on their nests at this time of year.'

'I'm curious. The sanctuary is important to Joe, otherwise why would he put excellent farming land under covenant and spend so much money on the fence?'

'Your point is?'

'Why hasn't he noticed the hole before now?'

'That's way above my pay grade, but it is funny you should say that. He has been distracted lately, and you're right. The hole has been there long enough for the predators to get in and he should have picked it up.' Sandy replied. 'I work on the assumption rich people have expensive hobbies and it's not my place to comment.'

Euphemia caught herself before saying what she wanted to say. That Joe wasn't rich. That the farms weren't making money and that the sanctuary was a luxury he couldn't afford. She didn't know Sandy well enough to trust him. He might be outrageously good looking, but so was Ted Bundy, the serial killer.

Knowing Arthur's accident was no such thing changed everything. Joe was missing. The sanctuary had been sabotaged and so had the ATV. It was sheer luck a super woman had found Arthur before it was too late, otherwise she wouldn't be going to a hospital later - she would be taking Josh to a funeral parlor.

'What happens if we don't replace the mesh on Friday?' she asked.

'More predators, I guess. The temporary repairs can't hold forever and before you ask, I don't have time to do regular patrols.'

'I'll talk to Arthur and Ally and let you know their decision tomorrow.' She got up, pulled down Westward Ho, and the door swung open. She waited for Sandy to precede her, but being an old-fashioned gentleman, he was waiting for her. Confusion reigned along with the dance of several miss-steps until Euphemia decided valor was the better part of honor and exited first.

CHAPTER 21

Josh twisted his hand free from Euphemia's grasp and started running. It didn't matter he was in a hospital and supposed to respect the right of patients to peace and quiet. He wanted to see his father. He sprinted down the corridor, sliding to a stop outside each room to check the occupant, until finally he spotted Arthur in a room by himself at the end of the ward. By the time Euphemia caught up with him, Josh was sitting on the bed beside his father demanding to know when he was coming home. Arthur was awake, his hair and face were still streaked with dried mud, and there were IV lines in both arms, but he was upright, talking and making sense. That's what really mattered.

'Not today, son,' said Arthur, ruffling his son's hair. 'Maybe tomorrow.'

'Does that mean I get to stay at the New House again tonight?'

'As long as Mrs Sage doesn't mind?'

'I don't mind,' Euphemia said. 'I'm happy to help. Where is Ally?'

'She's at a friend's place in town. She went to school here, so as soon as her friends found out what happened, offers of places to stay came flooding in. It wouldn't happen in Hong Kong. I believe I owe you a debt of gratitude for saving my life. She told me what you did. Thank you, too, for looking after Josh. Jane's brother is. Well, you know.'

'Uncle Kevin is you know what?' Josh asked.

'Your uncle,' said Arthur firmly.

Josh winked knowingly at Euphemia and giggled. She ignored him.

'You don't mind looking after Oakhill, do you? I need Ally with me. She can talk to the doctors better than I can. She remembers what they say. My head's a bit wonky. But look, I'll understand if you have to go back to Wellington.'

'No, we'll stay. We're happy to. There are some things we need to discuss. In private.'

Josh glowered at her and folded his arms across his chest. 'I'm private.'

'No, you're not.' Ally said. She walked in and swung Josh off the bed for a hug. 'You're the least private boy I have ever met. How would my son like to take me to the café for a coffee? And as a reward for being nice to your mother, you can have anything you like.'

'Anything?' Josh sounded as if he didn't believe her, but was prepared to entertain further negotiations.

'Anything.'

'As much cake as I want?'

'Within reason.'

'You said anything.'

'Okay. You drive a hard bargain. Don't blame me if all your teeth fall out when you're twenty- three.'

Euphemia watched the promise of endless cake battle it out with Josh's desire to hear what she was going to say to his father. The cake won but only by the slimmest of margins. He flung her a warning look as he let his mother lead him away.

'My son is either going to discover the cure for cancer or blow up the world,' said Arthur, fading back into his bank of pillows.

'He is a unique little boy.'

'I've heard him called a lot of things but unique sums him up nicely.' There were dark rings under Arthur's eyes and his skin was a light shade of yellow. He winced as he moved to get comfortable.

'I'll save you the trouble,' he said. 'The accounts look awful and Oakhill is, for all intents and purposes, broke.'

'Add to that two acts of sabotage that we know of and your brother is missing.'

'Sabotage?'

'One, the hole in the fence and two, I think someone deliberately loosened the brake cables on the ATV.'

'I thought that when they didn't work.' He bit his lip. 'I thought I was going to die.'

'You very nearly did.'

'And if you hadn't got there in time, I would have.'

'It was a team effort. You know there's been no work done at the Lake Farm all year.'

'Yes.'

'And there's no winter feed for the stock.'

'Yes.'

'And the fences are broken?'

'Yes.'

'And there is almost no capital left?'

'Yes.'

'Would you stop saying yes?'

'Yes. I mean, I know.'

'You do?'

'The farm was another reason for us to come home. We came back so Elizabeth could get treatment, but after Charlotte ran off with the manager, we knew things would go downhill. Joe pretends he's a farmer, but he knows diddly squat about running the station. He only stayed for the sanctuary. Derek and Charlotte were the real farmers- they kept the place running at a profit. And rightfully they got angry when Joe spent money on the sanctuary rather than reinvesting it back into the station. But he wasn't. He was helping us.'

Euphemia was surprised to see tears in his eyes.

'Do you want to hear the truth? We didn't come came back so much as we got out while we still could.' Arthur gulped. 'It wasn't safe for us to stay.'

'And Joe knew this.'

'It was his idea. Now he's missing.'

'Why was he helping you?'

Arthur looked out the window. Euphemia followed his gaze. It was a dull day. The sticks poking out of the damp earth had a month ago been vibrant shrubs. A blackbird hopped amongst the dead leaves, its yellow beak poised to drag out any worm traveling too close to the surface.

'Our daughter,' sighed Arthur, 'she got in with the wrong crowd. Kids with too much money and whose parents were too wrapped up in their careers or their social lives to take any notice. We didn't pick up on it until it was too late. By then, she had emptied our bank accounts to pay for her drugs. We thought we'd got her the help she needed. She told us she was feeling better. She started putting on weight, but on her first day out of the unit, she ran off. Have you ever been to Hong Kong?'

'Only to the airport.'

'There are so many places to hide. We were desperate to find her before they took her into China. We hired every private detective we could. We sold our apartment and cashed up whatever we had left in the market. It was Joe who finally tracked her down, but she came with baggage. She owed money to one of the triads. A lot of money. Do you know how much interest they charge?'

'I can imagine.'

They sat in silence for a while, and then Arthur spoke again. 'We had to sedate her before they would let us bring her home. The facility in Auckland has locks on the doors. They tell us things happened to her in Hong Kong and it's going to take a long time before she'll get better. If she gets better. It's our only hope, and it's taking everything we have.' A tear ran down his cheek and he wiped it away. 'Do you know what it's like to lose a child to drugs? To see your little girl dragged so low you don't recognize the baby whose chubby arms used to wrap around your heart when you got home from work? All that's left is...,' he broke off. 'I can't say it out loud. We want our Elizabeth back and we'll do whatever it costs.'

Euphemia gave a silent thank you to the universe for keeping Kezia and Nicky safe.

'Joe has been magnificent. There was never any question about the money. He's been paying off her debt because he knows what will happen to her and to us if he doesn't.'

'So that's where it was going?' Euphemia said. 'Charlotte never suspected?'

'I don't think so. She blamed the sanctuary. Do you know the triads monitor the police radio and Internet channels? They will know if you report my brother is missing. They said Josh was next if we did anything silly. You haven't seen what they do. I thought coming home would keep us safe, but it hasn't. The triads don't forgive and they don't forget.'

'Okay,' she said. 'Now I know what's going on, I promise no police. Not yet.'

Arthur reached over and gripped her arm tightly enough to hurt. 'Promise me you will keep Josh safe until we get home.'

Euphemia extracted her arm and stood up. 'I promise.'

'I'm sorry you've got caught up in our mess.'

'I'm not. And it's not hopeless.'

'I know that. We've been through the options. We don't have to sell Oakhill as long as the planning permission for the retirement village comes through. It's so damn slow. You know, the village was really Joe's idea. He knew the sanctuary would be a unique selling point. He knows these people, the green oldies, and he knows it will appeal to their altruism and their need to save the planet one last time before they die. He was going to discuss it with you when he saw you, but now it may be too late. I am terrified the triad has him.'

'Leave it with me,' she said, standing up.

Arthur burst out laughing. 'That's the funniest thing I've heard since this nightmare started. With all due respect and please don't take this the wrong way, but I hardly think a Hong Kong triad is going to take any notice of you.'

'You'd be surprised,' Euphemia replied.

CHAPTER 22

'S{\small EE} {\small THAT}?' S{\small ANDY} {\small POINTED} {\small TO} {\small A} {\small PATTERN} {\small IN} {\small THE} dust. 'That's a ferret's footprint—an adult judging by the depth.'

They were part way up one of the rough tracks inside the sanctuary. It was not only rough but narrow and even though someone had cut steps into the hill in some parts, in others; they had to grab whatever branch was closest and haul themselves up. Sandy led the way, followed by Josh. Euphemia brought up the rear, providing the boy with a boost from behind when his short legs couldn't reach the next step. Tree roots and crumbly rocks added to the obstacles in their way— it was slow going and hard work. Cool under the trees, Euphemia was pleased she had won the battle with Josh to get him to wear a jacket.

Had the girls been as difficult as this little boy? She didn't think they had been, but maybe time had smoothed over daily disagreements and pointless battles? He couldn't always be like this, or was he being a brat because of his father's accident? Whatever, it was tiring to be around him, especially when she had more important things to think about.

'He needs a treat,' Jane had said in the hospital car park after they said goodbye to his parents. 'How about McDonald's for lunch?'

'Who needs the treat?' asked Euphemia, knowing Jane had a particular fondness for chicken nuggets and barbecue sauce.

'We all do,' she replied.

They ate inside at one of the not so clean tables, gorging on fries, nuggets, and Big Macs followed by a chocolate ice-cream sundae for Josh and black coffees for the grown-ups. Euphemia realized how hungry she was when she ordered a large size of everything with extra fries. The food brought back fond memories of taking the girls for Happy Meals at the age was Josh was now. Somewhere amongst the junk in the attic, there was a shoebox of McDonald's plastic toys. The girls had grown up and left home, but when she suggested the box should either go to the dump or the op shop, they greeted this with howls of outrage. How dare she get rid of their treasured mementos of childhood? Easily had been her reply. 'Certainly easier than getting you to take it away.'

Already this afternoon, they had seen the footprints of two rats, lots of mice and worst of all, a mature ferret. She hoped it wasn't a pregnant female. The bush was depressingly silent and there was no sign of the birds. If they didn't act to eliminate the predators soon, they would decimate what was left of the sanctuary. Joe's hard work, the money he had spent to save his precious bush and its bird life would be for nothing. Worse, the retirement village was rapidly losing its unique selling point.

'This is boring,' said Josh, slashing a manuka bush with his hand. 'Why did I have to come? I want to go home.'

The whine in his voice has the same effect on Euphemia as fingernails being slowly dragged down a blackboard. She tucked her hands into the pockets of her vest and, under her breath, counted slowly to ten. Had Kezia and Nicky been as irritating as this boy? Maybe. Maybe she made exceptions for them because they were her children and she was hard wired not to mind when they were annoying? Or maybe the passage of time had diminished her tolerance and eroded her patience. Whatever, she was regretting her commitment to Arthur to look after him. If he kept up the whining, she would personally hand him over to the triad.

Fortunately, Sandy was more patient. He crouched down beside Josh, one finger to his lips. When he had the boy's attention, he pointed to a branch in the just bashed bush quivering beside him. Josh squinted his eyes focusing where Sandy was pointing, but seeing nothing, he snorted. There was a movement, a flash of blue followed by a tiny bark. Sandy pointed again. By now Euphemia was as curious as the eight-year-old and bent over to see what they were looking at.

'Oh,' said Josh. Excited, he turned and tugged on Euphemia's vest to make sure she could see it too.

A tiny lizard - black eyes, and a flickering of skin where ears should be, colored green with spots of white, was clinging to the branch. It was so well camouflaged, even Euphemia, with her enhanced visibility, found it hard to distinguish the creature from the spiky leaves surrounding it.

'What is it?' whispered Josh.

'That is a Wellington green gecko,' whispered Sandy. 'You are very lucky to see it. Normally, they live higher in the canopy. And they are the most marvellous creatures. I much prefer geckos to birds.'

The gecko opened its mouth and barked again.

'Look,' said Josh. 'Did you see that?'

'I did.'

'He's got a blue mouth.' Josh jiggled up and down with excitement, hopping from one foot to the other. With a flick of its tail, the gecko was gone.

'Is there another one? I want to see it,' Josh demanded.

'Look then,' Sandy said. 'But stay on the track and be back here in ten minutes. There's something I have to show Mrs Sage.'

'Call me Euphemia,' she said as Josh disappeared around a bend up ahead. Should he go off alone? He was only eight, and it was a big sanctuary. What if he got lost? What if he fell and hurt himself? Arthur and Ally didn't need anything else to worry about.

'He'll be fine.' Sandy said reassuringly. 'He is so busy searching for geckos, he won't go far. He is also eight. It's time he started doing things for himself without an adult around. That boy has been mollycoddled far too long.'

'Mmm,' she said, half listening. The other half was concentrating on Josh's footsteps in the leaf litter twenty feet ahead. He was making slow progress because he stopped to scrutinize each bush before moving to the next one. Sandy was right, he wasn't going far. She tipped her head at an unfamiliar sound. Higher, and towards the middle of the sanctuary a harsh white noise, a click, then nothing. She stood perfectly still, waiting. It had lasted for less than a second. Sandy didn't seem to have heard it. Had she heard it? The replay in slow motion confirmed it had been real and when she added the location, it had come from roughly the same place where the flash had been this morning. She was about to plunge into the center of the sanctuary to find out what was going on when Sandy grabbed her arm.

'Come and see this,' he said, pulling her off the track towards the fence. She had no choice but to follow and look at what he was showing her; broken stalks among the ground ferns, leaves trodden into the earth. 'Someone has been here,' he said, pointing

'How did they get in? There are only two keys. You have one, and Joe has the other. Right?'

'Right. But look over here.' Sandy showed her an area on

the other side of the fence. 'See those holes in the dirt? I reckon a ladder made them. And look at this,' he knelt down next to an area of flattened grass. 'It's rectangular - a box? It's possible the predators didn't get in through the hole in the fence. Maybe someone brought them inside and released them. On purpose.' He walked over to one bush and lifted its branches off the ground. 'See this?' He picked up a stick and pointed at a lumpy line of black droppings, the length and width of a finger with twists at each end. 'Ferret droppings. And there.' He pointed at more poop further under the trees. 'There's two of them. I don't need to tell you what that means.'

'Two females would be better than a pair wouldn't they?'

'Not if both females are pregnant. It's April now. There could be twenty-four ferrets by September if I don't find them.'

'And five months after that - five hundred and seventy-four,' she added.

'That was quick.'

Such white even teeth, such twinkling eyes, such a good-looking man. A handsome man who can survive in the wild and who cares deeply for the environment and who possesses the most wonderfully beguiling, charismatic smile is an awfully attractive human being. Euphemia closed her eyes and thought of Kenneth.

'Who do you think is doing this?' she asked when her traitorous heart calmed down.

'Someone who hates Joe or the Kincaides? Don't like birds? Maybe they hate Oakhill Station and what it represents? Take your pick,' Sandy said. 'Whatever their reason, it's not good enough. It's environmental vandalism. I'm going to find the bastards and make them pay.'

Euphemia thrust her hands into her pockets. There could be a range of reasons for the sabotage, each one as plausible as it being a warning from a triad. But why would a triad bother to destroy a bird sanctuary when, by simply loosening a brake cable on an ATV, they could send a very direct message to the Kincaides? Releasing pests into a sanctuary was surely too subtle for any self-respecting member of a Hong Kong triad to be bothered with? Not that she knew any triad members, self-respecting or otherwise. But what would be their point? The hole in the fence might have gone unnoticed for months if Euphemia hadn't seen it by chance on her run.

'I'm back.'

Josh's reedy voice carried the hopeful expectation of an answer.

'Don't worry. We're coming,' said Sandy.

Handsome. A body to die for. Responsible. Good with children. And married to the ghastly Jocelyn.

CHAPTER 23

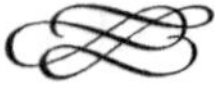

'Hardly anyone gets to see a Wellington green gecko,' said Josh. 'At least not in the wild, because they are so well camouflaged. They live in the upper branches of kanuka and manuka bushes, are active during the day and can live for twenty-five years. And, get this, they give birth to live young, not eggs like other reptiles. I have to go back. I didn't see any babies. The Wellington Green gecko is also called the barking gecko, and I heard it bark. Twice. Jane, are you listening?'

'Uh huh,' Jane murmured.

'I'm going to take off all my clothes, smear myself in peanut butter and roll on the sofa.'

'Uh huh.'

Josh shook his head and returned to his iPad. They were sitting in the study, Euphemia and Jane at their respective desks and Josh on a chair in the corner overlooking the valley. Relieved he had found something to occupy him, Euphemia looked again at the accounts. She estimated Joe and Arthur had diverted almost a quarter of a million dollars to the triad, mostly through a series of accounts on the dark net, and most of it in crypto-currency. No wonder she hadn't found it before.

So far Joe had liquidated family assets and worse, he had taken out mortgages on the Lake Farm and the grazing block near Featherston, the only properties which turned a profit. Oakhill Station had once provided a good return on capital, but as the wool price had dropped and with the price of lamb in the doldrums, the good times had ground to a halt fifteen years ago. Then a drought two years ago made things worse. Joe had been focused on the sanctuary and then on the construction of the New House, and hadn't diversified. Worse, he hadn't kept up with maintenance. The triad put the screws on at exactly the wrong time - if there ever was a good time for a blood, thirsty international gang of insane criminals to come into any life.

It reminded Euphemia of Hemmingway's description of financial ruin in one of his novels,

"How did you go bankrupt?" Bill asked.

"Two ways," Mike said. "Gradually and then suddenly."

A man she respected and liked was about to be brought low by events beyond his control. Joe could have hardened his heart and sacrificed Arthur's family to the triad, but that wasn't the way he thought or behaved. Family is family and we stick together in good times and bad, he had said on more than one occasion.

She made the last entry in the spreadsheet, applied the formulas, and groaned when the results appeared in the relevant cell. If the Kincaides were to keep anything, then the retirement village had to go ahead and quickly.

She called Ally and asked for the name of the person in charge of consenting the development at the council. Next, she wanted to know her if they had a developer in mind and got his name too. By the time she finished talking to everyone, it was almost dark. She closed her laptop, stretched, and wondered if she had time to fit in another run.

Josh looked up from his iPad. 'Jane, I need to talk to Mrs Sage. Alone, if you don't mind.'

'I'll make us something to eat, shall I? Maybe Kevin could join us. He's been alone in that great big house all day.'

'Let's all make dinner,' said Euphemia, getting up and pulling down Westward Ho. 'I'm starving.'

'But what about you-know-what?' asked Josh trying hard to wink and failing.

'You're not in a hurry?'

'Sort of.'

'Tomorrow then, after breakfast?'

'Promise?'

'Promise,' she replied. 'After breakfast' could mean any time between now and Christmas next year. It felt ridiculously good to outsmart an eight-year-old blackmailer.

CHAPTER 24

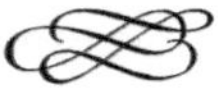

PETAL AND BRUTUS SLEPT THROUGH THE ARRIVAL OF the diesel SUV. They didn't react to the slamming of doors, followed by strange male voices wondering if they had the right place. At the first overly loud knock, however, both dogs leapt to attention and hurtled out of bed, barking furiously to let everyone know what they already knew. They had visitors.

Jane opened the door and two inspectors from WorkSafe, the agency responsible for investigating accidents in the workplace, introduced themselves, took off their boots and came inside in their thin city socks.

'Magnificent view,' said the older of the two men, walking over to the window.

'I'm Jason Shaw and this is my boss, Allan Hardcastle,' said the younger man. Allan tipped her a jaunty salute, and Jason pressed two business cards into Jane's hand. Both men wore zipped fleece jackets, the WorkSafe logo emblazoned on the left breast, over black turtlenecks and blue jeans. Allan had twenty years on Jason and a large beer gut, but otherwise, they looked the same.

Josh remained hunched over his bowl of cereal at the kitchen bench. He was muttering under his breath about yet another delay to the promised talk with Euphemia.

'Jane, would you take Josh to the homestead while I look after these gentlemen?' suggested Euphemia. Jane whisked the cereal bowl away, dumped the contents in the compost bucket, put the bowl in the dishwasher, then shooed Josh out the door - the dogs, sensing the men were no fun, trotted along behind.

'First, I'd like to ask you some questions. Then, if you can take us to the accident scene, that would be very helpful,' said Allan.

'You wouldn't like a drink?'

'We had coffee before we left, thank you,' said Jason. He opened his compendium, and pen raised, sat poised to take down her answers.

The inspectors were very professional. They listened as she explained what had happened, and what she had seen when she arrived and found the ATV overturned. They took it in turns to ask questions about when the vehicle was last serviced and by whom, as well as the names of the people on the farm most likely to drive it. These were questions she couldn't answer, so she referred them to Arthur when he was well enough or Joe when he got back. They tut-tutted when she said Arthur hadn't been wearing a helmet and shared meaningful glances when she confirmed there was no roll bar on the ATV.

'This is the third ATV accident in as many months,' said Jason. 'The other men died. Mr Kincaide was lucky you found him when you did.'

Allan grunted and stood up. 'Time we had a look.'

Euphemia travelled up to the accident site in their SUV and walked them through what had had happened. Jason took photos while Allan wrote in his notebook.

'A few more photos and I think we've got all we need,' said Allan. 'My guess is, Mr Kincaide lost control on that steep slope, the brakes locked up, and the thing rolled as soon as it hit the bank of the stream. Textbook case.'

Euphemia checked to see if he was joking. 'What about the loose cables?'

'Textbook case.' He clicked his pen and tucked it into the spine of his notebook.

'Yip,' Jason said. 'See it all the time. I wish farmers would stop thinking they were Vin Diesel and start wearing the appropriate gear.'

'You're not going to take the ATV away and get it checked by a mechanic?'

'We don't have the budget for fancy stuff,' said Allan. 'I've been doing this all my life. I know what happened. I'll submit a formal report after I get back to the office. Tell Mr Kincaide not to worry. He'll get a caution about his lack of safety gear and he will be required to do a health and safety course. But it's online and won't take long. I won't recommend a fine as it's a first offence and there were no employees put at risk. I think that covers it.'

Euphemia's eyes widened. The gobble-de-gook he was spouting with such conviction made no sense. 'Look at these again,' she said, waggling the brake cables back and forth. 'And these,' she said taking the filed off nuts from her pocket.

'You've investigated a few accidents, have you?' Allan shot a knowing smirk at Jason as he rocked back on his heels, his arms folded across his chest.

'No, but I can tell sabotage when I see it. Can you?'

Allan let his arms drop and drew himself up to his full five foot four inches, his stomach popping free of his belt as he puffed out his chest. 'I understand you're concerned. You women get so emotional when something like this happens. You lose all objectivity. That's what experienced investigators like me and Jason are here for—to put your mind at rest and to provide calm, rational answers. The cables came loose after the machine fell over the drop, caught on a fencepost most likely. Stop worrying and look after young Josh. You're doing a good job.'

'What if it didn't happen that way? What then?'

'That would be a matter for the police, not WorkSafe.'

'I'll call them.'

'And they'll call us and I will tell them it was an accident.'

'Why would you do that?'

Allan sighed and looked at his watch. 'You're a guest here, aren't you, Mrs Sage? You live in the city? Am I right? You know nothing about ATVs, about farming or about farms.'

Euphemia spoke, but he held up his hand, palm towards her. 'Let me finish. It's nice that a lady such as yourself is taking an interest, especially when you're still upset. I have examined the scene, and I am satisfied my findings are correct. Have I made myself clear?'

'Perfectly.'

'Excellent,' said Allan. 'Ready, Jason?'

'Yes boss,' Jason replied, walking around to the passenger side of their SUV. Allan climbed into the driver's seat and closed the door, his arm resting on the window ledge, his fingers tapping the steering wheel while he waited for Euphemia to climb into the back seat.

'Nice watch,' said Euphemia. Allan whipped his arm inside and pulled his cuff down over the brand new Tag Heuer.

He leaned out of the cab. 'Thanks. A present from the wife.'

'I'll walk, thanks. I have to check on the steers,' she said. 'Shut the gates, won't you?'

He nodded and swung the SUV around in a wide loop.

Euphemia heard Jason say, 'I thought your wife went off with Ron from accounting?'

'She did,' said Allan. He clenched his jaw and smiling at Euphemia through gritted teeth, he waved again.

CHAPTER 25

IT TOOK FORTY MINUTES BEFORE EUPHEMIA SPOKE to a real life policewoman. First she had to get past the chat-bot, the human receptionist, and the civilian volunteer trained to listen and utter sympathetic noises, but not much else. The policewoman too listened politely and said she would call back after making inquiries. That was it. No time given, just that she would call back.

Euphemia counted how many times they had offered her a number to call for support to help manage stress. Four. The chat-bot was programmed for rote empathy, too. She would have preferred to talk to a detective who would take her concerns seriously. But the preset hierarchy of calls made no provision for an urgent escalation to someone who could actually help. She cursed the science of process management but did her best to remain as optimistic as the young constable took down her number after spouting a litany of platitudes about people usually turning up. She then assured Euphemia they were taking her concerns seriously, but they couldn't act until more time had passed. 'I've talked to Mr Kincaide's brother, and he said not to worry,' said the policewoman when she phoned back fifteen minutes later. 'You may not know this, being a guest at the house, but Mr Kincaide regularly disappears for a few days and he always comes back.'

Euphemia pressed End.

If only she could talk to Nicky. Her daughter would believe her. For the seventh time, she called Nicky's phone and for the seventh time got the same message. *This number is not currently in service.* She could always call her daughter's old boss Detective Inspector Dave Richards, but after seeing how affectionate he had been to Nicky at Kezia's wedding, she felt awkward. Their relationship was new and at a tricky stage and she didn't want to put him off the family.

Nicky, her career-driven tomboy daughter, had been cautious when Euphemia spoke to her the day after the wedding. 'I like Dave,' she said. 'I might even love him. Whatever love means.' Nicky did that annoying quote mark thing with her fingers.

'Dave deserves better than the Prince Charles get-out-of-romance-free card. He's a good man. We like him. Put him out of his misery and tell him how you truly feel.'

'I would, but then he'd want us to live together, or get married or...' She chewed her lip and twisted a strand of her curly dark hair around one finger just like she had done as a child when something was worrying her.

'Tell me,' Euphemia said.

Nicky took a deep breath. 'I have wanted to be a detective for as long as I can remember.'

'Uh huh.'

'I'm doing well and I aced my exams. I'm working for a unit I've been trying to get into for a while. I'm in the best job I've ever had. But. It's secret. I can't tell anyone about it. Not you. Not Dad, not even Dave. The hours are long. I get called away at a moment's notice and I have to go. And the kicker is I'm about to go undercover and I won't be around for months. I shouldn't have even told you that. Don't tell Jane or it will be around the office in no time.'

'What are you saying?'

'Even Dave, who understands what I do, would not put up with a partner who is never there. What if he wants kids?'

'I see. You realize kids come with a nine month stand-down period,' said Euphemia.

'Hilarious. I need to slow things down for both our sakes. Being away will do that. He'll probably have hooked up with someone else by the time I get back. Jackie in comms is always flirting with him. She'd be a better wife to him than me. She stays in one place and has regular hours.'

'Your job is not the problem.'

'I thought you were listening.'

'I was listening. I am listening. Your problem is you haven't talked to Dave. You have made assumptions and followed them to the only conclusion you can think of. You. Not him. There are two of you in this relationship and before you start.' Euphemia held up her hand. 'You are in a relationship already. With him. That's what he thinks and what he wants. You have to talk to him and tell him what you're worried about. Remember, there is always more than one solution to any puzzle. Always.'

Nicky started to speak. Then stopped. She started to speak and stopped again. The lip chewing and the hair twisting resumed, but this time Euphemia detected the hint of a smile at the corner of her mouth.

Now Nicky, her second daughter, her sporty no-nonsense courageous little girl, was working undercover somewhere in the country for goodness knows how long. She would be in danger and she would love it. Euphemia had no say in the matter. She had to trust Nicky had been well-trained, and that whoever was in charge would not put her in danger beyond her capabilities. That's the thing about children, she thought.

They grow up and leave. They make their own decisions and all a parent can do is to be there as their touchstone when they need to come home so they can recover from whatever has happened before they go back out and face the world again.

Of course she worried. Mothers worry about their babies from the moment they find out they are pregnant until they draw their last breath. It is both the blessing and the curse of parenthood. She had learnt to put her worries aside whenever Nicky was on an assignment. She filed away her fears in a mental drawer marked 'not-now'. Otherwise, they would develop a life of their own and crowd out the problems in front of her, the ones she could actually do something about.

Problems like where that very annoying high-pitched buzzing was coming from. She walked onto the balcony to see if a swarm of bees was heading towards the house. Petal sat up and tilted her head from side to side listening too.

In the distance, a black dot flew up the valley, getting larger and larger as it approached the house. It stopped and hovered ten feet away, level with her face. A lens focused, then receded back into its casing and advanced again, Euphemia's bendy face reflected on its surface. The drone turned three hundred and sixty degrees on its vertical axis, waggled up and down, took off, and flew out of view. The hum-buzz faded, then grew louder, this time on the other side of the house before stopping.

Euphemia heard giggling, followed by shushing and more giggling. She opened the front door, picked up the drone, turned off the battery power, folded its arms back into its body and carried it downstairs.

'Yours?' she asked.

Josh and Jane sat huddled over the remote, trying to figure out why their new toy had stopped responding. They leapt off the bed when they saw her, Josh dropping the remote as if it was the murder weapon in a thriller. Jane smoothed her hair and straightened her shirt. Brutus yawned.

'Awesome isn't it?' said Josh.

'Where did you find it?'

'In Joe's room,' Jane said. 'I thought it was a video camera, so I asked Josh to show me how to use it because I wanted to make a video for Justine. I thought it would be a nice for her to see where I am.'

'Why were going through Joe's things?'

'I was looking for clues. To find where he might have gone.' Eyes down, Jane fiddled with the sapphire rings on her right hand.

'Did you find any?'

'What?'

'Clues.'

'No.'

'It was my idea,' said Josh, stepping forward.

'Sweet child.' She hugged the boy back against her.

Josh grinned at Euphemia, then poked out his tongue.

Euphemia was about to reply in kind when she had an idea. 'Does the camera work at night?'

'I don't know, but I could find out. Why?'

'I'll tell you later. Are there any other gadgets in Joe's room?'

'It's full of stuff. Come and look,' said Jane, leading the way into the bedroom.

'Josh has got you wrapped around his little finger,' said Euphemia.

'Don't listen to her Josh, she's a mean old witch.'

'You promised you wouldn't tell,' said Euphemia.

CHAPTER 26

Joe's cupboard was a veritable treasure trove of electronic gadgets, most still in their original packaging. His heavy hand on the Amazon 'buy-with-one-click' button, was yet another reason why Oakhill was going broke. There were enough solar powered electronic gate openers, soil moisture monitors, ear-tag barcode recorders and water-trough level meters to stock ten farms. None of them used. Jane volunteered to sort the boxes into piles according to function, price and the date of purchase. 'We could sell the newer ones to raise money for the cause,' she suggested.

'Good idea,' Euphemia said, but her eyes were on the boxes stashed on the top shelf. 'I want to tell you my idea. But let's have lunch first.'

* * *

'Venison sausage and gouda sandwiches. Who would have thought the combination would taste so good?' Jane said.

'Would anyone like those?' asked Josh, eyeing the last sandwiches on the plate.

'Go ahead, you're a growing boy.'

Euphemia put the plunger of coffee on the table along with the mugs. 'Now, for my plan.' Jane and Josh listened as she set out what they were going to do. They smiled and nodded enthusiastically as they asked questions and added suggestions.

'What sort of maniac would purposely try to kill geckos?' Josh asked. 'No one has seen a Wellington Green gecko here for three years. I looked it up. They're an endangered species.' He finished his sandwich, reached over and took the last one chewing slowly as shook his head in disbelief.

'Effie, you should call the police again,' said Jane. 'We might be dealing with an international wildlife poacher—an armed and dangerous international poacher, or worse poachers, plural. Didn't they catch two Germans stealing geckos in the South Island?'

Josh's fingers flew across the screen as he searched for information on his iPad. 'Got it.' He read, 'Back in 2012, they caught a guy with 16 jeweled geckos packed into tubes. New Zealand geckos are prized because they are active during the day and give birth to live young. They are sold at a wildlife market in Germany for huge prices.' He stopped and looked from Euphemia to Jane. 'This has to be stopped,' he said. 'This is my heritage they're stealing.'

'Don't you mean our heritage?'

'You need to be young to have a heritage,' he said.

'We're young,' said Jane.

Josh gave her a withering look.

Jane put her shoulders back and upped his wither with a haughty raise of her head. 'Our heritage,' she said, 'won't get much protection from two middle-aged women and an eight, year old boy. We need a man for this job. What about Sandy? Or,' she hesitated. 'Kevin?'

'Kevin didn't help with Dad,' said Josh.

'He's afraid of heights.'

'He's afraid of work,' Josh muttered, then seeing the look on Jane's face followed up with, 'Mum said that. Not me.'

'I'm not sure we can trust Kevin to keep this to himself,' said Euphemia.

'We're in the country. Who would he tell?'

'He has a phone, and he's on it an awful lot.'

'Yeah,' said Josh. 'How come he's allowed to use his phone all the time and I'm only allowed to use mine after I've done my homework? It's not fair.'

'He's an adult. You are eight. It's perfectly fair,' Euphemia said.

'The Children's Commissioner might see it differently. Just saying,' replied Josh.

'You're both being mean,' said Jane. 'Kevin does his best.'

'I'm sure he does. But time is short and there's a lot to organize. We're agreed two to one? Kevin is not an option?'

'Agreed,' said Josh.

'Okay,' said Jane. 'But we still need a man.'

CHAPTER 27

THINGS WERE GOING BETTER THAN EUPHEMIA
expected. Even without the man, Jane insisted they needed.
They had gone to bed earlier than normal - Josh protesting
loudly that he should be allowed to stay up until Euphemia
explained that if the saboteur or saboteurs did come, they
would need to be alert when it came time for action. Grudg-
ingly, he climbed into bed. Brutus nestled upside down beside
him. Josh fell asleep as soon as his head hit the pillow.
Euphemia was not so lucky. Jane's snoring kept her awake.
Typical Kevin — he was never around when she needed him.

Josh pushed Euphemia's door open at one o'clock in the
morning. 'She woke me up,' he said pointing to Jane's room.

Euphemia sat up and turned on the light. 'Try these.' She
held out a pair of earplugs she had found in the bathroom.
Josh didn't look hopeful, but took them and went back to his
room. Euphemia heard him whispering to Brutus, then
silence. She tried to doze off, but it was no good, so she lay in
the dark and pretended she was somewhere else. That didn't
work either. She tried counting sheep, she visualized the

spreadsheet for the Lake Farm, and she wondered how Kezia and Ben were getting on in Tahiti. Barbara had lent them her villa on an outer island for their honeymoon. In the photos, it looked fabulous, but isolated. On the drive to the airport, Kezia made her mother promise not to contact them unless it was an absolute and dire emergency. Euphemia agreed, but added that it would be great to hear from them no matter what. As there had been no calls, texts, or emails, she assumed they were enjoying themselves and left it at that. But it hurt. More than she would admit to anyone. To be excised from her daughter's life, even if the cut was only temporary, was painful. *Am I a clingy parent, after all?* The possibility shocked her, and she refocused her thoughts on a flock of sheep lining up and hurdling fences in order of size.

At two thirty, the red light beside her bed started blinking. *'Action stations,'* she thought, relishing the familiar surge of adrenalin coursing through her body.

It had been a long time since she had used her powers properly. She didn't count the stampede. In fact, she preferred to forget the whole embarrassing incident. Her misplaced bravado had caused her to be injured unnecessarily. It was a painful lesson in not getting too big for her proverbial boots, but more importantly, it reinforced not to use the powers as a plaything. In future she would use them only as they were designed to be used- carefully and with forethought.

Sun Tzu, the Chinese warrior and philosopher, had put it best when he said 'he will win, who knows when to fight and when not to fight'. Of course by he, he also meant she. He wasn't stupid.

Wrangling the steer to lift the ATV off Arthur was something she had to do. Carrying him to safety had required strength and a bit of speed, nothing else. There had been no unusual risk to life associated with saving him, and it was nothing she hadn't done before. Tonight shouldn't be stressful, not the way she had set it up. But unknown unknowns can foil any plan, and she needed to be on the lookout for them. It felt delicious to be on hyper-alert again.

She had gone to bed wearing her best black merino running gear, so all she had to do was to pull on her trainers and double knot the laces. There was a half moon languishing in the sky, so she pulled her black beanie down over her head to prevent any reflection from her dark blonde hair. A lack of clouds meant there could be a frost later, depending on how long it took to catch the saboteur. Euphemia hated being cold, so she pulled on an extra vest and zipped it up to the neck.

She checked the time. The first set of motion sensors was at the turnoff two kilometers away. This gave her enough time to work out if the vehicle triggering them belonged to the saboteur or to an innocent country person. Keen not to wake the others until it was absolutely necessary, she tiptoed upstairs and checked her laptop. They had set cameras at regular intervals along the road to the station gates. Sure enough, a compact car was driving slowly towards the sanctuary with its lights off.

Bingo! She rubbed her hands together. Tonight was the night. When the car pulled off to the side of the road near the gates, she rallied the troops.

Jane woke with a start, mid-snore, her eyes flaring in the darkness until she worked out where she was and sat up. 'I need the bathroom before I do anything,' she whispered. 'See you upstairs.'

Josh, jittery with excitement, had leapt out of bed at the sound of Euphemia's footsteps. Fully dressed, he jiggled on the spot until Euphemia placed a restraining hand on his shoulder. Including him could be a mistake, but what choice did she have? Jane might be proficient at using the remote control for her smart TV, but that was the extent of her technical knowledge. The plan required someone smart enough to co-ordinate the technology on her command. Josh, brought up with an iPad in his basinet, was better able to handle this part of the plan. Like most children, his understanding and use of the Internet was innate. In a fluid and possibly dangerous situation, it would also be intuitive. She further justified his involvement by telling herself he would be safer at the house, overseeing the feedback from the different sensors. There was little risk to the boy as long as he did as he was told. He had sworn his obedience by making a series of complicated gestures which involved crossing his heart, tapping his eyes and turning three times on the spot. 'All the kids at school do it,' he said when she looked at him. 'A painful and slow death comes to those who break the scared oath.'

'Do not open the doors to anyone,' she said.

'Not even you?'

'Ha ha. Even me, unless you hear my signal, do not open the door.'

She left him sitting at the kitchen counter, three laptops open in front of him, and a walkie-talkie at his side. He gave her a two thumbs-up, perhaps the happiest eight-year-old boy she had ever seen.

Jane took up her position at the end of the drive. She too was wearing black, and a hat pulled down over her hair. It startled Euphemia to see the stripes of black paint Jane had added to her face. 'You look like Rambo,' she whispered.

'I feel like Rambo,' Jane replied ducking down behind the wall.

'Make sure your headphones and body-cam are on,' Euphemia said.

'B Baker to Baker base. Testing. Over,' Jane whispered.

'B what?' Josh's voice pierced the night.

'Turn the sound off,' Euphemia hissed. She pulled her

microphone close to her mouth and instructed them to keep radio silence until she gave the all clear.

'Affirmative,' said Jane.

Euphemia rolled her eyes, tapped Jane on the shoulder, and hand-signalled she was going in. Jane made the heart signal with both hands and blew her a kiss.

Ducking low, Euphemia crossed the road, unlocked the gates to the sanctuary and went in. The bush absorbed her immediately. Josh's breathing was in her ear as she made her way along a track, taking her to the perimeter fence. She did not know where the saboteur might try to enter, so she had to start at the beginning and follow the fence around hoping she saw them before they saw her.

She was counting on the fact they would not want to carry their stuff up the hill. The average ferret weighs between two and four pounds. Add to that the cage and the ladder, both of which would be unwieldy and heavy. The ladder imprints in the dirt outside the fence had been approximately three hundred yards from the road. Ladders were especially awkward to carry uphill and over rough terrain during the day, let alone at night.

Fervently hoping there would only be one saboteur, Euphemia ran through her senses one by one, making sure each was ready to work at full capacity. Her eyes, now they were used to the dark, were more sensitive than any vision goggles, her hearing better than a microphone. She prayed smell and taste would not be needed. To better concentrate, she switched off the others and leaned against a tree breathing quietly while she waited. It was beautiful in the bush. Peaceful. Black branches silhouetted above her against the star sprinkled sky, the crescent moon's silver light creating sharp shadows on the surrounding undergrowth. A hedgehog trundled into view and she nudged it with her foot. Instantly, it curled into a ball of spines and she tipped it, sending it rolling away and out of harm. She knew hedgehogs were a threat to native insects, but the thought of murdering Mrs Tiggywinkle was too terrible for words.

Perfume - bergamot, lemon, and jasmine. Rose too and vanilla. Patchouli? She wasn't sure about the last one, but she recognised the smell from Christmas presents given to her ten years ago. Their saboteur was either a woman, or a man with a penchant for Chanel No. 5 - nothing could be ruled in or out. Whatever, whoever, the person had stopped one hundred yards away. An aluminium clink sound was followed by another as they propped a ladder against the fence. Swearing followed. The saboteur was definitely a woman. And not a very happy woman judging by the panting and cursing.

Euphemia moved away from the shelter of the tree, edging forwards, making certain there was nothing under foot to give her away. The woman was talking so loudly to herself, she need not have worried. A herd of elephants could have tiptoed through the undergrowth and she would not have noticed.

'Ew! Ew! Ew! Ew! Eeeeeeeeeeeeeew! Yuck. Yuck. Yuckity yuck yuck!' Pause. Euphemia heard little claws scratching the floor of the cage, a squeaking mewling sound and a banging as something ran against wire rattling a metal catch.

A stifled scream followed by, 'Ew! Yuck! Yuck! Yuck! Yuck! This is so disgusting.' The woman shuddered and stamped the ground finishing with a last burst of 'Yuckity Yuck Yuck Yucks.'

Euphemia moved closer. A thin cloud crossed in front of the moon, darkening her surroundings. She crouched low behind a large manuka bush directly in front of the woman, who was now sitting on the ground, her back against the mesh. Beside her was a cage, the sort which Euphemia's neighbour used to take his cat to the vet. It was plastic, about three feet high, with a handle on the top and a little wire door bolted shut at the front. Euphemia counted two heads inside it, their teeth bared, their noses sniffing furiously, as their little hands gripped the wire.

The woman sighed, stood up, and shuddered from head to toe. She had a balaclava over her head, covering her face. All Euphemia could see were her eyes. She was slim and wearing dark overalls, a long-sleeved polar-fleece and trainers. Most surprising were the length and colour of her fingernails. In the semi-darkness, her bright red talons on jewel ringed fingers stood out as they gripped the handle on top of the cage.

'Yuck! Yuck! Horrible Yuck.' She said and put the cage down. The scrambling inside increased and there was more mewling and squealing as it rocked from side to side on the unsteady ground.

The woman re-positioned the ladder against the fence, found two small rocks to wedge the feet in place, braced herself, picked up the cage and, one step at a time, climbed. The top of the ladder stopped two feet from the top of the fence. More swearing. She hoisted the cage up and let it rest on the ladder while she re-adjusted her grip.

Euphemia clicked on her body cam and headphone. With all the clattering and swearing going on, she doubted the woman could hear her. Next, the woman readied herself and the cage and embarked on her final push to the top. She hauled the cage and its struggling occupants the last little way and had balanced it precariously on the top of the fence when Euphemia called 'Now.'

Five body lights aimed directly at the woman lit her up. She hoped Josh was getting a good recording of both her and the cage. Her hand went up to shield her eyes from the bright lights and in that one movement, one of her feet slipped out from under her, the cage slid off the top of the fence, the bolt on the door slammed back, it swung open and two screaming scrabbling ferrets sensing freedom, jumped. In opposite directions.

One hit the ground beside Euphemia, looked at her and prepared to make its escape. Euphemia's reactions were quicker. She grabbed it behind its head. Try as it might to escape and it tried - ferociously gnashing its teeth and swinging back on itself to wriggle out of her grasp - she pinned the ferret to the ground. But what to do with it? She couldn't bring herself to kill it, so she did the next best thing. She shrugged off her vest, wrapped the creature tightly inside it and tied a knot in the bundle well and truly immobilising the varmint. Unfortunately, the disgusting animal discharged its bladder all over her. How can you get away from yourself? Gagging to get rid of the stench, she re-visited the kill option, but it was too late.

She had been so busy wrestling the ferret she didn't at first understand what was happening above her. The second desperate animal had landed first on the woman's head before launching itself into the air and thence into the paddock, then disappeared into the night and freedom. The woman screamed, her hands reached up and in her confusion she dropped the cage directly onto the base of the ladder dislodging a rock. The foot of the ladder slid out, the top juddering down the mesh as the ladder fell away and landed with a clatter on the ground below.

The woman stayed where she was. The back of her fleece had caught on a loose piece of wire suspending her from the top of the fence. Euphemia watched as the woman swung slowly around to face her. She opened her mouth under the balaclava to speak, but no sound came, the noose of her jacket constricting her airway. They made eye contact, Euphemia calm and assessing - the woman panicking and terrified.

'Help?' she rasped.

The fence was over twenty feet high. The ladder and the woman were on the other side. Euphemia couldn't reach her, much less lift her up and relieve the pressure on her neck.

There was no tree, nothing she could climb. The cloud moved away from the moon and in the brightness Euphemia saw the woman's eyes bulging in their sockets at the same time as the veins in her neck stood out like thick cords under her skin. Each time she struggled to get a hand or foothold, the noose tightened.

'Do something.' Josh yelled in her ear. Euphemia had forgotten she was still transmitting and that the woman's distress was being relayed in horrific detail to an eight-year-old boy sitting alone in a kitchen. She switched off her body cam and headphones. He'd seen enough. He certainly didn't need to see what was going to happen next. Eight-year-old boys should never see a super woman (two words lower case) in action. Especially not eight-year-old boys as enterprising as Josh. Most especially not eight-year-old boys with recording equipment.

Euphemia squatted down. Then, like a jack-in-a-box released from captivity, she jumped straight up. High enough to reach the top of the fence where she hung for a second, face to face with the saboteur. The woman blinked furiously as she got the full blast of eau d'ferret. Her struggling intensified. Euphemia hooked a leg over the top of the fence and pulled herself up to sit astride it. With one hand, she grabbed the collar of the polar fleece and lifted the woman off her hook, then balancing herself with the other hand, Euphemia lowered her to the ground. The woman lay where she landed, gulping air, her hands feeling for the raw skin on her neck.

Below Euphemia, the bundle containing the captive ferret moved. While Euphemia had been saving a life, the ferret had been gnawing through the fabric of her favorite vest. A paw emerged, then whiskers. Damn it, she had not gone to all this bother for the bloody animal to escape and wreck mayhem on whatever bird-life remained. The woman didn't look capable of going anywhere fast, so Euphemia swung her leg back over the fence, jumped down and grabbed the bundle. A quick twist, another knot, and the escape was foiled.

Which was when the woman leapt up and ran straight down the hill.

Euphemia sighed and activated her microphone. 'Jane,' she said. 'I need you to do something.'

CHAPTER 28

As she emerged from the undergrowth, the woman checked her surroundings, dropped into a crouch, scuttled across the road and climbed into her car. Jane waited as she discovered the key was not where she left it. Head banging on the steering wheel followed. Three times. She got out and on hands and knees; she searched the ground around and under the vehicle. When the woman burst into tears, Jane stepped out of the darkness, grabbed her wrist, circled it with a zip-tie and double backed it around her own.

'You're coming with me,' she said. The woman pulled away and the thin plastic cut into them. Jane yelped, and the woman cursed. 'Behave,' said Jane, tugging her towards the gates. Jane stopped in her tracks when Euphemia walked across the road carrying the cage with the ferret safely locked inside.

'Go back,' Jane yelled. 'Go. A. Way. Now.'

'Do not come near us,' ordered Jane. 'You are not, I repeat, NOT to come to the house smelling like that.'

'It's only urine,' Euphemia muttered.

'It is not ------- ONLY urine,' yelled Jane. 'It is THE most putrid, disgusting thing I have ever smelt in my whole, entire life.' Breaking into a jog and pulling her prisoner behind her, she hurried through the gate first and up the drive, the light from her headlamp jiggling in front of them. 'Quickly,' she hissed, tugging at the retching woman's arm. 'She's gaining on us.'

Euphemia followed at a discrete distance until she reached the empty manager's cottage. Thankfully, the hot water hadn't been turned off. More wasted money. Stripping off, she soaped up and let the water run over her head and body. The aroma of panicked ferret is, she discovered, very difficult to remove. It was still strong after she repeated the soap/rinse cycle several times. Her best running gear was totally beyond redemption. It would have to be double-bagged and binned, if not doused in petrol and incinerated. With no clean clothes to put on, she wrapped a tiny towel around her and walked semi naked and shivering up to the New House. The hardened acorns and sharp gravel under her bare feet recalled painful memories of stepping on Lego when the girls were young.

Jane was sitting on the sofa attached to the woman, who was still wearing her balaclava, when Euphemia opened the front door. Josh, awake and alert, was tapping merrily away on his laptops, organizing video clips and checking sound levels. His excitement contained, but only just. Petal took one sniff and tail between her legs skulked off behind the sofa. Brutus did a double take. With a faraway gleam in his eyes, he sidled over to Euphemia and rubbed against her bare leg before circling and inspecting her ankles with his nose. Suitably primed, he reared up and wrapped his teeny tiny front legs around her calf, then humped her vigorously.

'Brutus, bad dog.' Josh ran over and pulled the Chihuahua away by this collar. 'He hasn't been fixed. Mum says he's anti-social, and he has to have the chop. Dad says he is a boy and entitled to his fun.' Brutus, embarrassingly aroused by the remnant of eau de ferret strained against Josh, his tongue lolling maniacally to one side, his eyes not leaving Euphemia for a second.

'Outside. Now,' ordered Euphemia. Josh swept the rampant Brutus onto the veranda where he paced backwards and forwards, his eyes fixed lasciviously on Euphemia through the glass.

'You still stink,' said Jane. 'Not as bad as before, but enough. Take another shower and use more soap. I'll make coffee while you get dressed.' She stood up, forgetting the saboteur was attached. They both yelped in pain as the plastic tie cut into their wrists again. 'Pay attention,' Jane said. The woman got to her feet and shuffled meekly behind her to the kitchen.

'If I cut this off, will you promise not to escape? I warn you I am a runner and I will catch you!'

The woman nodded sheepishly.

Josh had his hands wrapped around a mug of hot chocolate when Euphemia returned dressed in her second best black merino leggings, zip up sweater and shoes.

'The perfume helps,' said Jane. 'But not much.'

'I found it in the bathroom cupboard. It's old, so I wasn't sure it would work. Look,' she said. 'Brutus has stopped seeing me as the mother of his unborn puppies, so it must do something.' Brutus, his big eyes pleading, stood quivering in the cold on the other side of the door. Rather than detour to Euphemia, when he was let in, he rushed to check the food bowl.

Euphemia sipped her coffee then walked over to their captive. 'Let's get a look at you.'

Her head down, the woman pulled off the balaclava and, shaking the hair from her face, looked up.

Euphemia stepped back, surprised. 'Charlotte!'

'Charlotte?' Jane and Josh asked together.

'Let me introduce Charlotte Kincaide,' said Euphemia. 'Joe's ex-wife and Josh, your erstwhile aunt.'

'What does erstwhile mean?' Josh asked.

'It means former as in not any more,' Jane answered.

'Well?'

'I don't have to explain myself, least of all, to you,' Charlotte said.

'I'll call the police. You can talk to them.'

'You always were a tedious bitch, Euphemia Sage. I never understood why Joe kept you as a friend.'

'And I never understood why he married you,' replied Euphemia. 'You had nothing in common and tonight proves it. Sabotaging his sanctuary? Wait until he finds out.'

Charlotte, her lips pinched tight, folded her arms across her chest and stared defiantly up at Euphemia.

Josh drained the last of his hot chocolate with a loud slurp, a brown smile curving up from the corners of his mouth when he took his face out of the mug.

'You don't like ferrets, do you?' he said. 'I heard you saying 'ew' and 'yuck', when you were climbing the ladder.'

Charlotte erupted. 'Of course, I don't like them. Who in their right mind likes ferrets? They are disgusting. Whoever brought them into this country needs to be shot.' She smirked at Euphemia. 'That dog will hump your leg for a week. It takes that long to get the smell off, no matter how much of my old perfume you douse yourself in. I got sprayed a month ago, so I know. I could bloody well murder Joe. This is his fault.'

'Joe made you sabotage the sanctuary?'

'Of course he didn't. Are you dim as well as tedious?'

Euphemia bit her tongue hard enough to taste blood. The pain stopped her from doing something she would regret. On second thoughts, why not give this woman what she deserves —strictly in the interests of conservation. On third thoughts Jane might understand, but Josh was only eight. He was too young for what she had in mind. She bit her tongue even harder.

'What fabulous nails,' Jane said.

Euphemia stopped biting her tongue. Even Josh stopped what he was doing. Charlotte looked up from her sulk and studied Jane's face to see if she was being serious. Satisfied, she extended her hands, rippling her fingers to show off her nails.

'A woman in Wellington does them.'

Jane plumped down on the sofa next to Charlotte and held up her own hands in comparison. 'You're so lucky. I have terrible nails. See, they're short and cracked.' She was wearing her blue sapphire solitaire ring and three white gold bands with diamond insets, the stones twinkling merrily as she displayed her nails.

'Your nails are awful but what fabulous rings,' Charlotte said and reached over to take Jane's hand to better study the sapphire. 'Ceylonese. Emerald cut. Gorgeous.'

'You know your stones,' said Jane.

'Doesn't every girl?' She glanced across to see what Euphemia was wearing. 'I've never understood why people bother with star sapphires.'

'Neither have I,' said Jane.

'You have to catch them in exactly the right light, other-wise they look like a cheap piece of jade.'

Jane shifted to avoid meeting Euphemia's eyes. 'Tell me the name of the woman who does your nails. Would she do mine?'

'I don't see why not. She's not cheap, but she does an excellent job. My poor hands have taken a real hammering in the last three months hauling cages of stinking ferrets out here and look,' she held up her hands again. 'As good as new.'

'Ahem,' said Josh. 'You were saying about the stinking ferrets.'

'Three months,' said Euphemia. 'No wonder there aren't any birds left.'

'They'll come back,' said Charlotte.

'Will they?'

'Of course they will. Joe will sort it. It'll be fine. A temporary glitch.'

'A temporary glitch?' yelled Josh. 'Explain that to the geckos. Do you know how rare the Wellington Green gecko is in the wild? No. You don't. You only care about your stupid nails and stupid rings. You're a... a... murderer!'

'You're a Kincaide all right,' said Charlotte. 'Until I married into this family, I didn't realize righteous anger was a genetic trait. Geckos. Pah! Glorified lizards. Who cares?'

'Me. I care,' yelled Josh.

'You're a child. You don't count.'

'You're the child.'

'No. You are,' said Charlotte, standing up.

'You are.'

'No. You are.'

'One more you are than you can ever say you are.'

'You're the child.'

'I already said infinity. You're the child and so you are.'

'Enough,' said Euphemia.

Silence ensued until Jane shook herself. 'It's creepy when you do that thing with your voice.'

'I do nothing with my voice, Jane. You are mistaken.'

'You do nothing with your voice. I am mistaken.'

'It's three-thirty,' said Euphemia. 'We need to get some sleep. Charlotte, you sleep in Joe's room.'

She poured herself a glass of water, watching them as they followed each other down the stairs to bed. When she checked a few minutes later, they were fast asleep. Blessedly Jane wasn't snoring.

CHAPTER 29

'I FOUND A SUITCASE OF MY OLD CLOTHES IN THE wardrobe,' said Charlotte when she appeared for breakfast the next morning. She was wearing tan chinos, a blue denim shirt, under a patterned vest and a pair of tan ankle boots. She had tucked her dark hair, freshly washed and blow-dried, behind her ears from which hung drop pearl earrings. She looked like a model in a Ralph Lauren advertisement.

Josh huddled over a bowl of cereal, saw her, and swiveled away.

'Coffee?' asked Jane.

'Thanks. I hope everyone slept as well as I did.'

Josh spooned down the last of his cereal before pushing his bowl across the bench into the sink, where it landed with a clatter of porcelain and cutlery.

Charlotte was unfazed. 'Waking up this morning and seeing the valley in its autumn colors reminded me of how beautiful the farm looks from here. Joe was right to move out of the homestead.'

'He had little choice after you ran off,' said Euphemia, sitting down beside her.

'He did so have a choice. Joe moved out because he wanted to live in a smaller eco-friendly house and you know it. He hated the old place. I should know. It was me he moaned to for years about how much energy it used. How most of it was seeping into the atmosphere through gaps in the walls and roof, adding to global warming and increasing his carbon footprint on the planet. You only saw his jovial host's face. You never saw him grumpy. He was determined to build his perfect home and be done with the homestead. All credit to him, he's done a great job. It's fabulous.'

Charlotte was right, but Euphemia wasn't in the mood to let her get away with her self-serving version of the breakup.

'He was a mess after you left.'

'Was he? I heard he was more upset about Derek leaving than me. Good farm managers are hard to find. Isn't that what he told you?'

'Whoever said that only told you half the story. It devastated him. Because he loved you. He couldn't believe it when you betrayed him.'

'I didn't,' said Charlotte.

'Is that what you tell yourself?'

'I didn't betray him.'

'Derek would tell a different story.'

'Derek wouldn't. He helped me. He saw how upset I was and he helped me. That's all.'

'So you didn't run off with him?'

'I didn't sleep with him, if that's what you're asking. I did run off with him. It was to make a point.'

'I don't have time to play games. There are more important issues than you to deal with.'

'Like how many geckos you killed,' muttered Josh.

'I can assure you, I killed no precious stupid geckos.'

'They are precious and they're not stupid. You're a murderer.'

'I am not.'

'Ferrets are murderers and you're the one who put them in there, ergo you are a murderer.'

'Ergo?' said Charlotte, turning to look down at him. 'Ergo? What sort of dumb word is that for a kid to use?'

'You're dumb if you don't know what ergo means,' said Josh. 'Ergo is an adverb which means, therefore. Ergo, you not knowing its meaning, means it's you who is dumb - not ergo.'

'I know what ergo means. I said it was a dumb word for a kid, ergo you, to use.'

'I can use any word I like.'

Euphemia got off her chair and stood between them. 'I never thought I would have to say this again in my life, but the two of you are acting like children and only one of you is actually a child. Stop it. Josh you have homework to do. Do it.'

'I didn't start it.'

'Maybe not, but I am finishing it. If you want to see your father later, do your homework. Now.' Josh slid off the stool and stamped across the room, pulled down East of Eden and disappeared into the study.

'He's an eight-year-old boy, Charlotte, who thanks to you, got very little sleep last night and whose father nearly died. He's come back from Hong Kong, the city he grew up in to live in the Wairarapa countryside and he has no friends. You're the adult. Start acting like one.'

'Okay.'

'Okay what?'

'Okay, I'll be nice to him,' she said, drumming the red nails of one hand on the bench top.

'Stop that.'

'You're not the boss of me,' Charlotte said.

'No thank goodness, now drink your coffee and tell me what you meant when you said there was nothing between you and Derek. You lost me.'

'I didn't understand that part either,' said Jane, refilling everyone's mugs.

Charlotte gave an enormous sigh. 'It was a scheme we cooked up. To get Joe's attention. He was more interested in the sanctuary than me or the farm. He couldn't stop talking about it, and the money he wasted was beyond ridiculous. I wanted the old Joe back, the man I married. Oakhill Station-Joe was fun. Sanctuary-Joe was boring. Derek agreed to help because he was sick of running the place with no money. I helped, but he got stuck with all the heavy work. He thought Joe needed a proverbial kick in the butt. I thought if I left, Joe would miss me and would come after me. We could go back to the way we were.'

'How long before you realized he wasn't coming after you?'

'Before I knew he loved that blasted sanctuary more than he loved me, you mean? About a month.'

'What happened to Derek?'

'He got a job down south. If Joe asked, he would come back to Oakhill in a heartbeat. He misses it as much as I do.' She got up and walked to the window.

"Oh, what a tangled web we weave..."

'I know,' she said. 'When we practice to deceive. I didn't mean to kill his precious birds...'

'What about the Wellington Green Gecko?' Josh yelled from the study. 'It's an endangered species.'

'I only wanted to get his attention.'

'By destroying the thing he loved?'

'By destroying the thing he loved more than me. Yes.' She pushed open a door, stepped onto the balcony and shut it behind her. She was crying.

CHAPTER 30

'I DIDN'T KNOW YOU HAD COMPANY,' SAID KEVIN. HE walked in without knocking and went straight to the kitchen. 'Make some more. There's a love,' he said, waggling the empty plunger at Jane.

'Make it yourself,' she said and went downstairs.

Kevin, unperturbed, put beans in the grinder. He smiled at Euphemia over the noise and when it stopped, tipped his head towards Charlotte, who was standing with her back to them on the veranda. 'Who's that?'

'Charlotte Kincaide.'

'The prodigal wife? Well, well, well. Joe will be surprised to see her when he gets back.' Euphemia tried to remember the German word for people who delight in the misfortunes of others. Schadenfreude, that was it. Kevin oozed schadenfreude.

'Is there a reason you dropped by?' she asked as she tidied away the dishes and wiped down the bench.

'I came to see Jane, but she doesn't seem to be in the mood for visitors.'

'No, she doesn't,' said Euphemia. She squirted a spray of

cleaner onto the bench in his direction and followed with the cloth.

'I found an animal in a cage,' he said. 'It was making a hell of a racket outside the manager's house.'

'Thanks. I'll let Sandy know.'

'I already brought it up. It's outside.'

'You really didn't have to do that, Kevin.'

'No problem.' He walked across the room, knocked on the window, and waved when Charlotte turned around. 'Kevin, Ally's brother. We've met before.' he bellowed.

Charlotte put her hands over her ears and shook her head. Rather than taking the hint, Kevin pulled open the door.

'Remember me? I'm Ally's older brother, Kevin. We met at a Christmas party one year.'

'Did we?'

'We had a dance. *Heart on my Sleeve.*'

'You've got a better memory than me.' She walked past him into the room.

'When did you say we were going to see Arthur?' she asked Euphemia looking at her watch.

'Any time is good for me. Need to give old Arthur a bit of family support,' said Kevin rubbing his hands together. 'Don Luciano for lunch afterwards will round off the morning nicely.'

'Aren't you needed here?' said Euphemia, taking the hint.

'For what?'

'Joe ordered wine. It's in his diary to be delivered today. Someone needs to open the cellar for the deliveryman. Ten cases of last year's vintage - Dry River Pinot Noir. This morning is the only time they can drop it off. I'll understand if you can't stay.'

He scratched an eyebrow. 'Joe keeps his cellar locked tighter than the high security wing at Paremoremo Prison. He promised to show me what he's got down there, but the timing has never been right. It's a pain, but someone has to be here, I suppose. I could always visit Arthur tomorrow.'

'What would we do without you? I'll drop the key in on our way past.'

'You've heard from Joe then?'

'No, have you?'

'Not a word,' said Kevin.

'I assumed he was in town with Arthur and Ally?' asked Charlotte.

'We haven't seen or heard from Joe for days have we, Effie,' said Kevin. 'What did the police say?'

'The police?' yelled Charlotte. Petal and Brutus got up and slunk off to the study, their tails between their legs.

'He always answers his phone,' said Charlotte. 'Why didn't you say something?'

'I was about to tell you when Kevin arrived. And my name is Euphemia, not Effie.'

'I have a right to know he's missing. He is my husband.'

'You're separated.'

'Not officially.'

'Yes, but….,'

'But nothing. Where is he?'

'I wish I knew,' said Euphemia. 'He was going to the Lake Farm and said he'd be back the next day. That was two days ago. I've tried calling, left messages and emailed him, but nothing.'

'Have you been to the farm?'

'Not yet,' replied Euphemia.

'Why not?'

'Let me think. Jane and I finished the accounts. Arthur had his accident. We've been looking after Josh. Then some idiot broke into the sanctuary and released a lot of nasty predators.'

'Looks like I'll have to go then,' said Charlotte. 'I know

where his shack on the Pounui Lagoon is. There's a colony of Royal Spoonbills he's been following and the last of this year's chicks will be fledging. His phone will be off so he doesn't disturb them.'

Euphemia was beginning to understand why Charlotte had left. If Kenneth had ever disappeared for days at a time, and not answered her calls, she would have been furious. Actually, that wasn't true. Hurt, irritated, extremely disappointed, followed by angry and then, as a last resort, then she would have been furious.

It was a relief there was a rational, if somewhat selfish, explanation for Joe's silence. A bigger relief to know Spoonbill chicks were the reason behind his disappearance and not a Hong Kong triad.

Had Joe always been this self absorbed? Why hadn't she noticed? He had neglected his wife she sabotaged his sanctuary to get his attention. He had been neglecting not only his wife but their farm and the people who worked for him. Allan could have been right. Mechanical failure might explain Arthur's accident, after all. Joe had probably neglected the maintenance of the farm equipment, along with everything else. Could she stop imagining the worst and relax?

'I'll fetch Joe and bring him home. You take the little monster to see his father,' said Charlotte.

'I heard that.'

'Ergo. You are a monster. Well-mannered children don't eavesdrop. And if they do, they don't tell.'

The trip into town was almost uneventful. Arthur was much the same as the day before, but better rested and in less pain. To Euphemia he still looked more yellow than he should, but her color vision was so refined she reasoned she was noticing something that under normal circumstances would not be a problem. The doctors obviously weren't concerned, having opted to observe him rather than do further tests. If his condition remained stable, they planned to send him home the following day. The interim report from WorkSafe had been emailed that morning. He was relieved to learn there would be no formal charges, but was frustrated to be told he had to complete an ATV skills course.

'I've been riding the damn things since I was a kid,' he complained. 'I should teach these courses, not be forced to attend them.'

Ally was enjoying her time with old friends after the relative isolation of Oakhill Station, but she was looking forward to coming home to her kitchen and to sleeping in her own bed. Josh tucked up beside his father listened to this exchange of information. Dark rings under his eyes were the only clue to the tightly coiled excitement he was trying so hard to suppress. After a few minutes, it was clear he was losing the battle. The tugs on his father's sleeve became more insistent the longer the conversation went on, until finally, he could stand it no longer.

'We caught Aunt Charlotte putting ferrets inside the sanctuary. She says Uncle Joe doesn't love her, so she's trying to kill the Wellington Green geckos and the birds. The geckos are an endangered species, and I saw one.'

'Okay, calm down,' said Arthur, putting his arm around his son and hugging him into his side. 'How about letting Mrs Sage tell us what's happened?'

Euphemia explained the events of the night before, significantly downplaying the role of their son. Josh protested, but stopped when she raised an eyebrow and shook her head.

'Where is Charlotte now?' asked Arthur.

'She's gone to look for Uncle Joe,' said Josh. 'At Lake Farm.'

'The Pounui lagoon actually,' interrupted Euphemia. 'Apparently, he has a shack there so he can watch the birds.'

'That's good news.' said Ally. 'It means there is a perfectly innocent explanation and there's nothing to worry about.'

'What were you worried about?' asked Josh.

'Nothing.'

'Then why were you worried?'

Ally ignored him, and using the tried and true parental tactic, changed the subject. 'You should be back at school, young man.'

Josh wilted, then rallied. He reached up and, holding her face in his hands, said, 'Please don't make me go back. I hate it. The other kids are morons and I'm not learning a thing.'

'You're going, and that's an end to it. Mrs Sage will drive you down to the bus tomorrow morning. Look at these dark rings under your eyes. You need an early night,' said Ally firmly.

The mood in the room had taken a turn for the worst, so Euphemia and Jane made their excuses and left. Josh continued to moan that it wasn't fair and he shouldn't have to go back to school yet, as they left him to spend quality time with his parents.

The supermarket was close by and quiet in the middle of the day. They stocked up on essentials then leaving the car in the car park went across the road to the Lake House café in Queen Elizabeth park. The café was in an original 1920s building beside a large pond filled with ducks and pedal boats. After ordering, they moved outside to sit at a table on the wooden veranda overlooking a well-manicured cricket lawn on one side and the pond on the other. Two men in a boat shaped like a giant swan paddled past and gave them a cheery wave. Jane waved back.

Local Maori and some of the early settlers had gifted the park to the town over one hundred years ago. Trees, both native and introduced, planted at the time of the gift, had matured, providing beauty and shade. Shrieks of enjoyment from the small children in a nearby playground added to the cheerful atmosphere. The waitress had just put their coffees and muffins on the table when Euphemia spotted Daryl. He was watching them from behind the small grandstand on the other side of the cricket ground. His low-slung trousers, black oversized hoodie and sloppy high tops - his signature look meant it couldn't be anyone else. Surely he would not make another attempt on Jane's handbag? That would be too ridiculous for words. She buttered her cranberry muffin and when she looked up; he was gone.

'Did you see Daryl?'

'Where?'

'He was over there behind the grandstand.'

Jane put her hand up to shade her eyes. 'I can't see anyone that far away.'

'Never mind,' said Euphemia. 'He's gone now.'

When they returned to the car, Euphemia asked Jane to wait while she checked it for fingerprints. Still not trusting Daryl, she got down on her hands and knees and looked underneath.

'My friend lost her earring,' Jane explained to a woman who stopped to see if they needed help. Euphemia stood up and dusted off her hands.

'She's lost both of them,' replied the eagle-eyed shopper. 'Hope they weren't valuable.'

'She doesn't have any valuable jewelry,' said Jane.

The woman smiled. 'Sadly, neither do I,' she said and pushed her shopping trolley to a battered Toyota at the other end of the car park.

Euphemia unlocked their car, and they got in.

'You have enough expensive earrings for us both,' said Euphemia. 'You suit them.'

'I do, don't I?' said Jane.

They drove to the hospital and collected Josh who was so exhausted after last night's events and the excitement of seeing his parents he slept all the way back to the station waking only when Euphemia turned off the engine. They had just finished carrying in the bags of groceries when Kevin appeared.

'The wine never arrived,' he said. 'Not that I would have been much use if it had because you forgot to leave the key.'

'I was sure they said today. Let me check.' Euphemia tapped her phone and scrolled down to the correct message. 'I owe you an apology. It's next week. I guess with all the excitement of last night, I misread the date.'

'What happened last night?'

'Nothing,' said Jane.

'Nothing,' said Josh.

'Nothing,' added Euphemia.

'I don't believe you.'

'It's been a long day. We're worn out after the trip into town,' said Jane, taking charge and hustling Kevin to the door. 'Josh needs his dinner so he can go to bed. The good news is Arthur and Ally will be home tomorrow.'

'The day after,' said Josh, yawning and stretching at the same time.

'I was hoping we could, you know.'

'Not tonight, Kevin,' said Jane. She shut the door.

CHAPTER 31

Barbara answered after the second ring. It was 1 AM in Sydney, 3 AM in New Zealand.

'I'm sorry to wake you,' said Euphemia. 'Tell me if you can't talk. It's nothing serious. I need to understand more about the powers and you're the only one I can ask.' Euphemia wasn't in the habit of waking people in the middle of the night. She usually managed her fears, otherwise fondly referred to as the 'three o'clock horrors', by either going for a run or by snuggling into Kenneth and letting his warmth soothe her.

Tonight, she doubted if either of these coping mechanisms would calm her. Questions had been building up for months and now stuck in the country, away from Sage Consulting, thoughts of the future dominated her thinking.

Until she developed the powers, she always knew what each day, month, year would bring. She was organized. Life was predictable. The most exciting thing that happened to her was achieving a personal best on a long-distance run. She had a pleasant home, a good job, an excellent income, and a splendid marriage. Her daughters were grown up and independent. Yes, life was boring, but it was first world boring. She had choices and she could afford to indulge them. She knew how lucky she was when she watched the news and saw disasters unfolding in other countries. New Zealand had had its share of pain and suffering to be sure, but each time something happened, everyone knuckled down, did their best to help and life got back to normal — for people like her.

Jane being kidnapped, then Barbara's attempted murder had shown her she had been skating along the surface of what was happening around her. Was it wilful ignorance or naivety on her part that she hadn't gone beyond the white picket fence of her cozy, safe life and seen the world and the people in it for who and what they really were? Once she was exposed to evil, she couldn't in all reality go back to her superficial existence. Not when she had the power to help.

Barbara was the only person who understood. The Sydney businesswoman and ex-socialite might be older and more sophisticated than Euphemia, but she, too, was a descendant of Rachel. Her only daughter had died young like Fredericka leaving her to bring up her granddaughter Abbey. Tragically young and having recently completed a doctorate in music at the University of Sydney, Abbey was killed by a drunk-driver. Heart-broken Barbara withdrew from public life focusing her energy and funds on the RS Holding Research Foundation in Mauritius. When she heard about Euphemia's adventures in Wellington, Barbara reached out. The bond between them forged when Euphemia stopped a lawyer who had been embezzling funds from the Research Foundation, from throwing Barbara off the top of the Sydney Harbour Bridge.

Barbara had been a treasure trove of family information. Brought up by her maternal Aunt Maree, Euphemia was thrilled to meet a relative. Barbara was only too happy to answer her many questions, telling Euphemia as much as she could about the history of their family and the foundation in

Mauritius. Finding out about the powers they shared proved more difficult. Barbara was not always forthcoming.

'I wasn't asleep,' said Barbara. 'I'm pleased it's not an emergency.'

'I'd be pleased if it was.'

'Is that a rip-roaring case of the post midnight blues I hear?'

Euphemia switched the phone to speaker and pressed it against the wall. Jane, right on cue, let loose a spectacularly loud burst of snorts and grunts. 'Not only do I have to listen to that, but my flushes are worse. One change of pyjamas already tonight and it's only three o'clock. I'm tired. If I'm not using my powers, I might as well take HRT and be done with it.'

'Where are you?'

Euphemia explained the events of the last three days. They seemed so pathetic when she told her story out loud.

'You're away from the office and the people you know and you're disappointed that nothing exciting is happening when you thought it might be about to.'

'I know I shouldn't be, but that's part of it. I'm staying in a beautiful house with a good friend who snores and keeps me awake. Kenneth is having a wonderful time with Roger in Malaysia. Tomorrow, hopefully, I will drive back to Wellington when Joe and Charlotte return. There are no triads, no foreign saboteurs, nothing exciting happening. The hole in the fence is a domestic dispute and not sabotage. It makes me wonder if there is any point in having superpowers. I barely use them and then only for the most mundane reasons when I do.'

'What if I told you I'm still trying to work that out myself?'

'If that's true, I'm seriously going to look at HRT. I can't stand the hot sweats or the skin crawls. The lack of sleep and the roller coaster of emotions makes life unbearable, and for what?'

'I understand.'

'If HRT gives me back my body but deactivates the switch, then so be it.'

'You're right. I thought the same.'

'This could go on for years.'

'It could.'

'How long?'

'I don't know. Every woman is different. The symptoms and, by association, the powers have lasted a couple of years in some of us and for others, decades.'

'And you?' Euphemia asked, feeling some of the tension leave her muscles as she settled back into her pillows.

'I still use them, but the situation has to merit it. My powers take longer to get going. My body doesn't respond as quickly or with the same intensity as it used to. I don't know if I can still trust the powers to do what I need them to do. If they do work, then it's horrible because, like hangovers as you get older, it takes longer to recover. I wish I had your youth. The only benefit of being my age is the hot flushes aren't as bad.'

Euphemia thought about this for a moment. 'Do you have one power that works better than the rest?'

'At my peak, I would say yes. My hearing was superb, but now not so much.'

'I think my voice control is a strength, but my problem is I don't get the chance to practice in real-life situations, so I can't be sure. I tried using it to get Kenneth to take the rubbish out and he just laughed.'

'I never had much luck with that one. Based on the records we have accumulated so far, voice mastery is a talent few of us have had.'

'There are records? That's fantastic. Can I read them? Is there a link you can send me?'

'I wish,' said Barbara. 'We keep everything in the library in Mauritius. We haven't digitized.'

'Why not?'

'Security. The fewer copies of the information there are, the less likely they are to fall into the wrong hands.'

'Encryption technology being what it is, that doesn't make sense.'

'You're right. It's something the council needs to discuss.'

'There is a council? Who is on it?'

'I can't tell you. Not on the phone.'

'When then?'

'Soon, I promise.'

'It has to be soon. I can't do this alone. I keep coming back to the same issue. What's the point of having super powers? Wonder Woman, Spiderman - they use their powers for the good of humanity. Together, they save the world, cities, the planet. Me, I wrangle a bolshie steer into the mud in a paddock in the middle of the night. Big deal.'

'And if you hadn't?'

'Yeah, sure, Arthur might have died. Or I might have. Or Ally, but you know what I mean. It's hardly big picture stuff. It's not saving the planet from climate change or starvation or pandemics. The powers are personal, not global, so what's the point? One person can't change the world. Is it really worth the sacrifice?'

'This Spiderman. Have you told him what a good job he's doing?'

'Of course not. He doesn't exist.'

'Wonder Woman then.'

Euphemia sighed. If she had been standing up instead of snuggled under the duvet, she would have kicked the ground in front of her.

'It was better in the old days,' said Barbara. 'Then you could glimpse the strings holding Superman up as he circled the papier mâché earth in the movie studio,' Barbara said. 'Competing with CGI is a bitch.'

'I suppose.'

'What do you think you should do?'

'I don't think I should be stuck in the country doing the accounts for an old client. I should use the powers to rescue people from floods, or forest fires, save them from terrorist attacks, or stop slavery or stop avalanches. I have powers, but I feel powerless.'

'Floods, fires and terrorist attacks are easy enough, as long as long as you are there when it happens. None of us had much luck with avalanches. Snow is hard to control once it slides down a mountain. Miriam, your fourth cousin on my side, tried once.'

'What happened?'

'The village at the bottom of the valley got smothered and her with it. It took her twelve hours to dig herself out and her healing powers couldn't save her left great toe from frostbite.'

'Tell me she saved the villagers.'

'No. She didn't. They evacuated to safety an hour before it came down. A complete waste of the powers, but Miriam isn't a woman who likes to be told.'

'At least she tried.'

'The powers are to be used with a modicum of common sense. That's one reason they are activated only after a series of steps. The first is as you know being the first-born daughter, the second is giving birth to a daughter and then bringing her up and the third is reaching menopause - events, which not only require an ability to get along with fellow humans but patience, judgment and a sense of humor. Miriam unfortunately started menopause too early. Her judgment suffered because she still had to cope with her teenage daughter.

Annabelle was a piece of work in her teenage years but has thankfully since settled down. Anyway, you can tell Miriam from the rest of us, but you can't tell her much.'

Euphemia waited for Barbara to stop laughing at her own joke. 'So which one of us stopped slavery?'

'No one stopped it,' said Barbara. 'There are more slaves in the world now than in the recorded history of mankind. Anna saved some. An ancestor on your side she was travelling to the colonies in the seventeenth century. She discovered the Captain and crew had a sideline business and had secreted ten slaves in the hold. She bought all ten and gave them their freedom when they landed in Virginia.'

'She used her money. Not her powers.'

'She did what had to be done. I don't think the Captain or crew wanted to sell for the price she offered them. They were also a little miffed to be set ashore on an uninhabited island in the Caribbean with only the rations meant for their cargo.'

'Cute story.'

'Cute? Yes. Brave? Yes. Anna did what she could. Time and place, you see. The powers don't give us x-ray vision. We can't fly or tele-transport ourselves to far-flung outposts of the planet or the universe with Superman. We can't stop time with a golden lasso like Wonder Woman or heave trucks over our shoulders like the Incredible Hulk. At a pinch, we could climb up the outside of a skyscraper, but that would draw too much attention and there are smarter ways of doing things. Oh, and we may be smart, but we don't know how to defuse a nuclear weapon. At least I don't. I can't speak for everyone. We can only do what any normal woman would want to do, depending on the situation, she finds herself in. Because of what happened to Rachel, we're lucky to have more in our armory than our less blessed sisters. We can be brave and step up when they can't - something you should never under-estimate.'

Euphemia sighed. 'I guess you're right.'

'Right doesn't come into it. We live the lives we find ourselves in to the best of our abilities. That's all we can do.' Barbara paused. 'I've been thinking about what you said about Joe.'

'You're going to tell me I've been worrying over nothing.'

'No. I don't think you have. You're right to worry. I was going to ask if you had heard from Charlotte?'

'No,' Euphemia said. 'I tried, but her phone was off.'

CHAPTER 32

THE WESTERN LAKE ROAD RUNS BETWEEN THE BASE of the Remutaka Hills and a series of lakes, wetlands and farmland linking the town of Featherston to the coast. Euphemia had completely underestimated the distance when she set out to find Charlotte and Joe. She left a note for Jane and Josh telling them where she was going, but hoped she would be back with good news before they woke. There was little chance of that now. Dawn was breaking over the hills on the other side of the floodplain, and she still hadn't reached her destination. The narrow road slick with damp plus a series of one lane bridges meant she had to concentrate on her driving. Just as well, because she had forgotten the thermos of coffee she made before setting out. Thirsty and caffeine-starved Euphemia was in a grump, which no amount of morning scenery could improve. Worse, she had forgotten to fill the car with petrol and the needle was nudging empty.

The sign to the entrance of the reserve flashed past on her left as a van full of people, most of whom were leaning against the windows, asleep, passed by on her right. There was barely enough room on the road for both vehicles and she cursed silently as she narrowly avoided going into the ditch. Today was going from bad to horrible in a hand-basket. She turned the car around and found the entrance again. There was no road, just a two-wheeled track on top of a levee between two swamps. The muddy ruts on either side of the middle strip of grass looked deeper than her car could manage. She didn't want to get stuck in a place where rescue would be nigh on impossible, so she parked in front of the sign to the reserve, got out and locked the door.

Thankful for the extra layers of her merino running gear, she pulled her beanie down over her ears and zipped up her jacket. Tucking her chin down into the high collar, she thrust her hands into her pockets and set off. The lagoons bordering the levee were ringed by reeds and tall grasses. Ducks, swans, dabchicks and gulls peppered the surface of the waters, bobbing in and out of the mist. She didn't see any spoonbills, chicks, or adults. There was no wind, but this early in the morning, the muddy track was freezing and it didn't take long for the cold to soak through her shoes and into her socks. She tried not to think of the other warmer things she could be doing, as damp seeped into her bones.

After walking for half a mile, she reached a right-angle turn in the road leading inland. A fenced paddock higher than the lagoon with a few mopey cows at one end, lay to her right. There was still no sign of a shack, much less the red Tesla or even Charlotte. There were no footprints in the mud, no tracks, no clues to show anyone had been here. Euphemia, standing alone on a levee rising from the middle of a swampy lake in the cold damp mist of early morning, felt foolish. Why hadn't she waited until Jane, Josh or even Kevin at a pinch could have come with her? Super-vision was all very well, but two or three pairs of eyes were always better than one.

Having come this far, she figured she might as well follow the road to the end to see where it took her. On the bright side, she was seeing a part of the country she would be unlikely to come back to - no matter how exotic the bird life might be. A pukeko ran across the track and down the bank to her left, squawking in alarm. These purple-blue birds with their bright red beaks and long red legs were supposed to be quite intelligent. An urban myth, judging by the behaviour of this one; it was still squawking long after she passed by.

She turned back to see why it was still making a fuss. It made one last cry and disappeared into the grasses. There, tucked under a cabbage tree, was a wooden building, its tin roof camouflaged by netting and branches. She kicked herself for missing it.

A slatted wooden path jutted from the base of the levee across the grass leading to the back of the hut. Midway up one corner of the building, a stainless steel bolt secured with a padlock held a door shut.

Half sliding, half scrambling down the grassy bank, she crossed the slippery planks to the hut. The bolt secured by a padlock held fast when she squeezed her fingers through the tiny gap between the door and the wall and pulled. She put one eye up to the gap. It was dark inside. There were no windows, just holes which, when they were un-shuttered, allowed the occupant to spy on the birds. It had almost no furniture apart from a bed, a stool, a chair and enormous chest secured by another padlock. No sign of Joe.

Disappointment diluted her attention when she turned to leave. Her foot met no resistance to what she assumed was solid land. It went straight through the grassy top, down into cold brackish water. The rest of her overbalanced and in she went, accompanied by a loud splash. Mud sucked at her feet as she tried to stand until leaning forwards she grabbed the netting on the side of the hut and pulled. It ripped free, and she fell backwards. Her head went under, her eyes stung by the salt, her sinuses flooded with pain. Gasping for air, she reached for and pulled again on the netting. This time it held. Hand over hand, inch by careful inch, she pulled herself towards the hut and climbed back onto the walkway. Her knees pulled up, her arms wrapped around them, teeth chattering, she sat and let the water drain from her clothes. An icy wind fresh from the Antarctic arrived as if on cue to add misery to her morning dip.

She needed to get dry and warm quickly or hypothermia would set in. Still shivering she climbed up the levee and stripped down to her underwear, wrung out her clothes and put them back on. She reasoned that with the excess water was gone, the woollen fabric would form its own thermal environment with her skin. It was now a simple matter to contradict her body's natural response of redirecting blood to her vital internal organs to conserve heat. She closed her eyes, envisioning her blood flowing to her skin, its heat drying the damp layers of wool from the inside. By adding short bursts of energy in the form of turbocharged shivering, she warmed up and soon dried out enough to carry on.

The funk she had been in earlier, was gone, Euphemia ran and this time she paid proper attention to her surroundings, focusing on every bent blade of grass, every hollow in the mud, every sound of every bird in the whole goddamned desolate wetland. Five minutes passed. She pulled up at an unmarked gate, set back from the road. Behind the gate was another gravel road which lead towards a building whose roof she could see over the tops of scrubby trees. There were muddy splash marks on bushes and wet tire tracks at either end of puddles in the dips. She hoped the vehicle which made them had been leaving rather than arriving. Snooping was better without witnesses.

She ran towards the barn, for that is what it was, using the trees as cover. A rusty blue tractor, its tires flaking rubber into the dirt, was parked next to a small window in a sidewall. If someone was inside and saw her, she could use the 'pathetic woman- I got lost' routine if anyone challenged her, but only as a last resort. Challenges were better avoided. With her back flat against the rotten boards of the barn wall, she listened. Scratching noises, followed by a series of comforting clucking.

She swivelled around and peered through the window. A hen jerked its head back in fright. The clucking got louder and broodier. Dark, beady eyes met Euphemia's blue ones. Its head cocked to one side, a claw froze in midair, it waited then moved off pecking at the ground, tossing aside old straw with its feet as it meandered over to the red Tesla parked inside the barn.

CHAPTER 33

A PADLOCK SECURED THE BOLT ON THE BARN DOORS. Did anyone use anything else apart from padlocks in the Wairarapa? Luckily, the hinges had rusted. Euphemia landed one swift kick on the saggiest door and it caved in. The chicken darted through the gap in a flurry of feathers and alarmed clucks. She waited. No sounds to show she had been heard, so she slipped inside.

The Tesla sat in the middle of the barn, a fine layer of dust coating the fire-engine red paintwork. There was no mud on the wheels so someone had cleaned it. Joe, in full eco-warrior mode, had insisted on showing the Sages what every button and switch was for, so there was nothing Euphemia didn't know about the vehicle. Peering through the driver's window, she discovered why Joe hadn't answered his phone. It was lying on the wireless charging console between the front seats. She tried the doors. Locked. More to the point, the alarm hadn't gone off. Someone had either disabled the sentry function or the battery had run out of charge.

She circled the interior of the barn, noting the hay bales

stacked neatly against the end wall and an old plough rusting into the dirt floor.

'Is anyone there?'

She cocked her head to listen. The question had come from behind the hay bales. When she tossed them aside she found a door. Like every other door this morning, it too was bolted padlocked. It was also steel and part of an old shipping container. With a simple twist and a hard yank, she ripped a metal strip from the old plough. Next, she wedged it behind the bolt and, with one foot braced against the wall of the container, pulled hard. A series of satisfying noises followed as the screws popped free from their sockets releasing one end.

The door swung open. Weak light from a lantern torch revealed Joe lying on the floor handcuffed to a chain bolted. A bucket lined with a thick plastic bin bag sat in the corner behind him - the smell identifying its function. A shelf stocked with packets of food, bottles of water, and a couple of books had been fitted halfway up the far wall.

Joe put his hand over his face, squinting at the sudden bright light, and sat up. His blue cashmere jersey was filthy and ripped at one shoulder, his hair hung lankly across his face. 'Euphemia?'

'The one and only,' she said. 'You've got to get out of here.'

'What day is it?'

'It's Thursday. Where's Charlotte?'

'No idea. Why?'

'She came to look for you.'

'Oh God,' he said. 'I haven't seen her.' He tried to stand, but the chain was too short and he only made it to his knees.

Euphemia used the metal strip to liberate Joe from the wall. It was quicker and easier than doing it at his end. Looping the chain over his shoulders, she helped him to his feet.

'Can you walk?'

'Now I can,' he said. He got up slowly and stretched each leg.

Euphemia pushed him ahead and out the door. 'Go as fast as you can down the drive. Hide in the trees until I come and find you.'

'What are you going to do?'

'No time. Go.' She pushed him. He stumbled but recovered and soon broke into a shuffle. When he had disappeared into the bushes, she closed the door, found the screws and fed them back through their holes in the bolt plate, twisting them into place and sliding the bolt closed. Next, she re-stacked the bales exactly as she had found them. Snapping a branch from a bush outside, she swept away the hay stalks and footprints on the floor. Only when she was satisfied the place looked undisturbed, did she run down the drive. It was easy to find Joe. She smelt him long before she reached him.

CHAPTER 34

'Please shut the windows. It's freezing,' Joe said. The chain across his shoulders rattled with his shivering.

'Not long. We're almost there,' she replied.

Joe poked his head up from the back seat and looked out the window. 'We're not almost there. We're only at the rail trail turnoff.'

'Keep down.'

'Only if you wind up the windows.'

'Only if you promise not to stink.'

He lifted a blue cashmere arm and sniffed. 'Stink is harsh.'

'Truth is harsh. Now stay out of sight. When we get closer to town, you're going to get out and hide.'

'I'm what?'

'I haven't got enough petrol to get us home. I don't want anyone to see you when I go to the gas station. Don't worry, I'll come back.'

'You'd better or I'll take my business elsewhere.'

'We need to talk about your business.'

'Now?'

'No, not now.' On reaching a straight stretch of road with a good view in both directions, she slowed down. There were no cars and no houses, but it was drizzling. 'Here is a good place,' she said.

Joe wasn't happy, but did as he was told. She watched in the rear vision mirror as he slid into a hollow, out of sight behind a stand of scrubby bush.

* * *

She was standing at the counter, paying for the petrol and two chocolate bars, when Daryl Mathews sauntered in wearing a plain sweatshirt. Not a hoodie. His trousers were at his waist and not sagging over his bottom, and he had even had a haircut. The most amazing aspect of his appearance was that it was only eight thirty in the morning and he was clean-shaven.

'Hungry?' He nodded at the chocolate bars.

'Always,' she said collecting her purchases and receipt.

'Seen Mr Kincaide lately?'

She paused on the threshold. 'No. Have you?'

Daryl smiled stupidly. 'Why would I?'

'I'll tell the police you were asking after him.'

He stopped smiling. 'I was only being polite. Jeez.'

'Tell them, not me.' She got into her car, noting the other vehicle on the forecourt was a brand new black SUV. She drove off, then turned back to park on a side street with a good view of the garage. Daryl climbed into the SUV and the bass beat of a Metallica song reverberated in her chest as he clicked it up to full volume before starting the engine. Taking care not to be seen, she followed him the short distance to the turnoff to the Western Lake Road.

* * *

'Why does everyone who comes through that door stink?' Jane asked.

'It's part of living in the country,' Euphemia said. She turned to Joe, who was following several steps behind her. 'Have a shower or three, get changed and we'll talk about what's next.'

Joe nodded, but at the top of the steps, he stopped. 'Joan, have you heard from Charlotte?'

'My name is Jane and sorry I haven't.'

'Hi Uncle Joe,' said Josh. He was sitting at the table doing schoolwork. 'You really stink. And you,' he said to Euphemia. 'You smell too. Not as bad as last time, though.'

'Manners, young man,' Jane said. 'Do your homework or I will tell Ally you pretended you were sick to get out of going to school today.'

'Why is Josh here?' asked Joe.

'We're looking after him while Arthur is in hospital.'

'Arthur is in hospital?'

'He's fine. An accident on his ATV. We'll talk later. Shower. Soap. Shampoo. Rinse. Repeat. Clean clothes. I'll fill you in after you're done.'

Euphemia was back upstairs before Joe. She was down to her third best set of black merino running gear. Her second best gear, she put in the washing machine. Joe looked and smelled like a different man when he reappeared. His soft olive green corduroy trousers and his oatmeal turtle-neck jumper hung loosely from his shoulders and hips. His wet hair was drying quickly, and he had shaved. Best of all, he was wearing a light cologne smelling of lavender and musk. He rubbed his hands together as he walked into the living room. 'Coffee and eggs, in that order, I think.'

'You do the eggs,' Euphemia said, pouring the coffee.

'I'll do the eggs,' said Jane. 'We've been worried, haven't we, Effie? When you didn't come back, we didn't know what to think. I said something was wrong. We called the police but they didn't want to know.' Jane filled a pan with water and set it on the stove, then took eggs and bread out of the fridge.

'Thank goodness they didn't,' said Joe, taking a seat on a stool.

'I agree,' said Jane. 'They only complicate things. I said that, didn't I?'

Euphemia frowned. 'Did you?'

The water was boiling loudly. Jane cracked the eggs into it one by one and, crushed the shells, before dropping them in the compost bin.

Euphemia sipped her coffee. 'How did you end up in a container?'

'How did you know where I was?' Joe asked, their questions overlapping.

'You first,' said Euphemia.

'Someone put a rag over my face when I got to the shack. I don't remember anything after that. The next thing I know, I am chained to a wall and having to shit in a bucket. Not my style at all. They took my watch, so I didn't know the time. Very disorientating. I don't recommend the experience. And if I haven't said this already, thank you. Now you tell me how you found me.'

'Charlotte told us about your shack. She went to fetch you home yesterday and we haven't heard from her since.'

'Why were you talking to Charlotte?'

'We caught her sabotaging the sanctuary,' said Jane, taking plates out of the warmer drawer. She slathered the toast with butter, lifted the eggs out of the water, let them drain and slid them onto the toast.

'What did you say?'

'We'll talk about that later. What matters is where is she now? Because whoever took you could have taken her.'

'Of course,' said Joe, cutting through the top of his

poached egg to release the yolk. 'Please tell me she didn't put rats in the sanctuary. She said she would do that in our last argument.'

'Ferrets,' said Jane.

'Oh God, not ferrets.'

'And rats.'

'As I was saying,' said Euphemia, glaring at Jane. 'We have to find her. The ferrets can wait.'

'Not if they are breeding females,' said Joe.

'Joe, listen to yourself. This is Charlotte we're talking about. She's your wife.'

'Ex-wife. She ran off with my best farm manager remember. I'm not sure I have any sympathy for her, to be honest. Ferrets. That's low even for her.' He put a heap of eggy toast into his mouth and chewed silently staring into the distance.

'I now understand why she pretended to leave.'

'She didn't pretend. She buggered off with Derek, the best farm manager I've ever had. The place has gone to rack and ruin since he left. As you obviously know.'

'Another long story and one we don't have time for. Concentrate Joe. Who took you and why?'

Joe was about to speak when Kevin walked in with a courier package. 'Hi Joe,' he said cheerily. 'I knew you'd be back. I said not to worry, but they wouldn't listen. Women, aye? See Jane, what did I tell you? You girls get yourselves all worked up over nothing. Men like Joe and me, we need time out now and then.' He held up the package. 'The courier delivered this to the homestead. Says it's urgent, and it's addressed to you.' He handed the small package to Joe and sat down at the counter. 'Excellent. Poached eggs. Pass me a mug, would you? There's a love. I desperately need coffee.'

Jane extracted a mug from the dishwasher, rinsed it under the tap. She was about to hand it to Kevin when she stopped.

Beside the open courier bag, scattered across the granite bench top, were ten bright red fingernails.

CHAPTER 35

EUPHEMIA TOOK A POSTCARD OUT OF THE BAG. ON one side was a color photograph of the Hong Kong skyline at night, and on the other was a message. "*Pay up!*"

'What's going on?' asked Kevin.

Euphemia slid off her stool, took Kevin by the arm and walked him to the door. 'I'm sure it's nothing serious. It's probably a joke,' she said. 'But in the meantime, you are a vital link in the chain of whatever is happening here and we need you back at the homestead to wait in case there are more deliveries?'

'If it is a joke, it isn't very funny,' he said.

'Which is why we need you to stay at the homestead in case there are more packages,' Euphemia said.

I'll help. Of course I will...,'

'Excellent,' she said, shutting the door before he could say anything else.

Joe was absent-mindedly chasing a nail around the counter with his finger and didn't look up when she returned. 'She would never give up her nails willingly,' he said.

'We know,' said Jane. 'Nails like this are expensive and only a proper artist can make them look natural. One would have been enough to send a message, but all ten! These people don't take prisoners.'

'Obviously they do,' said Euphemia.

'Has Arthur said anything?' asked Joe.

'He told me the entire story. I'm sorry.'

'We asked for time,' Joe said, not looking up. 'They agreed to extend the deadline by six months until we got approval for the subdivision.'

'They've changed their minds,' said Euphemia.

'Do you think it was the triad who chained me up?'

It could be. Someone sabotaged the ATV.'

'What?'

'It rolled on Dad and nearly killed him,' said Josh. 'If Mrs Sage hadn't lifted it off, he would be dead.'

Euphemia had forgotten Josh was there. She wasn't sure how much he knew and she didn't want to be the one who told him about his sister and the money the family owed to the triads.

'I don't think Mrs Sage lifted it exactly,' said Jane patiently.

'How else did she get it off? And she tied up the steer.'

'Don't young children have fantastic imaginations nowadays?' laughed Jane. 'It was dark Josh. We couldn't see what happened from where we were.'

'I did,' said Josh. 'I videoed it. I'll show you.' He took his phone out and started swiping frantically for the right app.

'Pass me your phone,' said Euphemia, using her voice. Josh stopped scrolling and put the phone on the counter. She turned it off and put it in her pocket, which she zipped shut. 'I would like to talk to your uncle privately. Would you go downstairs while I do?'

'Why? Do you think I don't know what Elizabeth did and why we had to come here? I'm not a baby.'

'Maybe not, but there are some things children shouldn't hear.'

'That's what Mum says. It's not fair.'

'Life is unfair. If you want to be a big boy and help, you will go downstairs. Now.' Josh was about to protest, but the tone of her voice overrode his objections.

How is Arthur?' asked Joe when Josh had gone.

'Ally called earlier. He's coming home this afternoon,' said Jane.'

'One positive,' said Euphemia. 'Joe, we have to call the police.'

'We can't. These people are ruthless. They have Charlotte.'

'Then the police will find her. Their forensic team can search the barn for clues. We can't.'

'No, I won't allow it,' said Joe. 'They'll kill her. I know it. You've both been a great help, but this isn't your fight. Go back to the city and forget everything.'

'I am not leaving you here alone,' said Euphemia. 'We're not leaving until we know Charlotte is safe. Jane agrees with me.'

Jane screwed up her face. 'I guess so.'

'I'm here,' said Josh, rounding the corner into the kitchen. 'He's not alone.'

'Spoken like a true Kincaide,' said Joe. 'All for one and one for all, aye boy?'

Josh flushed with pride, straightened his shoulders, puffed out his chest and looked at his uncle with the most manly expression he could muster. 'I know where you keep the key to the gun cabinet. We could arm up.'

'That's enough,' said Euphemia. 'When an eight-year-old boy talks about guns, you know things are out of control. Please Joe, call the police.'

'I know you mean well, Josh,' Joe said, 'but promise me you won't ever, ever, ever open the cabinet.'

Josh's shoulders sagged and tears welled up in his eyes. 'I promise.'

Euphemia waited. 'That's it?'

'I will not call the police while they have Charlotte, and neither will you.'

'We don't know who has her.'

'Ten clipped fingernails and a postcard of Hong Kong, not enough of a hint?' He got up and walked over to the window.

'Okay,' said Euphemia. 'Let's say you're right. "*Pay up*" doesn't give us much to go on. When, how much, to who?'

'To whom?' corrected Josh.

'Thank you. To whom?'

'We have to wait,' said Joe.

'How long?'

'I don't know Euphemia. As long as it takes.' He turned around.

'I saw Daryl...,' said Euphemia. 'When I was filling the car in Featherston this morning.'

'That little weasel,' said Jane. 'Did he apologize for trying to steal my bag?'

'What do you think? No, he didn't. But it was strange. He looked almost respectable, and he was driving a brand new black SUV.'

'Did you see where he went?' asked Joe

'Funny you should ask. I had to wait for him to drive past your hiding place before I could pick you up. He was heading out to the coast on the Western Lake Road.'

'I don't know why. He lives in South Featherston with his mum. Completely different direction,' said Joe. 'Jocelyn tried everything to make him leave home, but he won't go. No one will give him a job, so he's on the benefit. He refuses to leave unless she pays his rent.'

'You don't mean Sandy's Jocelyn?'

'That's her. Daryl's father disappeared early on in the

piece. She did her best, but it can't have been easy. The lad was trouble from the word go. Sandy tried to get him interested in helping with sanctuary, but it was pointless. Couldn't or, rather, wouldn't listen. The boy prefers petty thievery to honest work.'

He tried to steal my handbag,' said Jane. 'I had to fight him off.'

'You were very brave. Most women would have run a mile.'

Jane smiled modestly. 'I'm not most, women.'

'I can see that,' said Joe.

Jane flushed as they made eye contact holding it until Josh pointedly cleared his throat.

CHAPTER 36

'No,' whispered Jane. 'You go. I'll stay here.'

'You have to go,' Euphemia said. 'You know Kevin. I don't.'

'You do so know him.'

Not as well as you,' Euphemia said.

'If I go, he'll get the wrong idea.'

'If you go, you can break it to him that your relationship is over.'

'It was a mistake, not a relationship,' said Jane. She twisted the sapphire on her ring finger. 'If it makes you feel better, you were right all along and I should have listened to you.'

'It makes me feel much better.'

'Gloat all you want,' she said, switching her fidgeting to her diamond pendant. 'You were right. Which is exactly why I should stay here in case Joe wakes up and you should be the one to check on Kevin. Pulllleeeese Euphemia.' Jane looked over to make sure Josh really was reading his book but turned her back to him in case he wasn't and whispered again, 'Joe is the first man I've met in ages who is halfway decent.'

'He is decent, and he is still married,' whispered

Euphemia. 'He still cares for Charlotte, and she still cares for him. I care about you and I don't want you to get hurt again.'

'I won't get hurt. I get there are issues between them. All I want is for him to get to know me before he makes any rash decisions—that's all. Puuleease. One chance?'

'He's asleep, so how he's going to get to know you? And you are not to wake him up. He's exhausted.'

'I wouldn't. I won't.' She crossed her heart and pointed skywards. 'I want to be here *in case* he wakes up. And I don't want to fight Kevin off again. He won't leave me alone. He says I drive him crazy, and he has to have me.'

'Stop. You've made your point. All right. You win. You stay here. But do not wake Joe up. Got it? Do not.'

'Got it.' A tiny skip accompanied this last statement.

'Josh,' said Euphemia, 'Your parents are coming home and we need to make sure everything is ready for them.'

'You mean we have to check on Uncle Kevin?' He shot a dark look at Jane. 'Why do I have to go? I want to stay with Jane and Uncle Joe.'

'Your parents will want to see you as soon as they walk in the door. They must have missed you so much,' said Jane. She took his book, snapped it shut, and dropped it on the sofa. 'Plus, we should check there hasn't been another delivery.'

'Uncle Kevin said he'd do that.'

'Silly. Uncle Kevin is having his afternoon nap. Now, off you go, both of you,' said Jane. She shooed them up the steps. Petal and Brutus brought up the rear just in time to get through before she closed the door.

Euphemia walked down the drive, her shoulders hunched, her hands tucked into her jacket pockets. 'Are you warm enough?' she asked Josh.

'Yip,' he replied, bending down to pick up a stick. He tossed it onto the grass verge, but the dogs ignored it.

'Petal never was a stick dog,' said Euphemia. 'Not even when she was a puppy. What about Brutus?'

'Food yes. Sticks no,' said Josh. 'We lived on the fifteenth floor in our building in Hong Kong. He was always an inside dog.'

'Do you miss it? Hong Kong I mean.'

'I miss my friends but I miss Anna the most. She was our amah. She looked after me when I was a baby. I'm saving up to go back and see her.'

'Is that why you want ten thousand dollars?'

'Yip.' He slowed to step on an acorn and crush it into the dirt.

'You know I won't pay you, don't you?'

'Sort of.'

'Sort of?' She laughed. 'Hear me. I will not pay you.'

'You should see what I'm selling before you say that.'

'Fair enough. Show me then.'

Josh held out his hand for the phone. She took it out of her pocket and gave it to him. He turned it to landscape mode, tapped the screen, and handed it back to her.

She could hear the restless sounds of cattle, as their shapes became easier to see in the dark.

'I adjusted the filter there. See?'

'Very good,' said Euphemia. Memories of the animals' warmth, their breath steaming in the cold air, flooded back. She watched as she grabbed the beast by the horns and wrestled him into the mud. Josh was right. She was clearly recognizable. He had captured everything in perfect detail.

'I look quite good, don't I?' she said, pressing pause.

'Not bad,' Josh said. 'Ten thousand dollars' worth, I reckon.'

'There has to be a better way for you to get back to Hong Kong Josh - a more honorable way. You're a Kincaide.'

'So is Elizabeth. Look what she did. She ruined everything.

If she hadn't taken drugs, I wouldn't have to go to this stupid school and sit on that stupid bus with those stupid kids. Dad wouldn't have nearly died. I hate it here. It's cold, and it's…,' He burst into tears.

Euphemia put her arms around him. He slumped against her, sobbing. Brutus, trotted over and sat as close to the boy as he could get. Petal plopped down and licked her bottom.

'Have you told your parents how you feel?' asked Euphemia.

'Noooooo,' wailed the boy.

'Don't you think you should?'

'Noooooo.'

Euphemia bent down and crooked her finger under his chin to make him look at her. 'If I was your mother, I would want to know. So I could fix it.'

Josh gulped and sniffed a line of snot back up his left nostril, then wiped the tears from each cheek with the heels of his hands. 'We can't go back because of Elizabeth. She's not well,' he said. 'And even if she was okay, then the triad would get her.'

'She'll get better,' Euphemia said, 'and when she does, then you could go back without her, maybe.'

'What about the triad? We can't go back if they're trying to kill all of us.'

'We can sort them out.'

Josh laughed and made a face. 'The triad? You don't know what they're like. My friend David told me they cut off your fingers if you look at one the wrong way. He said if you owe money, then they cut off parts of your body until you pay them back. He said they pour hot oil into your ears slowly, one ear at a time, and if you owe a lot of money, they cut out your eyes. One by one.'

'Your friend David has an overactive imagination.'

'It's the truth. David told me. So did Sammy.'

'These are the school mates you want to go back to Hong Kong and see so badly?'

'Yes.' He paused. 'I haven't really put the video on TikTok.'

'I know.'

He looked at her, amazed. 'How did you know?'

'Because you're a nice boy Josh and because I checked.'

He shifted from one foot to the other and, trying not to smile, bent over and rubbed Brutus behind the ears. Brutus snuggled into his leg for a moment and then, sensing he was no longer needed, sauntered off to nuzzle Petal, whose leg was still in the air.

'Not that this isn't worth ten thousand dollars, Josh. You are a talented iPhone cinematographer. Few people could get such a clear image in the dark.' Euphemia tapped the screen and replayed the clip.

'I want to make films when I grow up. Hey,' he said, pointing at the screen. 'What's that? There.'

Euphemia paused the clip again. 'Show me,' she said and examined the white dot he had pointed at more closely.

'I think it's a face,' said Euphemia, increasing the resolution. 'Higher up the hill, on the other side of the stream.'

'Do you know who it is?' asked Josh.

She studied the screen. 'I think I do,' she said and smiled. ' Can I delete this?'

Josh screwed up his face as he thought about it, took a deep breath and said, 'Yeah, okay.'

'Thank you,' said Euphemia. 'One day I will make it up to you, I promise. Come on. Let's find Kevin.'

CHAPTER 37

THE BACK DOOR WAS WIDE OPEN WHEN THEY arrived. Brutus and Petal ran inside, jostling each other out of the way to get to the dog bowls by the stove. Petal licked one, then the other, to make sure they really were empty, Brutus followed along behind. Job done, they nudged open the door to the pantry on the off chance the bag of dog food was open. Disappointingly, it wasn't. They slumped down in a patch of sunshine - tongues out chests panting after their stroll down the hill.

There was no one in the kitchen, the library, or the sitting room. This morning's paper lay spread open on the dining room table, a cold half cup of tea beside it.

'It's like the Marie Celeste, but in the country,' said Euphemia.

'What's the Marie Celeste?'

'A ship. They found it floating in the middle of a calm ocean with no one on board and the lifeboats still on their racks. No one knows what happened to the crew.'

'Spooky,' said Josh, taking a step closer to Euphemia. 'Look upstairs. You go first.'

'Hello,' called Euphemia, as they climbed the staircase. There was no reply. 'You look that side. I'll check this side.'

'I'll stay with you to make sure you're all right,' said Josh, taking her hand. She opened the doors to the guest bedrooms, but they were all empty. They doubled back and checked Josh's room, Elizabeth's room, and finally the master bedroom. All empty.

'Where does Kevin stay?' asked Euphemia.

'In the old servants' quarters,' said Josh. 'Up there on the third floor.' He pointed to a narrow door at the end of the corridor. The wooden floorboards creaked loudly as they walked towards it. Josh's hand gripped hers tightly. Outside, a magpie called to its mate, and the trees rustled in the breeze. In the far distance, sheep bleated. A curtain billowed silently at the window at the end of the hall. Josh gripped harder.

A scramble of paws on floors—a cat snarled and hissed then fled past them, its hackles raised as it cut a corner then looped back around their legs and made a dive into Josh's room - two tiny dogs slavering at the mouths ran after her in hot pursuit. Josh screamed. Euphemia didn't—but nearly had.

'It's just a game,' said Josh, relaxing his grip on her hand. 'Snoopy lets them know when he's had enough.' As if to verify this, Snoopy, his ears flat against his head, raced past them, taking the stairs four at a time, the dogs following but with less gusto than before.

The door at the end of the corridor swung out before Euphemia could open it. Kevin emerged, smiling as if he had been expecting to see them. He nodded, shut the door, turned the key in the lock and pocketed it. 'I don't know about you, but I could kill for a cup of tea,' he said and proceeded down the stairs.

Josh and Euphemia exchanged glances. 'Must have been having that nap.'

'Guess so,' said Euphemia, but she put her head against the door and listened.

'Anything?'

'No.'

'Look what I found on the back step,' Kevin said pointing to a red and white courier bag on the table when they entered the kitchen.

'It wasn't there when we arrived and I haven't heard a vehicle,' said Euphemia. 'Haven't seen one either.'

'Nor me, but it was there when I came down,' Kevin said taking mugs out of the dishwasher and setting them on the bench. 'It's addressed to you this time. Not Joe. Aren't you going to open it?'

'We should call the police,' she said. 'So they can take fingerprints, or swab for DNA. They can ask the courier company who sent it.'

'Uncle Joe said not to,' said Josh.

'I think he's wrong.'

'You don't know what's in it yet,' said Kevin. 'Could be something completely unrelated.' He handed her a mug of tea.

She took a sip, the scalding hot liquid burning the roof of her mouth. The plastic envelope lay between them on the table. Josh picked it up and felt it gingerly. He shook it. 'There are no body parts in this one,' he said.

'You really should be at school,' said Euphemia. She found a pair of scissors in a jar on the windowsill and neatly snipped the top off the envelope. A folded piece of plain paper landed on the table. She used the tips of her fingers to hold the corners, opened it out, and read the message.

'*If you want to see Charlotte Kincaide alive, leave thirty thousand dollars in unmarked bills in the mailbox at midnight. Call the police and she dies. Slowly.*'

There were ten bloody fingerprints beneath the message.

'This makes no sense,' said Euphemia.

'Which part?' asked Kevin.

'All of it. Why is it addressed to me? And it's Saturday.'

'They know you're here?'

'Okay, but it is still Saturday.'

'The triads don't work business hours.'

'No, but banks do. How do we get thirty thousand dollars in unmarked bills from an ATM? On a Saturday?'

'Ah. I see your point.'

'I know where Dad keeps his money,' Josh said.

'Where?' asked Kevin.

'In the safe in the study. I'll show you. I know the combination.'

'You wonderful, wonderful, boy.' Kevin put his hands on either side of Josh's face and kissed him on the forehead. 'We're saved.'

Josh furrowed his brow. 'Who are we?'

'I meant us. Charlotte's saved, that's what I meant. The words came out wrong.'

Josh moved to stand beside Euphemia.

'Let's see if there is enough there to pay the ransom,' Kevin said. 'I volunteer to put it in the mailbox. It's the least I can do.'

'That won't be necessary because we're not paying it.' Euphemia rummaged in a drawer and found a plain zip-lock bag. She used her fingertips to pick up the note and then the courier bag and deposited them inside the bag. 'Evidence,' she said sealing it.

'Aren't you clever?' Kevin said. 'I would never have thought of doing that.'

'We'll show this to Joe. He should decide what we do.'

'Or,' said Kevin. 'We have the ransom money, thanks to little Josh here. I can take care of this quietly. Charlotte comes home, surprises Joe and everybody wins.'

'It's an idea,' said Euphemia. 'Just not a good one. Come on, Joe needs to see this.'

CHAPTER 38

Euphemia led the way, followed by Josh carrying the evidence bag in front of him like a pageboy bearing a ring at a wedding. Kevin, overtaken by Brutus and Petal, brought up the rear.

'Who are you?' Josh said at the top of the steps.

'That's not how you greet a visitor Josh,' said Joe. After his nap, he looked a different man entirely from the creature Euphemia had rescued from the barn. His blue eyes sparkled, his face had lost its sallowness and he was smiling at his nephew. 'This is Alastair,' he said. 'He cycled all the way from Wellington to see Mrs Sage and Mrs French.'

Josh, still holding the envelope in front of him, stared at Alastair, who, clad in a full length bright green lycra bodysuit, was standing beside his uncle.

'Over the Remutaka's?' asked Euphemia. 'That's quite a feat.'

'I came over the rail trail. Doesn't take long that way and there are no cars until you get to the Western Lake Road. Nearly got bowled by some idiot in an SUV who came out of nowhere. I ended up in the ditch.'

'How awful?' said Jane from the kitchen. 'You must be starving.'

'Coffee would be marvelous,' said Alastair. 'I brought a packed lunch and ate it on the way, so don't worry about food.'

Jane set to filling the kettle. Again. Alastair slid over to the kitchen in his stocking feet. 'Need any help?'

'What?' asked Jane. 'No. Sit down and relax. It's such a surprise to see you.'

Undeterred, he leaned on the counter beside her. 'How are you?'

'Fine.'

'The office hasn't been the same without you.'

Jane flicked a glance at Joe to see if he was watching, and when she saw him talking to Josh about something in a plastic bag, she leaned over to Alastair and muttered. 'You shouldn't have come.'

'I wanted to see you,' said Alastair.

'You only saw me four days ago.'

'It seems much longer,' he said.

Jane spooned coffee into the plunger and poured in the hot water. She started to push the plunger down when Alastair reached over and put his hand over hers to help. She jumped and took her hand back. 'Anyone else like coffee?' she called, edging past Alastair to see what Joe was looking at.

'Oh my God, is that blood?'

'Yes,' said Josh. 'Aunt Charlotte's.'

'We don't know that for sure,' said Euphemia. 'Good to see you Alastair.'

'Of course, it's Charlotte's,' said Kevin. 'Who else do we know being held hostage?'

'Hostage?' asked Alastair.

'We don't know that either, Kevin,' said Euphemia.

'Josh says there's enough money in the safe to cover the

ransom demand,' said Kevin, trailing after Joe, who had moved back to his usual position by the window.

'I doubt that,' said Joe. 'And even if there were, we can't touch it. It's Arthur's money.'

'Joe, please call the police,' said Euphemia. 'Please.'

'No,' said Joe and Kevin in unison.

'Please.'

'If the kidnappers find out, they will kill her,' said Kevin.

'That is exactly why they should be involved. Joe. You can see that, surely?'

'How do we know it's not a scam?' asked Joe.

'Why would it be a scam?'

'Something doesn't feel right.'

'Was it a scam when they locked you up?'

'I'm not sure. I never saw who did it,' Joe said.

'We know someone wanted you out of the way. If we find out who that was, then maybe we can find out why and that could lead us to Charlotte? Try to remember what happened. Miss nothing out, no matter how small.'

'I received a text the spoonbill chicks were fledging,' Joe said.

'Who was it from? Have you still got it?'

'I didn't recognize the number, but I don't always. I figured it was from another twitcher because there was no name. That's not unusual, so I'm afraid I deleted it. I drove to Pounui, parked the car, walked to the hut and the next thing I remember is waking up in the dark.'

'Where did you park? Did you see anyone? Another car?'

'I left the car at the entrance where I normally leave it.'

'Someone knew that's what you would do,' Euphemia said. 'Go on.'

'When I think about it, I do remember hearing a car drive past. I didn't take any notice, but I heard it stop further up the road.'

'Color, make, driver?'

Joe rubbed his chin. 'Black, I'm certain it was black, and it was going fast, which is why I remember it stopping. I heard the brakes.'

'Were you in your car, or standing beside it?'

'I had changed out of my shoes, pulled on my gumboots and I was halfway to the hut by then.'

'Think carefully,' Euphemia said. 'Did you hear footsteps? Was anyone following you?'

He closed his eyes and breathed out. 'I heard the sea roaring. There was a storm the night before, and the waves were pounding the beach.' He stopped. 'Now I remember. The door to the hut was open. I assumed the wind had blown it open and went in, not thinking anything of it, then someone grabbed me from behind and put a wet rag over my face. Foul smelling stuff - alcohol. Next thing, I'm chained up where you found me.'

'You saw no one.'

'Behind the door, there was a man behind the door. I turned, but he got me before I saw him properly. Just a shape, really. He was stronger and taller than me.'

'You poor thing,' Jane said. 'You must have been...'

Euphemia held up her hand, interrupting her. 'You're certain it was a man?'

Joe thought. 'Yes,' he said. 'I remember his shoes. They were soaking wet. I remember thinking the guy had to be an idiot wearing trainers in a swamp.'

'Concentrate, Joe. Can you describe them? Color? New or old?'

'He's doing his best, Effie. Stop hounding him.' Jane went over and put her hand on Joe's arm.

'And you're distracting him when I need him to concentrate.'

'He is concentrating,' Jane said.

Joe patted Jane's hand and moved away from her. 'Euphemia, you're really helping. I thought I didn't remember, but I do. I'm pretty sure they were Nikes. Old ones.'

'Anything else? Did you see them again? Anything from the room?'

'I'll try writing it down and see if I can remember it better that way.'

'That rules out a triad,' said Josh.

'Why do you say that?' asked Euphemia.

'David told me the foot soldiers dress to blend in, so they wear trainers. But they always wear new shoes so they don't leave wear patterns in the blood when they cut bits off you. He said, they get a special deal from the manufacturers in Shenzhen. His father works for Nike, that's why he knows. His father said the triads were some of his best customers.'

'Who is this David?' asked Joe. 'He sounds rather ghoulish.'

'He was my best friend,' Josh replied. 'Anna said his father is one of them, a triad guy, but I don't believe her.'

The adults looked at Josh and then at each other.

'Charlotte,' Euphemia said, breaking the silence. 'What are we going to do?'

'I vote we wait,' said Joe. 'If Josh is right, the triad doesn't have her and the more I am convinced this is a scam.'

'How can you say that?' asked Euphemia.

'Because I know my wife.'

'Ex-wife,' said Jane. 'An ex-wife who sabotaged your sanctuary.'

'Hm?' Joe wasn't listening. Instead, he turned to Euphemia. His face lit up. 'I just remembered. The food in the chilly bin - the bread—it was a sourdough. There's only one person who can make bread like that.'

'The baker in Martinborough,' said Euphemia.

'The baker in Martinborough,' echoed Joe. 'It's Charlotte's favorite bread and mine.'
'That means the kidnapper is a local.'

CHAPTER 39

Euphemia's phone rang. She answered it, listened, then passed it to Joe. After a moment, he nodded and went into the study. Euphemia knelt down in front of Josh. 'That was your mother,' she said. 'Your father won't be coming home today after all. He was getting ready when he collapsed. He will be all right, but he needs an operation.'

Josh took a deep breath and tried not to cry. 'Can I talk to him?'

'I'm afraid not. Your mother said they are getting him prepped for surgery. But she wants you to come into town and be there when he wakes up.'

Joe emerged from the study and handed Euphemia her phone.

'They said he was better,' Josh said. Brutus came over to the boy and rubbed against his leg. Josh picked him up, burying his face in his fur.

'A small set back - that's all,' Joe said. 'Your father will be right as rain in no time. Kincaide men are made of sturdy stuff. Don't forget that. Come on, grab your things and I'll drive us into town.'

Euphemia helped Josh into his jacket, while Jane retrieved his iPad and put it into his backpack.

'You heard your uncle,' Euphemia said as she walked him to the door. 'Your father is going to be fine.'

'Give them our love,' Jane said. She helped him into the ute and did up his seat belt. Alastair stood on one side of Jane, Kevin on the other as they lined up to wave goodbye. Josh's face was pale and serious as he stared at them through the window. Jane blew him a kiss. Joe revved the engine, leaving a shower of gravel in his wake as he fishtailed down the drive.

'That poor kid,' said Alastair. He attempted to put his arm around Jane's shoulders, only to find Kevin had beaten him to it. There was a slight tussle on the front step before Jane shrugged them off.

'I'm going for a run,' said Euphemia, when they were inside. 'I need to think.' She disappeared downstairs to get changed.

'Good idea,' Jane said. 'I haven't been out in days. I'm going for one too.'

Alastair raised his eyebrows. 'When did you take up running?'

'I have always been into fitness. I don't parade around in Lycra like some people. Exercise makes me feel alive. It's good for you.' She started running on the spot as if to prove her point. 'Running is more honest than cycling,' she added, trying not to puff. 'Your body does the work, not some machine.'

'But the machine only works if you use your body.'

'A bicycle is an enhancement, like hormones. It makes you go faster.'

'It's nothing like hormones.'

'I don't want to argue with you, Alastair. You have your views and I have mine. That my exercise is natural, and yours relies on technology is beside the point. If you'll excuse me.'

'Women,' said Kevin. He was lying on the sofa, reading an *Architectural Digest* magazine.

'What do you mean?'

'I mean, women are not the logical sex,' said Kevin. 'Men are. I can say that to you because you're a man.'

'If that were logical, which it isn't, explain why you think you can only say it to a man.'

'Sorry? Look mate, us blokes should stick together.'

'Or what?'

'Or the girls will take over the world, that's what and I don't know about you, but I don't fancy being told what to do by a pack of sheilas.'

'Remind me again which century we live in,' said Alastair.

'Oh I get it,' said Kevin, throwing aside the Architectural Digest and standing up. 'You're one of them - a metrosexual. I should have known when you arrived on your bike in those tight clothes and silly backwards shoes. I bet you drink lattes and Marlborough Sauvignon Blanc and go for massages on Saturdays.'

'What if I do?'

'I knew it.' Kevin slapped his thigh. 'You are one of them. No wonder Jane doesn't know how you feel about her. You're waiting for her to give you permission to say something rather than telling her what you want like a real man would.' He advanced towards Alastair, his index finger straightened and poked him in the chest to reinforce each word which followed. 'Like. A. Real. Man.'

Alastair waited until he finished speaking, until Kevin's chin jutted in front of his face. The he calmly brought his fist neatly up under that same chin, just hard enough to lift him off his feet for a fraction of a second.

'Do you?'

Alastair turned to see Jane standing at the top of the stairs in her bright pink running gear. His hand hurt, but he couldn't rub it now.

'Do I like you? Yes. Jane French. I do.'

'Oh.'

'Is that all right?'

Kevin waggled his jaw from side to side. 'I'm calling the police and have you charged with assault,' he said, rubbing his chin. 'Jane. You saw what he did. You're a witness.'

'I had my eyes closed because I didn't see a thing after you poked him four times in the chest.'

'Pokes in the chest hardly compare to a punch'

'You think so? Quite frankly, Kevin, I don't give a damn.'

Alastair, his heart bursting, watched the little pink pompoms bouncing over the back of her shoes as she pulled open the door and ran down the drive.

CHAPTER 40

KEVIN AND ALASTAIR HAD BEEN TOO BUSY PLAYING duelling stags to notice Euphemia slip out of the house. Far be it from her to interfere in the mating rituals of middle-aged men. Firmly on the side of Team Alastair, she hoped he would get rid of slimy-Kevin once and for all. Alastair might not have the attributes Jane prized in a man. He wasn't wealthy; he hadn't gone to an elite school, and he wasn't in a high-paying job. He preferred cycling to cars, but for all that, he was a decent man and he would treat Jane with the love and respect she deserved - if only she would give him a chance. Why Jane was attracted to bad boys and not particularly bright bad boys was a mystery.

First Justin, then Kevin. Now she had an unrealistic gleam in her eye whenever Joe was around. Joe might not be a member of the same bad boy club as Justin and Kevin. But he was self-centred, in a way that he hadn't been at university. There he had been caring, funny, and always entertaining. But she thought, that must have been a veneer. The older she got the more she realised that age like power reveals the person under the surface.

Charlotte is still the perfect foil for Joe, and if she is still alive, they have to get back together. Jane will be better off with Alastair, even though she doesn't think so yet.

Euphemia hurdled the fence across the road and ran up the hill beside the sanctuary. The weather hadn't decided what it wanted to do — one minute the sky was overcast and the next it was blue and sunny. Inside the fence, the bush was silent, the brooding trees unleavened by the sound of birds. Bloody Charlotte, and her bloody ferrets. Sabotaging the sanctuary was such a wicked thing to do. Could Joe be right about her disappearance being a scam?

Euphemia shook off her doubt and doubled her speed. There was nothing she could do about it now. She had to clear her head of the confusion of the past few days and think about nothing other than the world around her and her feet hitting the ground. She ran down into the next valley, straight up the hill on the other side and on past the top fence marking the boundary of the sanctuary. The rain two days ago had soaked down to the roots of the grass. Green shoots were poking up through the dry stalks of summer, the earth now darker and softer underfoot, was unlike the rock-dry surface of before. That hill topped, she leapt like a goat over boulders and gorse leaving the sanctuary below her, she ran for sheer joy - every muscle, every sinew working in combination with her lungs and heart to achieve perfection. She soared like a ballerina, her legs outstretched over a dry streambed at the bottom of the slope, landing halfway up the next.

Arms pumping, she ran to the top and stopped. From this vantage point, she could see the entire valley. The road wending its way along the bottom, and opposite her Oakhill Homestead, the New House, and the farm buildings and cottages with the home farm rising behind them. In the distance stood her erstwhile nemesis—the 'horned one' grazing peacefully with his band of merry steer mates. A flight of magpies cawed noisily in the trees around the home-stead, the sound contrasting with the silence in the sanctuary.

Could Charlotte really be to blame for such devastation? She knew how much the place meant to her husband. The hurt in her voice when she described Joe's neglect of her and their marriage had been unmistakable, as had the love in her eyes when she talked about him. Vain, and shallow she might be, but Euphemia had seen the disgust in her eyes, heard the revulsion in her voice as she hauled the cage of struggling ferrets up the ladder. Josh had picked up on it, too. Wait a minute! She hadn't given the boy's comments the attention they deserved.

Charlotte's utter distaste for the creatures meant there was no way she could have put the animals into the cage. She would have had to handle them to do that. Which meant leaving her comfort zone, a zone Charlotte never left. She would never have devised such a plan by herself. Someone was using her to do their dirty work for them. Is that why she had disappeared? Someone was worried she wouldn't keep quiet and would expose who was really behind the sabotage?

Euphemia could feel the temperature dropping on her back as the sun slipped towards the horizon, but she wasn't ready to return to the house and its bickering occupants. She needed more time to think without petty distractions. She lay down on the warm earth and looked up at the eggshell blue sky fading to the transparency of glass.

'Mrs Sage?'

Euphemia sat up. 'Sandy?'

'What are you doing here?'

'I could ask you the same question,' she said, getting to her feet.

'I was checking the fence,' he said. Dressed in camouflage bush clothing, he had pulled a dark beanie low over his head and he was wearing a full backpack. He was also carrying a very large rifle with an expensive-looking scope attached to it.

'Which doesn't explain why you are all the way up here,' she said.

'I guess it doesn't.' He was standing so close to her she could feel his breath on her cheek.

'A beautiful evening,' she said and stepped away from him, out of his reach. 'Doesn't it get dark quickly? I'd better be getting back. I don't want Jane to send out a search party.'

'No rush. I said you'd gone in to Masterton to see Arthur.'

Euphemia took another step back. 'Why would you do that?'

'So they won't worry about you.'

'What do you mean?'

'When you don't come back tonight?'

Euphemia didn't wait to hear what he had to say next. She gave him an almighty push and the steep hillside did the rest. He stumbled as he tried to recover his balance. His foot twisted in a rut and he overbalanced, a whoosh of air escaping from his lungs as he landed on his backpack. She vaulted him as he tumbled head over tail then kept running at full speed until she reached the back fence of the sanctuary, where she stopped. It was almost dark, and she waited for her eyes to adjust. She stilled her breathing to better listen for him. He was back on his feet and getting closer, moving quickly and heading directly towards her - in the dark.

She remembered the scope on the top of his weapon. If it was heat sensing, he could see her. She weighed up her options. She could easily outrun him, but she couldn't outrun a rifle round.

Last year when she actually caught a bullet in the building's foyer in Sydney, it had been fired from a pistol. A pistol round is slower, heavier and travels at less than the speed of sound. It had also been fired at midday in a well-lit foyer with white walls. A rifle bullet travels at two thousand feet per second, at supersonic speed. She was in open country and it was dark. The odds were stacked against her tonight. Her night vision meant she could see Sandy, but she would not see a bullet until it was too late. If she attempted to cross open ground to get to the road, he would use the scope and easily pick her off. She had to find cover.

'Mrs Sage,' he called. 'Stay by the fence. Then we can discuss what happens next, like civilized people.'

'I don't call hunting me down like an animal, civilized,' she called back.

'Who said anything about hunting?'

'Isn't that what you'll tell the police? That you were hunting rabbits? That you didn't identify your target and my death was a tragic mistake?'

He was getting closer, circling to her left so he could come up at her from the side. With her back to the fence, she could only move in one direction to get away from him, but it was away from the road, away from safety.

'You have been a nuisance since you arrived.'

'Tell me something,' she called.

'Anything. You won't be telling anyone.'

'Did Charlotte know what you and Daryl were doing?'

'All credit to the city girl for figuring it out.'

'It wasn't hard. Daryl and the black SUV were the giveaway.'

'He's not the brightest of lads, is he? When he told me he saw you at the service station on his way out to the lagoon, I knew you would make the connection.'

'Is that where Charlotte is? In Joe's hut?'

'Damn you're good.' He laughed. 'Stupid woman got caught, so we had to change the plan.'

'She didn't know what was she doing, did she?'

'No. She's not like you.'

'I still don't understand why. You helped Joe build the sanctuary, the fence. When you showed Josh the geckos, I could tell how much they mean to you. Why destroy it?'

'A woman like you would never understand.'

A twig snapped. He was getting closer. Euphemia, the fence against her back, edged away from him as she searched for the right spot to make her move.

'Try me,' she called.

'Jocelyn. Daryl. They deserve a better life than I can give them. The geckos were our ticket out of poverty. I was doing fine until Arthur came home. Next minute he and Joe were planning to build a retirement home for old greenies over-looking my sanctuary. Hundreds of old eco-warriors let loose in my sanctuary. Imagine it, green boomers used to getting their own way rebuilding my tracks, setting up houses for my wetas, checking my traps, counting the birds and no doubt documenting every insect in the place for posterity. On spreadsheets.'

'Worst of all,' he said. 'They would find my geckos. Not just the Wellington greens but the others, the rare ones I intro-duced and which are breeding. These people set up commit-tees and volunteer societies, fundraising groups and native plant nurseries. There would be school trips, open days, night visits, year round guided tours and documentaries. There wouldn't be a weed left in the place. Politicians would have to get involved whether they liked it not. I've seen boomers in action. Retirement doesn't slow them down, it turbo charges their desire to leave the world a better place. Look at you. You're old and the speed you run at is unnatural.'

'I've been training for an event,' Euphemia replied.

'The Olympics?'

'This isn't about me. Why would aging greenies threaten your life with Jocelyn and Daryl?'

The metallic sound of a bolt being pulled up back and

down interrupted the silence. Another twig snapped. His outline was getting closer. He raised the rifle to his shoulder, his finger was on the trigger and he was two hundred meters away and closing.

'Daryl and Jocelyn, Sandy?'

A rock crumbled under his foot.

'What has the sanctuary got to do with them getting a better life?'

He swallowed and relaxed. The rifle dropped to rest on his upper arm. 'The geckos sell for up to a thousand dollars each at wildlife fairs overseas. People love them because they live for a long time and they are pretty. You saw how Josh was when he saw his first one. A couple of years ago, a Chinese guy approached me in the pub. If I supplied them, he would get them out of the country. I have earned more money in the last three years than I have earned in my whole life. I look after the geckos and they look after me.' He re-shouldered his rifle and breathed out. 'Time's up.'

Euphemia leapt high, her hands gripped the top of the fence. She pulled herself up and rolled over the top to drop inside the sanctuary. Pushing aside branches and scrabbling over tree roots, she dived deep into the bush until she reached what she calculated was the middle. He cursed as he started running. From here, it would be a race to the road. He had a clear run around the perimeter. She had the bush to contend with, but she also had a useful dollop of super powers.

Every sense on full alert, her night vision allowing her to see what was ahead, she used her hands to swing from one branch to the next, her legs powering off the trunks. She was nearly at the gate - the bush had thinned out; the smells had changed from the closeness of dew-laden leaves to the smell of tar-seal cooling. Sandy had almost kept up with her, but in the last few seconds he had fallen, his feet sliding out from under him on wet grass, his curses meeting her ears as she reached the gates. One vault and she would be free to hightail it up the drive. One vault and this madness would be over. She bent her knees, ready to spring up and over. That's when she saw a hand in the mud beside her feet—palm up and lifeless, a hand missing its bright red fingernails.

CHAPTER 41

EUPHEMIA FELT FOR AND FOUND A PULSE, THEN DOVE under the cover of the bush and pulled Charlotte's hand out of view.

'I know you're in there. I'm coming to find you.'

A dog, probably Brutus, barked. Petal wasn't interested in making noise for its own sake. It took too much energy. In the distance, a door opened and Jane called him inside. They were such homely normal sounds. Euphemia wanted to come out of hiding and reason with Sandy telling him that no matter what he had done, she would help him sort it out. Nothing was worth what he was about to do. She might have tried if she had been alone, but now she had Charlotte to consider, she couldn't take the risk.

'Ridiculous animal doesn't belong here.' Sandy leaned his rifle against the gate, took off his daypack, and unzipped it, rummaging around until he produced a key. He inserted it into the padlock on the gate, rattling the chain when it didn't work. 'Damnation.' He took out the key, threw it on the ground, and pressed his face hard against the mesh. Laughing he called out, 'Don't run off now.' His lovely white teeth glistened in the dark.

His LandRover was across the road and he yanked open the glove box, hurling items onto the floor as he searched for the correct key.

'Charlotte, wake up,' Euphemia whispered giving her a good shake at the same time. It was no good. She didn't respond. Euphemia couldn't leave her, but she also couldn't vault over a twenty-foot fence carrying seventy kilograms of unconscious woman. Not quickly, anyway. They had to hide until she could think of a plan. Hoisting Charlotte over her shoulders, fireman style, Euphemia plunged into the bush and up the hill.

Back on the road, the door to the LandRover slammed shut, then more footsteps. This time when Sandy put the key into the padlock, it sprang open and the chain fell away clanking against the fence. The gate swung open. She heard twigs cracking beneath his feet and branches being pushed out of the way as he advanced up the hill towards them.

'I'm coming,' he called softly. 'Don't make this hard. I am a highly trained professional bushman. I know who you are, Mrs Sage. I will find you and I will kill you.'

She froze, unwilling to give away her position by making a noise. Even unconscious, Charlotte had a different idea. Her left arm slid from off Euphemia's shoulder and thumped against the trunk of a tree. Sandy gave a grunt of satisfaction and changed direction. There was no way to save herself or Charlotte unless she could move undetected. She had to stash Charlotte and deal with Sandy on her own terms. Further up the hill, she found an old log partly concealed by ferns. Quietly, she lay Charlotte on her side behind it, took off her jacket and draped it over her face so it didn't shine white in the moonlight. Free of her burden, Euphemia started towards the fence.

She heard him as he moved up the centerline she had mentally drawn down the middle of the sanctuary. Every few minutes he would stop, call her name and listen. She stopped when he did, waiting until she heard him moving again before she too moved, hoping his noise would mask her own. He had three advantages. One, he had the night scope and two; he knew the layout of the sanctuary. He knew exactly where the fallen trees were, where the low-hanging branches and rocky outcrops were, where there were loose rocks underfoot. And three he knew when he was going to halt and listen for her whereabouts. It was inevitable she would make that one step after him, which would betray her. She needed that step to be at a time and place of her own choosing.

By now, he was on her side of the sanctuary, almost level with her, separated by trees and undergrowth. He stopped. She did too, one knee raised, frozen like a stork in a pond, waiting. A full two minutes later, she heard his foot on wet leaves. She was ready. She stamped her foot straight down onto a rotten branch; the sound shattering the quiet.

'Got you!' he yelled, and he crashed through the bush straight towards her. The fence was twenty feet away, the trees close to it cleared to prevent animals from using them as a bridge into the sanctuary. She could go up the hill or down. She could hide, hoping he wouldn't find her. Or she could deal with him. Right here. Right now. Like the super woman she was - two words lower case.

She ran to the trunk of an ancient rimu, scrambling up it like a bear until she reached a thick branch twenty feet above the ground. Less than ten seconds later, Sandy stopped directly below her and looked around. She smelt the peppermint on his hot breath rising to her hiding place in the cool evening. He positioned himself one foot in front of the other; the rifle tucked into his right shoulder; he steadied the barrel with his left hand, his finger on the trigger, his right eye staring down the sight. He swung the rifle slowly through one hundred and eighty degrees, then turned to complete the circle.

'What the...?'

She heard the frustration, the anger in his voice. Euphemia exhaled and waited until he lowered the rifle. She counted to three and jumped.

CHAPTER 42

CHARLOTTE WAS SITTING ON THE LOG HOLDING HER head in her hands when Euphemia got back to her.

'What happened?' she asked. Her head lolled backwards and sideways, her attempt to look at Euphemia failing without the cooperation of her eyelids. 'Wooooooo.' She groaned, then slowly she slid backwards off the log, landing on her back with her feet in the air. 'Slippery. Don't just stand there. Help me.'

'Whatever you're having,' said Euphemia, grabbing her hand and pulling. 'I don't want it.'

'I've had nothing, nada, zip, nothing,' slurred Charlotte, releasing Euphemia's hand and sliding over the log again. 'Damn. Nearly made it. Come on Sage, put your back into it. Pull.'

Euphemia did exactly as asked, almost launching Charlotte into the air.

'Wow! You've got a good back. My head isn't working.'

'That happens when you get drunk.'

Drugged. Not drunk. I know drunk.' She hiccupped. 'This isn't it. Okay, I might be a little teensy tiny miniscule weeny, weeny, bit drunk. But in my defense, your honor, I was thirsty and the only thing I had to quench my thirst was vodka. And not the good stuff.' She opened her eyes wide and stared blearily into Euphemia's face. 'Not my fault. They locked me in and I've been here all day and all night.' She lifted her hand and promptly burst into tears. 'What have you done?' she wailed. She lifted her other hand, and the wailing intensified. 'How could you?'

Getting Charlotte to her feet was an exercise in patience, geometry, and engineering. No sooner was her weight transferred onto one leg than the other collapsed. Alcohol vapour hit Euphemia's nostrils like the perfume from an unlit flamethrower as she half-carried, half-dragged her to the gate. 'That's it. You can do it - one foot in front of the other. Good girl. Now the other one.'

'Walking is harder than it looks,' said Charlotte. 'How have I been doing this so easily all my life and not noticed?'

'I wonder. Let's go back to the house, get you sobered up and you can tell me all about it.'

'You're so nice,' said Charlotte, wiping tears from the end of her nose with the sleeve of her sweater. Her knees buckled and before Euphemia could adjust her grip, Charlotte fell forwards hitting the mud face first and lay there. 'I am so cold. Veeeery veeery cold.'

'Stand up.' Euphemia shook her. But the only response was a long, low, and very loud snore. 'All the women I know snore? I don't get it.' There was nothing for it but to throw the unconscious Charlotte across her shoulders again and set off.

EUPHEMIA PUSHED OPEN the front door with her foot and staggered into the living room, Charlotte still draped across her shoulders.

'You found her. Is she all right?' Jane asked.

'Cold and very drunk,' said Euphemia. She lay Charlotte down on the sofa. 'She's been outside in the bush for a night and a half. Can you find a duvet and then fill a couple of hot water bottles? We have to get her warmed up.'

Two of the many things Euphemia appreciated about Jane were that she was smart enough to understand a situation without the need for long, drawn out explanations and she didn't ask inane questions. She got on and did what was asked of her without making a fuss.

Kevin, in contrast, stood rooted to the floor. He hadn't moved from his spot near the study. He stared at Charlotte as if he'd seen a ghost. 'Why? Where did you...? How...?' He was giving an excellent imitation of a not very intelligent goldfish.

'Would you put the kettle on please, Kevin?' Euphemia had asked using her normal voice. He didn't move. She employed her command voice. 'Now. The kettle.'

Immediately, he went over to the bench and pushed the switch.

'Fill it first please, Kevin,' she called.

Alastair relieved Kevin of the kettle, filled it, and switched it on with a flourish.

'She asked me to do it. Not you,' Kevin said.

'But you weren't doing it. Coffee anyone?' Alastair, having successfully occupied the high ground at the sink, rinsed the plunger. Not one to give up, Kevin got to the beans first. There was a tussle over the grinder. Alastair won.

'For goodness' sake. Stop it, both of you,' Jane said when she reappeared with the duvet and the hot water bottles which she tossed on the bench. 'Fill these before you make the coffee.'

Euphemia pulled off Charlotte's wet shoes and socks and rubbed her feet dry with one of several towels Jane dumped on the floor beside her.

'Take her clothes off and dry the rest of her,' said Jane,

putting the duvet over her. 'She probably has hypothermia. Dan told me what happens when the core temperature drops. Was she disorientated when you got to her?'

'She wasn't the best,' Euphemia replied, now feeling guilty for blaming everything on the vodka. 'She had drunk a bottle of vodka.'

'Alcohol makes the body lose heat, which would make her worse,' said Jane. 'If she doesn't come around in the next half an hour, we'll call an ambulance.'

'Another one,' Kevin said. 'That will be the third ambulance in as many days.'

'And that is important. Why?'

Euphemia pulled and tugged under the duvet until there was a pile of muddy clothes on the floor beside the sofa. Kevin had, by this time, cunningly outmaneuvered Alastair and re-taken the sink. Rather than stand idly by, Alastair swooped over, whisked up the clothes and bore them triumphantly past his rival to the laundry.

'Kevin, fill the hot water bottles,' said Jane. 'Where did you find her?'

'In the sanctuary and it was sheer luck I did,' Euphemia said. 'She would have died if I hadn't.'

'How did she get there?'

'We won't know until she wakes up and tells us, but I think it might have been Sandy.'

'Sandy?'

'He tried to kill me.'

'Who tried to kill you? Why?' asked Kevin. He handed the hot water bottles to Jane. She wrapped them in towels and slipped them under the duvet.

'Sandy tried to kill Effie,' said Jane.

Kevin nervously looked at the door.

'Don't worry,' Euphemia said. 'He won't hurt you or anyone else. The police have him.'

'The police? How?'

'I can't go into how, other than to say a team has been monitoring his comings and goings as part of their investigation into wildlife smuggling.'

'Wildlife?'

'Specifically native geckos. There's been a resurgence in smuggling ever since the government disbanded the wildlife protection unit. Germans love our geckos and will pay big money for them.'

The duvet erupted, the hot water bottles slithered onto the floor and Charlotte rolled onto her side, vomited, and rolled back again.

'That's a good sign,' said Jane. 'I learned that at my first aid course. Don't stand there gawping, get a bucket and the paper towels.'

'Alastair. Get a bucket and paper towels. Quickly,' yelled Kevin.

'What's the magic word?'

'Please,' replied Kevin.

'You're grown men and you're acting like children.' Jane said.

'He is,' muttered Kevin.

'You both are. You're sure it was Sandy?' asked Jane. 'I mean, he's so good looking.'

'What's that got to do with it?'

'I'm just saying. What did you do to make him want to kill you?' asked Jane.

'Excuse me, what did I do? I can't believe you said that.'

'No need to get snippy.'

'I was not being snippy.'

'You were snippy, Sage,' mumbled Charlotte, her eyes still shut. 'Sandy is dangerous.'

Alastair handed the kitchen roll to Kevin, who refused to take it.

'You're just as capable of cleaning up vomit as I am,' Alastair said.

'You,' said Euphemia pointing at Kevin, 'clean up the mess. And you,' she said to Alastair, 'make the coffee.'

Kevin peeled ten sections of paper one by one from the roll and piling one on top of the other until he had a thick wad. He reached down and swiped up the mess with one hand while pinching his nose with the other. Then, holding the package by his fingertips as if it were radioactive, he rushed outside.

'Don't suppose you have a bucket?' asked Charlotte.

Jane shoved it across the floor just in time. Charlotte heaved, but there wasn't much left in her stomach after the previous effort. Gradually, her eyes cleared as the duvet and hot water bottles did their work. Her hair was awry and studded with branches and leaves, her face covered in mud. She looked from Euphemia to Jane, then wrinkled her face when she saw Alastair.

'Who are you?'

'I'm Alastair, I work at Sage Consulting. I came over to see Jane...'

Charlotte cut him off. 'My nails!'

'Who took them?' Euphemia asked.

'I allow two people near my nails - me and my manicurist. I had to do it, or Daryl said he would. Don't worry, I have an appointment in Wellington to see Stacy next week.' She looked at her hands again. 'If I can wait that long.'

Euphemia sat down in the chair opposite. Alastair handed her a mug of black coffee, which she took gratefully.

'Sandy wanted to convince Joe they meant business. He knows how important my nails are to me, and he was going to make Daryl do it.' She shuddered. 'Jane, you wouldn't be a love and bring me a glass of water, would you? A jug if you can and maybe some pills. I have such a headache.'

'You poor woman, what you have been through?' Jane said.

Charlotte blew her a kiss and crinkled her eyes. 'Aren't you wonderful?'

'She is indeed,' Alastair replied.

'Daryl, Jocelyn's idiot son, was waiting for me when I went to the shack.' She sat up, nearly dropping the duvet from under her arms tucking it up again just in time. 'Joe? Is he all right? Did you find him?'

'He's fine. He's at the hospital with Josh and Ally. Arthur needs surgery.'

Charlotte burst into tears. 'I was so worried. I couldn't bear it if anything happened to him.'

Jane paused on her return from the kitchen. A second later she straightened her shoulders and, taking a deep breath, put the glass, two white tablets and jug of water on the table in front of Charlotte, then she sat down beside Euphemia. 'Joe will be pleased to see you safe,' she said. 'He was worried about you.'

Euphemia put her hand on Jane's and squeezed it. 'You are a good person, Jane French,' she whispered.

'He was worried about me? Truly?' Charlotte asked.

'I'd say it was more that he was only a little bit worried,' said Kevin.

'And you would be wrong, Kevin, so keep quiet,' said Jane. 'He was really worried. He still loves you, Charlotte. And it's obvious you still love him.'

CHAPTER 43

'Daryl was at the hut,' said Euphemia. 'You're sure?'

Charlotte put the tablets on her tongue and swallowed them with the water. 'I'm sure. I reckon I could have got away if he had been on his own. He is such a weed, but he had another guy with him.'

'Who?'

'I haven't seen him around here before. A Kiwi based on his accent - Chinese. He kept yelling at Daryl that his boss was angry about the shipment being late.'

'So, Sandy doesn't call the shots,' Euphemia said.

'Who else could it be?' asked Jane.

'Someone who doesn't want to see the Sanctuary Village go ahead.'

'Why not?'

'Because they don't want a village of boomer eco-warriors bent on saving New Zealand's wildlife, interfering in their lucrative and illegal trade in geckos.' She stopped and looked across the room. 'Isn't that right, Kevin?'

'Why ask me?'

'Because you're their inside, man. How else would two courier bags arrive when none of us saw or heard a van? And,' said Euphemia getting up, 'you were the only one who could have told Daryl where Charlotte was going. You've been feeding them information all along.'

'Not me, I swear. The courier could have used an electric car, a small one. Green - which blended with the trees. You know how quiet they are. I swear I have nothing to do with any of this. It was all Sandy and Jocelyn's...,'

'You rat,' said Charlotte. 'I lost my nails because of you.'

'Not me. I told them not to go that far. I liked your nails.'

Jane marched over to Kevin, who was leaning against the bookcase. 'Tell.' Poke. 'Us.' Poke. 'Everything.' Poke. Poke. Poke.

'I won't.' He ducked out from under Jane's finger, went over to the dining table and sat down with his back to them, his arms folded in front of him.

Jane followed and sat opposite him.

'Tell us and I'll go easy on you.'

'No.'

Euphemia sat in the chair on his other side. 'If you tell us what you know, I won't tell the police.'

Kevin studied her face. 'Promise?'

'Promise.'

It was as if a dam had broken. Kevin started talking and didn't stop. 'When I first got here, I helped Sandy box up a shipment of geckos. He said they were for the Karori sanctuary in Wellington, otherwise I wouldn't have done it. Later, I found out they were really going to Germany. He said it was too late, and I was involved whether or not I liked it. He threatened to tell Joe unless I loosened the brake cables on the ATV. I knew it was getting out of hand, but I didn't want Ally to think her older brother had messed up again, so I did as I was told. I tried to stop Arthur from using it. Take the ute, I said, but he wouldn't listen. I haven't worked for over a year and Sandy paid me two thousand dollars for the first shipment. I needed the money. After that, they didn't pay me at all for the ATV. They have no honor. A deal is a deal. Daryl laughed and told me to do as I was told. When Arthur didn't come back, I knew what had happened. That's why I didn't come with you. I couldn't bear it if I had killed him. I wasn't really afraid of heights.'

'Is that it?' asked Jane.

'No,' he said. 'I'm sorry. I was going to tell Joe what I did, but you arrived and I couldn't.'

'Me?'

'When I saw you again, I wanted you. You know how I feel about you. We're so good together. That's why I took your jewels.'

'You did what?' roared Alastair.

'It's all right. Euphemia got them back,' said Jane.

'It's not all right,' said Alastair.

'I said leave it, Alastair. They're my jewels.' She turned to Kevin.

'I didn't want to disappoint the woman I love. Not again.'

'That wasn't love. You don't love me, Kevin. You love yourself and you use everyone else as an excuse when things go wrong.'

'I am a good man, Jane. Or,' he paused, 'I will be, if you tell me you love me.'

'I can't do that. I won't. Not now. I was stupid and really lonely. When we first met, I talked myself into the love part. I was infatuated, so I didn't see you for who you really are - a man who believes the world owes him more than he deserves.' She pushed her chair back and stood up. 'I deserve better. One day, the right man will come into my life. A man who loves me for me. And when he does, I will love him for the rest of my life.'

The loud clapping and cheering from Euphemia, Alastair and Charlotte, which followed this declaration stopped, when the front door swung open and Jocelyn marched in followed seconds later by Daryl.

CHAPTER 44

'What have you done with my husband?' Jocelyn demanded.

Side by side, the contrast between mother and son could not be more stark. Jocelyn was stocky, broad shouldered and big-breasted compared to Daryl's lanky frame and sunken chest. Her light brown hair, cut shaggy to frame her face, made her brown eyes stand out. Her light orange lipstick unintentionally highlighted the dog's bottom of smoker's lines around her lips. She was wearing a black polo neck jersey and ironed jeans tucked into knee-length flat boots, dangling earrings and a right wrist full of bracelets. Daryl had resumed his usual bogan attire; low-slung jeans, a faded black oversized hoody and grubby high-tops with the laces undone. His unwashed hair hung in curtains on either side of his face. A volcanic pimple looked ready to erupt to the left of his nose.

'Where is my husband?' demanded Jocelyn again.

'I thought it was a de facto relationship.' Charlotte stood up, the duvet firmly tucked under her arms.

'The lady bitch of the manor has come crawling home, I see?'

'No thanks to your son,' said Charlotte, swishing forwards and trying not to trip over the end of the duvet. 'I would have died if Euphemia hadn't found me.'

'Nothing to do with me,' mumbled Daryl.

Jocelyn rounded on him. 'Be quiet.'

Daryl's head retreated turtle-like into his hoody.

'Sandy came to shoot rabbits, and he hasn't come home.'

'He didn't tell us,' said Euphemia.

Jane, Charlotte, and Alastair nodded in agreement behind her. Kevin coughed into his fist.

'What was that, Kevin?' Jocelyn asked.

'She knows,' he said, pointing at Euphemia.

Jocelyn fixed her gaze on Euphemia and moved towards her. 'She knows what?'

'Where Sandy is,' said Kevin.

'Where is he?'

'The police have him in custody. We know about the geckos. Kevin told us Sandy asked him to fix the brakes on the ATV and that he duped Charlotte into sabotaging the sanctuary. We know about the contacts in Auckland. Kevin told us everything.'

'Not everything, I swear,' Kevin said.

Daryl shoved his hoody back off his head. 'He said it would be all right,' he yelled at his mother. 'That I wouldn't get into trouble. Sandy lied and you let him. It's all your fault Mum.' He ran to the door, yanked it open and was gone - swallowed up by the night.

'He lied to me, too. It's all his fault,' said Kevin. He stopped in the doorway and blew a kiss at Jane. 'Goodbye, my love. I know you don't love me, but no matter - we'll always have Palmerston North.' He left, and they heard him calling out to Daryl to wait for him. A slam of car doors and the sound of an SUV speeding down the drive followed. No one knew what to do, least of all Jocelyn. Presumably, she had no way of leaving now that Daryl had gone.

Charlotte rearranged the duvet under her arms, the air puffing out of the feathers when she resumed her seat on the sofa. Jane fiddled with a nail, still embarrassed at the mention of Palmerston North.

'Cup of tea, anyone?' asked Alastair.

'Please,' said Jocelyn, sitting down next to Charlotte on the sofa. 'I'm exhausted. I'm not cut out for this, not at my time of life. Oh God, here comes another one.' Her face flushed red as beads of sweat popped out on her top lip. She tried to haul her jersey over her head, but it got stuck on her bracelets. The more she tugged, the more stuck her sleeve became, the more desperate she became.

'Stay still,' said Charlotte. She unhooked the sleeve and Jocelyn pulled the jersey off.

'Thank you.'

'You're welcome.'

'Sorry about what I said before. I didn't mean it. One minute I feel fine and the next I want to machine gun the world and everyone in it. It would be helpful if I got a warning, but I don't.'

'I had that,' said Jane, sitting in the chair opposite. 'And hot flushes. Justin used to get so irritated with me turning the heater on and off again, throwing the duvet on and off. He told me if I didn't get it seen to, he would leave.'

'Who is Justin?'

'He was my husband. He died. Last year.'

'I'm sorry,' said Jocelyn, accepting a cup of tea from Alastair. 'Did you see someone?'

'The best thing I ever did,' Jane said.

'Yes. The doctor gave Miriam HRT. She was in the café when we saw you. Sorry about that too, by the way. Miriam said she got her life back and that I should try it. I've been too busy running around after Sandy to make an appointment.'

'I hate to interrupt this meeting of the Ponatahi menopause support group,' said Euphemia, 'but what about the sanctuary?'

'It can go up in flames and every damned gecko in it for all I care,' said Jocelyn. 'None of this was my idea. Sandy got it into his head that we should be further ahead than we were. If Joe Kincaide had paid his bills on time, none of this would have happened. Sandy didn't ask me. Just went ahead with his stupid plan and next minute some guy in Auckland is yelling at him on the phone telling us to stop the retirement village from going ahead.'

'How long ago was this?'

Jocelyn thought for a moment. 'It was when I changed my hair from blonde to brown to hide the grey. I remember because Sandy was too angry with Arthur and Joe to notice and we had an enormous fight.'

'How long ago did you change your hair color?'

'A year. Maybe two. Not long after you ran off with what's his name?'

'Derek and I didn't run off with him. He was helping me, that's all. We didn't have an affair. Like Sandy, he was sick of Joe not paying the farm bills. He wants to come back because he misses the place.'

'So is that why you called us and asked about Joe?' Jocelyn looked at Charlotte.

'Yes, and Sandy said the sanctuary was his life and maybe I would like to do something about changing that.'

'He lied to you, too.'

'I thought he was telling the truth. I wouldn't have sabotaged the sanctuary otherwise. Now I feel guilty about the birds.' Charlotte burst into tears.

Jocelyn put her arm around her shoulders and hugged her.

'The birds are fine. The ferrets were sterile. Sandy made sure before he let you have them. He wanted to get rid of the birds temporarily, not forever. They'll come back.'

Charlotte wiped her eyes with the heels of her hands and sniffed. Twice. 'You're not just saying that to make me feel better.'

'Why would I want to make the bitch lady of the manor feel better?'

This time it was Charlotte who hugged Jocelyn, forgetting in the process about the duvet, which slumped without support into a pile at her waist. Alastair turned bright red and glanced away.

'Ahem,' Jane said, pointing.

Euphemia had stopped listening when the hugging started. She was reading the text, which had made her phone vibrate in her pocket.

'Caught an earlier plane. Home tomorrow @ 3 pm. Can't wait to see you. K xx'

No sooner had she read this than her phone buzzed again. *'Fantastic honeymoon. Home tomorrow @ 3 pm. K & B xx'*

'It must be good news,' Jane said. 'You haven't looked this happy in days.'

'I haven't felt this happy in days,' Euphemia said. 'We're going home.'

CHAPTER 45

Horizontal rain and wind lashed Euphemia's little car as she drove along Cobham Drive to the airport. Wellington, the coolest little capital in the world on a good day, could be downright miserable the rest of the time. Never more so than when a southerly blast from the ice-sheets of Antarctica blew in to batter the city and those in it. It was still autumn, and this weather was both nasty and premature, but it still couldn't dampen Euphemia's spirits. A few weeks, nothing in the grand scheme of things, but it had seemed like years since she had last seen her husband and daughter. She had had time to rush home after the drive over the hill, dump her stuff, turn the heating to high and take a chicken out of the freezer to roast later.

Petal, pleased to be home, had rushed upstairs and down looking for and finding no one. A circuit of the sopping garden in which she flushed the neighbor's cat out from under the agapanthus by the compost bin followed. Exhausted by her exercise, she plopped down in her basket.

'Kenneth and Kezia are coming home,' said Euphemia.

'And Ben, we shouldn't forget him. He's a member of the family now.'

Petal smiled. At least that's what Euphemia told Nicky later.

Nicky, her magnificent, brave little girl, was coming home too, her undercover operation having concluded with the arrest of David Cho at Auckland Airport as he tried to leave the country. Sandy had given the police his accomplice's details when he was questioned after Euphemia handed him over in the sanctuary.

'How did you know we were here?' Nicky had muttered when she emerged from the undergrowth in full camouflage gear, branches and leaves poking out from her uniform and helmet. Three similarly decorated policemen emerged behind her daughter, all four of them armed to the teeth.

'I heard a radio discharge when I was here with Josh and Sandy. Oh, and you featured in a video he took.'

'The night you wrestled a steer?'

'It was very dark. I did no such thing.'

'You're lucky I was on recon alone that night,' said her daughter.

They handcuffed Sandy and led him away, but not before he had sworn at Euphemia and called her, an interfering old bat who poked her nose in where it didn't belong. She was relieved that was all he said. And grateful for the carotid death grip Barbara had shown her last year, which rendered someone immediately unconscious. She had been dying to try it out and who better than on a good-looking man like Sandy? He had gone down like a block of stone and didn't come around until after Nicky and her compatriots were standing over him.

'This is your mother? What's she doing here?' Nicky's colleagues asked in unison.

'She's a greenie,' Nicky replied.

'She jumped out of a tree onto an armed man.'

'Actually, I slipped and fell out of the tree,' said Euphemia. 'It was lucky he was there because he broke my fall,' she said, relieved it was dark and they couldn't see her face.

'What were you doing in the tree?'

'Like Nicky said, I'm a greenie. I was checking out a kaka nest. We heard a pair had come over the hill from Karori and set up house together. Sad to say, the nest was empty. Maybe next year.'

'But it's dark.'

'They sit on their nest at night. During the day they are out finding food. You haven't seen them, have you? My group in Wellington would be over the moon if you could confirm a sighting.'

'Hey guys,' interrupted Nicky. 'Enough chit chat. We need to question the suspect. We'll leave you to your kaka search, Mum.'

'Excellent,' said Euphemia. 'I do have some stuff to attend to before I lock up. Conservation work is never done.' No one laughed. 'Nicky, would you mind exiting the sanctuary on the right side? There's a nest which I don't want you to disturb by the gate on the left.'

'I think I heard the bird you're referring to an hour ago,' Nicky said. 'You're right, I wouldn't want any of us to disturb an endangered species.'

'That's my girl. See you at home.'

'Good night, Mrs Sage,' said the officers one by one as they left in a line, keeping a truculent Sandy in front of them.

CHAPTER 46

WHIPPED INTO A TANGLED SKEIN OF YELLOW AND red, the wand sculpture in the middle of the roundabout was bearing up under the southerly onslaught, but only just. Euphemia whipped around the corner, driving parallel to the airport's single runway, the windscreen wipers lost the battle against the wall of water coming at the car. She was relieved to find shelter behind the terminal, parking as close as possible to the building. White taxis queued outside the arrivals gate, their drivers staying warm in their cars instead of milling around, socialising outside like they normally did. There was no point in using an umbrella on the short run from the car to the terminal. Experience had taught her umbrellas were a hindrance in such winds and usually ended up blown inside out and jettisoned in the nearest rubbish bin.

Inside the terminal, young people buds in their ears, rested against walls and backpacks staring at their phones while above them the information board was a fluttering list in yellow of delayed or cancelled domestic flights.

The two international flights Euphemia had come to meet were expected to arrive on time. The flight from Tahiti via

Sydney arrived ten minutes before three, and the flight direct from Singapore, ten minutes after. She bought a coffee and drank it peering out the windows across the rain lashed runway to Lyall Bay, where the waves were breaking over the perimeter road. She consoled herself with the knowledge that so far there had been no disasters here despite the weather regularly hurled at it.

Only experienced pilots ever landed in Wellington on a day like today; those who had mastered the art of negotiating the violent cross winds and tricky updrafts resulting from the combination of challenging geography and horrendous weather. To the south of the runway lay Cook Strait, separating the North and South Islands of New Zealand and to the north was Evan's Bay, a long narrow inlet between two hills. Recommendations that the council make the runway longer and safer had disappeared into a budget hole two years before.

Euphemia drained the last of her coffee, tossed the cup in the bin, and checked the information board. The Sydney notification had flipped from 'On Time' to 'Delayed Five Minutes', without her noticing. Those extra minutes until she saw Kezia and Ben stretched in front of her. She toyed with the idea of another coffee but decided against it, not wanting to be going backwards and forwards to the bathroom for the rest of the afternoon. On her wander past the newsagent, she saw the headlines about the capture of an international gang of wildlife smugglers. Conservationists were over the moon and full of praise for the work by the police undercover team which led to the capture of the perpetrators.

Joe had called as soon as Arthur was safely out of surgery, not caring it was the middle of the night and that he was waking her up. Although shocked to learn of Sandy's involvement, he was delighted at the attention the sanctuary would now get from gecko and skink lovers around the country. Most of all, he was heartily relieved the triad had not been to blame after all and that he and Arthur could get on with their plans to restore the Kincaide family fortunes. When he eventually ended the call, Euphemia tried to go back to sleep, but Jane was in excellent form and it wasn't an option. She found Alastair reading an *Architectural Digest* magazine in the kitchen when she went upstairs to make a cup of tea.

'Does she snore this badly every night?' he asked.

Euphemia poured hot water over her ginger and lemon tea bag. 'Kind of.'

'It doesn't matter,' he said. 'I love her anyway… or I will when she lets me.'

'It could take a while,' Euphemia said.

'I know. She's worth it. I can wait.'

* * *

THE DOORS OPENED, and a weary young couple emerged, pushing an overloaded trolley in front of them. An older man rushed forward and wrapped his arms around the young woman, smiling and crying at the same time. Airport arrival areas hadn't been the same for Euphemia after seeing *Love Actually*, still one of her favorite movies. All that happiness and love in such a concentrated space was infectious. The doors opened again. A businessman this time, looking embarrassed there was no happiness or love for him, made a break for the doors before battling against the rain to the taxi stand outside.

Finally, the doors opened and through them came Kezia, then Ben searching but not seeing her at the back of the crowd. Her eldest daughter looked radiant, her hair bleached by the sun, her eyes clear and bright against her tanned skin as she scanned the crowd. When she saw her mother, she broke into a huge smile and, leaving Ben with the trolley, ran straight into her mother's arms.

'Guess what,' Kezia said when she stood back.

'You missed me,' Euphemia said, reaching up to give Ben a welcome kiss on the cheek.

'I did, but that isn't it. Ben, I know I said we should wait, but I can't.'

'You're pregnant,' said Euphemia.

Kezia's face fell. 'How did you know?'

'I didn't think I would be right.' She grasped Kezia by the shoulders to study her properly. 'You are. How absolutely, amazingly, wonderful.' She took the tissue Ben had ready and wiped the tears from her eyes. 'You clever, clever people. How pregnant? How many weeks?'

'Eight,' said Kezia. 'I thought I might be at the wedding, but I wasn't certain. Isn't it amazing?'

'Wait until we tell your father. He's on the plane after yours.'

'Let me tell him, won't you?'

'Of course I will. It's your news. Ben, have you told your father yet?'

'Not yet. We weren't supposed to tell anyone for another month, were we Kezia? Not until we were past the dangerous period? That plan just crashed and burned.' He hugged Kezia to his side and planted a kiss on the tip of her upturned nose.

A murmuring started at the back of the crowd and rolled forward like a wave picking up power, growing louder as it got closer. Not a kind sound or a comforting sound, it was the sound of panic thrashing through order. A sound of pure fear and it infected everyone in its path. Euphemia turned towards it - towards the news that a plane had crashed off the runway into the sea and that the emergency services were on their way.

The End.

DEDICATION AND ACKNOWLEDGEMENTS

Dedicated to my sisters, Jill, Prudence and Janet for their continuing support and encouragement.

Thank you to all those who make Indie publishing an exciting adventure: Mark Dawson and James Blatch (The Self Publishing Show), Joanna Penn (The Creative Penn Podcast for Writers) and Lindsay, Jo and Andrea at (Six Figures authors). Your podcasts accompany me on my daily walks and leave me feeling better every time. Craig Martelle at 20books to 50K, you are an inspiration of sensibleness. Peace, fellow humans.

And a huge shout out to Donna at dlrdesigns051185@ gmail.com for her fantastic cover designs.

ABOUT THE AUTHOR

Rosy Fenwicke lives in Martinborough, a village in the Wairarapa Wine Region of New Zealand. She has three grown children and two Jack Russells. She enjoys reading, writing (of course), gardening and swimming. Buster and Cookie, her dogs, take her for walks around the vineyards every day.

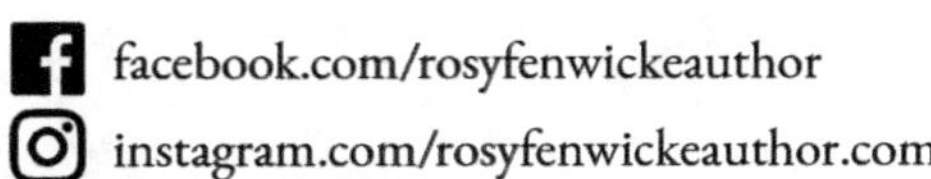

facebook.com/rosyfenwickeauthor

instagram.com/rosyfenwickeauthor.com

HOT FLUSH. BOOK 1: THE EUPHEMIA SAGE CHRONICLES

Hot Flush. Book 1. The Euphemia Sage Chronicles

Praise for Book 1 in the Euphemia Sage Chronicles: "Really enjoyed this book ...one of those that makes you want to carry on reading even though you have to get up for work the next morning !!!"
Amazon review: 5 Stars.

Switched Up. Book 2: The Euphemia Sage Chronicles

Follow Euphemia's adventures as she tries to get to grips with her super powers without being caught by Jimmy Abrahams, a pesky young journalist, determined to make a name for himself at her expense.

COMING SOON: NO RETREAT: BOOK 4: THE EUPHEMIA SAGE CHRONICLES

No Retreat: Book 4: The Euphemia Sage Chronicles

Why is all the food green? Jane and Sarah insisted Euphemia come with them to an expensive spa. When she finds out there is no coffee, Euphemia plans her escape but the owner is hiding something and lives are in danger.

COLD WALLET.

Cold Wallet

"A savvy, psychologically rich novel of tech-based intrigue." Kirkus Reviews.

Jess returns from her honeymoon a widow and the new owner of a cryptocurrency exchange. A doctor, knowing nothing about crypto, she turns to Henry. Will he help or will he destroy her?

DEATH ACTUALLY. DEATH. LOVE. AND IN BETWEEN

Death Actually. Death. Love. And in Between

"What a satisfying, interesting and very well written book! I loved this story and all of this characters. I strongly recommend this to absolutely anyone! This will be a terrific beach read, but you might not want to put it down to go in the water!" *GoodReads Review: Lucia. 5 Stars.*

9 780047 360949